THE KNOCKED UP PLAN

LAUREN BLAKELY

Copyright © 2017 by Lauren Blakely
Cover Design by Helen Williams.
Photo credit **Wander Aguiar Photography**

Also by Lauren Blakely

Standalone Male-POV books
Big Rock
Mister O
Well Hung
Full Package
Joy Ride
Hard Wood (October 2017)

One Love Series dual-POV Standalones
The Sexy One
The Only One
The Hot One

Standalones
The Knocked Up Plan
Most Valuable Playboy (August 2017)
Stud Finder (Sept 2017)
Come As You Are (January 2018)
Satisfaction Guaranteed (Summer 2018)
Far Too Tempting
21 Stolen Kisses
Playing With Her Heart
Out of Bounds

The Caught Up in Love Series
Caught Up In Us
Pretending He's Mine
Trophy Husband
Stars in Their Eyes

The No Regrets Series
The Thrill of It
The Start of Us
Every Second With You

The Seductive Nights Series
First Night (Julia and Clay, prequel novella)
Night After Night (Julia and Clay, book one)
After This Night (Julia and Clay, book two)
One More Night (Julia and Clay, book three)
A Wildly Seductive Night (Julia and Clay novella, book 3.5)
Nights With Him (A standalone novel about Michelle and Jack)
Forbidden Nights (A standalone novel about Nate and Casey)

The Sinful Nights Series
Sweet Sinful Nights
Sinful Desire
Sinful Longing
Sinful Love

The Fighting Fire Series
Burn For Me (Smith and Jamie)
Melt for Him (Megan and Becker)
Consumed By You (Travis and Cara)

The Jewel Series
A two-book sexy contemporary romance series
The Sapphire Affair
The Sapphire Heist

About

There are three little words most guys don't want to hear on the first date.

Not those…I mean these…"**knock me up**."

This single gal has had enough of the games, the BS and the endless chase. I know what I want most, and it's not true love. It's a bun in the oven, and I'm not afraid to hit up my sex-on-a-stick co-worker to do the job. Ryder is gorgeous, witty and wild — and he's also a notorious commitment-phobe. That makes him the perfect candidate to make a deposit in the bank of me.

I won't fall for him, he won't fall for me, and there's no way baby will make three.

Right?

* * *

There are four words every guy wants to hear on the first date — "**your place or mine?**"

When my hot-as-sin co-worker makes me a no-strings-attached offer that involves her place, my place, any place

— as well as any position — I can't refuse. After all, my job is like a coach and my latest assignment for the good of mankind is to create a fail-safe, battle-tested, proven guide of what to do or say to get a woman to fall into your bed — I mean, fall for you. So when Nicole says she's game to work through my list in a hands-on way, I take her up on her deal even with her one BIG condition.

There's no way I'll want more from one woman than any position, any where, any night? Except . . . what if I do?

This book is dedicated to W&W.
You were my plan.

Chapter One

Nicole

I fight back a tear as I listen to the radio caller. As I nod in the studio booth, my headphones on, I cover my mouth so I don't sob during my own show. I'm not even sure I can bear to repeat what she's told me out loud on air. But I'll have to when it's my turn to give Rachel from Murray Hill some advice.

The poor dear.

She hasn't had an orgasm with another person ever.

Have you ever heard such a tale of woe?

No. Just say you haven't. Because that, my friend, is a horror story.

That is fright night, all right.

"We tried all the positions that the Blue Steel site recommended, even the Crouching Cowgirl, which they said was a guaranteed path to an *O*, and that still didn't work."

The second she mentions Blue Steel, there's no more hint of rain in my ocular forecast. My spine straightens, and I'm no-nonsense as I jump in. "Rachel, let me ask you something—did Blue Steel recommend the Wheelbarrow in its list of positions?"

"Yes," she says, a hint of excitement in her voice. "How did you know?"

I shake my head. That man-centric site is too much. "Listen, love. Do you honestly think any woman is going to climax when being pushed like a big old gardening tool that's typically used for hauling rocks and dirt? And hey, if a lady can trip the light fantastic upside-down while doing a handstand, then I'm awarding her top honors in the Orgasm Olympics."

Rachel snickers.

"But here's the thing. Those positions you see on the men's sites—they're mostly about acrobatics and notches on a bedpost. A woman like you, who has struggled"—my tone softens, my deep and absolute sympathy for her as clear as day—"to achieve the ultimate in personal pleasure"—miraculously, I say this without breaking down into a pool of abject sorrow—"should look elsewhere. I would advise you to check out positions designed to maximize enjoyment for the woman."

I rattle off some top-notch bring-it-on-ers, as I like to call my five favorite positions for climbing the peak. "But Rachel," I say, propping my elbow on the desk and imagining I'm fixing this woman with a serious stare, even though my sidekick, Jamie, is the only one here, "if you're not into the guy, you're probably not going to visit the Promised Land. Do you like him?"

Dead. Silence.

There's nothing worse on air than a whole lot of nothing. I push her again. "Does he do it for you? Does he make your stomach flip? Does he give you butterflies? Do you feel it in your knees when he kisses you?"

"Ummmmm . . ."

There is no time for hemming and hawing on a live show, even if the bulk of my listenership comes from podcast downloads the next day. "I want you to think about the stomach-flipping factor of the equation, Rachel. I want you to ask yourself if he's the one you want. When you're all alone, your eyes are closed, and you're free to dream about whoever floats your boat, is it him? Does he make your toes curl? Because in my experience, a grade-A, top-choice, certified toe-curler is what'll get you over the O hump."

"No pun intended," Jamie chimes in from her spot on the other side of the desk, her silver laptop flipped open, too. I hold up a hand and mime high-fiving her, and we do a shoulder shimmy in tandem. Yes, we've got this down pat. Sometimes we even swing our imaginary lassos in unison when we're roping a most excellent point.

"I don't know if my toes have ever curled, Nicole. But you've given me a lot to ponder. Thank you. I always love your advice," Rachel says.

"And I love that you listen to the show. Now we'll wrap up this week's edition of Making and Breaking the Rules: Your Guide to Dating and Mating." But before we run through the closing credits, I have something to ask of my army of women listeners.

"Ladies," I say, in a serious tone. "Soldiers on the dating battlefield. Comrades in bras. Let's all say a prayer tonight. A prayer for Rachel." I bow my head. "If you've been lucky enough to climax with a partner, I ask that you send some of your orgasmic energy to Rachel in Murray Hill. Sisters in sexy times, we so desperately need all of your collective focus and energy on the great mountain ahead that Rachel seeks to scale, whether with her current partner or a brand new one." I look up, and Jamie still has her hands steepled together in plaintive prayer. "And just remember—sex is good, love is great, and when you bring them together they're even better."

How's that for a tagline?

After we play the credits and hit end on the recording session, I raise my eyebrows at Jamie in question. "Don't even tell me you had ten orgasms last night like you usually do."

Jamie laughs as she rises and walks around the desk. "Just two last night," she says, in her cheery, chipper tone that matches her bright blond hair and blue eyes, as well as the big, fat, sparkling diamond on her left hand. Ah, to be so young and hopeful.

I had a ring on my finger once upon a time.

I gather my notebook, laptop, and phone, and head for the door, leaving Jamie behind since she works on the next show. As I head down the hallway of Hanky Panky Love, the dating division of the lifestyle media giant I work for in a role that's expanded from columns to also include the radio show, a masculine voice calls out to me.

"Hey, Nicole."

A smoky, sexy, masculine voice, I might add.

Ryder Lockhart stands in the doorway of the studio next to mine, his arm resting on the door. That's one lucky door.

If someone needed a photograph for a catalog of the casual, cool, confident male, Central Casting would serve up this man. The white button-down shirt that hugs his delicious biceps is peeled up at the cuffs, revealing strong and worshippable forearms. The front can't hide how flat and firm his abs are. I must thank the maker of that shirt in my daily prayers. His black jeans are neatly pressed and fit just so yummily on his hips. For the record—yummily is not an adverb, but it should be. I'll work on my campaign to Merriam-Webster, starting tomorrow.

His eyes are full of naughtiness as he meets my gaze. "Clearly you haven't tried the Wheelbarrow with the right man," he says.

I tap a red manicured nail against my bottom lip as if I'm considering this. "You think that's the issue with the Wheelbarrow? Not the fact that I'd be upside-down during nookie?" I ask ever so innocently.

A lopsided grin shimmers across his fine lips. Yeah, they're yummy, too. He simply suffers from an extreme case of handsomeness.

"I do, indeed, think that's the biggest hurdle. There are certain advantages for the fairer sex when it comes to that position, but it requires a partner who knows exactly how to hold on properly," he says in that deep, gritty voice. He could read the phone book and make it sound like foreplay, which means everything he says makes you feel like a cat in mating season, even if he's talking about changing the toner in the copy machine. I'd probably have a dirty dream about toner if he did.

But his filthy-fantasy-inducing voice is only one-quarter of the assets he possesses for wooing the ladies. The other three quarters? A thick head of soft and wavy light brown hair, cheekbones carved by the gods, eyes that inspire dreams of tropical waters, a body handcrafted by his own rigid discipline, and a brain shaped and chiseled by Stanford.

Fine, that was more than four quarters. Well, what-the-hell-ever. He's got more than his fair share of chickadee-charming tools. It's my job to notice this stuff.

Balancing my laptop and notebook on my hip, I shove my copper-colored hair off my eyes. "Is that your way of inviting me to take your wheelbarrow out for a ride around the garden?"

His lips curve up in a mischievous grin. "Nicole, don't you know? You can ride this ride any time." That's where his teasing ends. "But holy smokes, the end of your show." He clutches his hand to his chest as if he's in pain. "Were you about to cry, too?"

"Oh, it was awful, wasn't it?"

"So sad," he says, shaking his head. "Almost makes me want to take on the job for Rachel myself."

"How thoughtful of you."

"I'm considerate like that."

"You'd be a Good Samaritan of orgasms, then?"

"Perhaps it's my true calling," he says, in a completely serious tone.

"Patron Saint of the Big O?"

He snaps his fingers and points at me. "Yes. That'll go on my new business cards. Maybe I'll even make house calls to administer my special brand of medicine."

I make a stop sign midair. "You're the worst. Seriously the worst."

"But I'm the best at Ping-Pong. Are you all set for the match later this week?"

"I'm always ready for the matches," I say, then pretend to whack a white ball with an imaginary paddle. We play on our company team in a tournament-style game that raises money for local kids' charities. Don't let anyone tell you otherwise—Ping-Pong is a game that, if played well, is great for your ass. "Incidentally, I have a tip on the guys at RBC that we're playing against. One of them has a powerful but ridiculously wide swing. So much that his teammate is constantly jumping out of the way."

Ryder's baby blues spark with strategic understanding. "Which means if we time it right when hitting to the teammate, we might find that the ball clatters to the floor while he's trying to avoid getting whacked by the guy next to him."

"Exactly."

"Brains and beauty," he says as he roams his eyes down my body.

He's not hitting on me. It's just his way. I give him a demure little curtsy as thanks. "Likewise."

"Also, for the record, there are many ways to bring a woman pleasure with the Wheelbarrow. If you're not enjoying it, he's doing it wrong." He steps closer to me, and I catch a whiff of his cedar cologne. He raises his index finger and moves it close to my lips as if he's going to shush me. "And don't let me hear those pretty red lips ever knock the Crouching Cowgirl again."

I roll my eyes. "It. Hurts. The. Feet."

"Boohoo. I bet it doesn't hurt the—"

I pretend to zip his lips and throw away the key. I shoo him into the booth where he records his show. "Go dispense your manly wisdom."

When it comes to on-air work, Ryder is basically, well . . . me.

But with a dick, and with the priorities that come with said appendage.

The funny thing is he was hired about a year ago, and his show was supposed to be a funny but earnest forum to offer dating advice to dudes. Lately, though, his show has been all about getting laid. It's still funny, but it's just different. A little crasser, if you will. Maybe it sounds like my show is about getting horizontal, too, but it's not. My goal is to maximize women's opportunities—for dating, mating, cohabitating, and, eventually, procreating.

"By the way, your show was great," he says, his tone stripped of bravado now. He smiles, and it's all genuine. "I always enjoy listening to it."

I blush. "Thank you. Same to you."

"Keep up the good work." As Ryder heads into his studio, I linger a bit in the hallway, shifting my laptop to my other hand, checking out the man through the window.

I like to think of myself as a woman of many talents. I know how to run at the mouth on air, I can craft a snappy column on the dos and don'ts of the most popular fetishes, I can dole out excellent trash talk at sporting events, and I'm also a top-notch appraiser of men.

Picture an art appraiser. That crusty old fellow in tweed and elbow patches, wire-rimmed glasses sliding down the bridge of his nose, cataloging the brushstrokes, the signature, the type of paint in a Van Gogh.

He wonders if it's fake or real?

Is it real or fake?

That's me when it comes to men.

I flip open my spiral-bound notebook with dogs in spacesuits on the cover. I uncap my pen and scribble some quick notes.

Nice jawline. *Check.*

Strong arms. *Check.*

Height. *Check, check, check.* Because, you know, height is some kind of Holy Grail.

Charming and likable. *Check-a-rooney.*

The Stanford pedigree makes him especially appealing, though. Empirically, of course. I'm only jotting down thoughts for my ongoing research into the male species.

I head to my office to work on my latest column on the best knots to use in your scarves for binding your wrists together in front, behind, or above the head, as well as for tying to the bedpost, a chair, or the fridge.

Fridge bondage. It's a thing. Who knew?

When I'm done with my tips for avoiding freezer burn in the process, my mind drifts back to checklists, attributes, and the best features a gal could want in that special someone.

And to Ryder Lockhart.

Chapter Two

Ryder

I adjust my tie, smooth a hand over my crisp light blue button-down shirt, and survey the crowd.

If you could call the half-dozen or so attendees here today a crowd.

More like a Chia Pet's early hair covering. A few sprouts that barely cover a bald man's head. I sigh, wishing for the days when I strode across the stage, grabbed the mic, and commanded a standing-room-only crowd of utterly rapt dudes, eager for my heartfelt and passionate advice.

As the Consummate Wingman, I can claim credit for more than forty-five marriages and engagements that have led to easily a dozen kids. I've been invited to countless weddings, been the first person toasted at most of them, and I've happily raised my glass in return to celebrate all those satisfied clients—men who needed a little help talking to the ladies.

That's what I gave them. A boost of confidence, born from my once-upon-a-time belief in happily ever after back when I was Manhattan's very own Hitch.

Wait. Excuse me. I think my lunch is coming back up. Happily ever after is a cycle of bullshit, love is a medley of lies, and marriage is a thing that can only go wrong.

But hey, that's between you, me, and the lamppost because right now I've got to be the guy who can help hitch any man's wagon to his dream woman's star. I suck in a breath, square my shoulders, and walk into the room, imagining I'm shushing the crowds who are wildly applauding their hero.

Like I used to do.

In reality, I'm greeted by a few clammy-handed, barely audible claps from the twenty-something guys.

And that's how the next hour of this seminar on dating and mating in the modern age goes. Did I mention it's being held in an exercise room at a gym on 14th Street? Yup. A couple hours ago, this room hosted a crew of sweating fitness warriors, squatting and lunging. Now, I've got the last slot of the night. No more keynotes at posh hotels. No more swanky, elite sessions at the Yale Club. No more client list a mile long.

The beanpole man in the front row, parked on the metal folding chair, raises his hand and clears his throat when I call on him.

"Fire away. Hit me with your question," I say, mustering the most enthusiasm I can dredge up.

His voice is reedy thin. "Is it true that I shouldn't post on Instagram right after I do it with a woman I met online?"

The beaky-nosed guy next to him shakes his head. "The new rule is wait an hour. Same goes for Facebook, Twitter, and checking Tinder for other chicks."

I groan as I scrub a hand over my jaw. This is like teaching remedial math. "Actually, gentlemen, I appreciate the sharing, but allow me to dispel some of that misinformation. Shockingly, you will find that checking *any* form of social media shortly after sex is a pet peeve of most women."

An auburn-haired, goateed man in the second row furiously jots something down in a notebook. Perhaps I'm getting through to him.

"The same holds true for passing out after sex, recounting the act of intercourse as if you're a play-by-play announcer, mentioning your mom during a post-coital snuggle, asking the woman you slept with to make you a sandwich, and calling her an Uber within the first fifteen minutes of finishing."

The guy with the goatee raises a tentative hand. "Same for Lyft?"

I laugh lightly and slash a hand through the air. "Yes, and for the old-fashioned yellow cars known as taxis, too."

He nods and mouths a *thanks* as he lifts his pen to his notebook.

I pace across the wood floor. It's streaked with sneaker marks. "Want to know the biggest post-sex pet peeve of all?"

All the men raise their faces. Eager acolytes.

"Asking her if she came. Because if you can't figure out whether she took a trip to the stars or not, then guess what the answer is."

"Um," the beanpole stammers.

"She might be shy about it," the beaky-nosed one offers.

"She might be quiet," a dark-haired guy suggests.

"What if she's one of those women who is just really subtle when she comes?" another dude asks.

Screw remedial math. This is kindergarten. "Seriously? Shy? No. She's not shy. If she comes, you will fucking know. When a woman comes, it's like an earthquake. Do you miss an earthquake?"

"No?" Beanpole asks.

I shake my head. "No indeed. The earth's fault lines don't split open subtly. The earth is not quiet when it rattles land masses." I start shaking from head to toe. I drop my mouth open in a huge *O* in my best approximation of the exquisite torment of a woman's pleasure. "If she's not doing that, it means you're not doing your job." I point at each of them as if they're all culpable. "It means you're huffing and puffing, but the wolf didn't blow the house down. Got it?"

I take my time meeting the gazes of the guys, making sure they're clear on this point. If I can't get them down the aisle anymore, then maybe I can help them identify a motherfucking female orgasm. Lord knows, the men of the world need some help—I had a caller yesterday on my show who presented with the same fucking dilemma, and I gave him the same advice. "The house falls, she came. The house is still standing, she didn't."

The pen moves at lightning speed, and my money is on goatee-man as the first to find the G-spot.

"Here's the bottom line. Do you want to get laid?" They set a world record for nods. "Then, if you want to get laid again, you will make sure she comes."

The room goes silent, and that's when I realize my mistake. I've dropped the "get laid" bomb. That's basically the worst combination of two words that a dating coach can utter. I scrub a hand over my jaw and try desperately to reroute myself. "What I mean is, if you want to have a healthy, lasting, long-term relationship with a woman, it would be great if you treat her like a queen in and out of the bedroom."

I flash a winning smile, showing off my straight, gleaming choppers. I look like a million bucks, and I have the pedigree to back up all these statements.

Correction: I *had* it.

Now I'm the guy coaching the Tinder-using crowd on how not to fuck up a hookup.

Chapter Three

Nicole

My girls are shocked.

As we round the trail curving along the reservoir in Central Park, Penny nearly stumbles on a twig, while Delaney shouts, "You're kidding me."

Penny's little dog, Shortcake, stares up at her mistress with a look of utter concern on her furry features over the near-fall. "I'm okay, sweet little darling," Penny coos to her butterscotch Chihuahua mix as she regains her footing. Then to me, Penny says, "You're not joking?"

Admittedly, during our morning jog might not have been the best time to drop my giant-pumpkin-sized news. But sometimes you have to rip off the Band-Aid. Especially if it's a plan of the life-changing variety. "I'm completely serious. This is something I've always wanted," I say, as my Irish Setter mix Ruby jogs by my side. The calmer I am about my news, the more likely my friends will understand. And I need them to understand. Their support is like air to me.

Penny smooths a hand down her red pullover as we continue our run on this September morning. "*Always* meaning in the last twenty-four hours?"

"It does seem like your sense of *always* might be a tad off, considering this is the first we're hearing about it," Delaney says, her brown eyes trying to drill a laser hole in me. It's a tough feat while running, so she's unsuccessful.

"Always as in always. But lately, I've been thinking more and more about my long-term portfolio approach, and it seems like the time is now." My heart speeds in my chest. I wonder if its pace is from the run or from the admission. But I pride myself on keeping cool and collected in matters of the heart.

"Portfolio?" Delaney scoffs at my word choice.

I smirk since I chose that word for effect. "I have a vision for how I want my future to unfold, and I want to take the necessary steps and make the best investments to ensure it happens."

Penny snorts. "I cannot believe you're using asset allocation strategies."

"Would you say you've been considering this massive, life-changing plan for longer than a week, longer than a year, or so long we need to tackle you for never breathing a word to us before?" Delaney tosses out, as her arms swing neatly by her sides. She's the only dog-free member of our pack. I've always hoped she'd adopt a small little mutt from Penny's Little Friends Animal Rescue, because I think a dog is pretty much as close to a soul mate as one can ever get. Plus, we'd all be perfectly paired then, girl and mutt. No such luck. But Delaney finally opened her home to a four-legged creature a few months ago when she adopted an orange, six-toed cat named Crazypants.

"To answer the *have I always* question," I begin, turning to Penny as Ruby and I maintain our pace along the leaf-strewn path, "it's sort of like—how did you know you wanted dogs? You just knew, right?"

Penny nods as she brushes off a strand of brown hair from her cheek. "I've always loved dogs. I can't remember not wanting one."

I shrug as if my situation is as easy to understand. "It's the same for me."

"And you don't want to wait any longer to meet the right guy? To make sure you don't want to do this with a partner?"

I slow as we weave around the tip of the water. "Ladies, I'm thirty. I'm not getting any younger, and the pickings aren't getting any better. I've been on the dating merry-go-round for far too long, and it just keeps spinning. It's making me dizzy. Plus, let's not forget I'm immune to love. May I present evidence in the form of Greg?"

Delaney sighs sympathetically. "He was such a nice guy."

"He was extraordinarily sweet and quite good to me, too," I say, recalling my ex from a few years ago. "And I didn't feel it. I'm like a defective part. I'm the balloon in the bag that doesn't blow up."

Penny furrows her brow. "I've never come across a balloon that doesn't blow up. Is that a thing?"

"Fine. I'm the bad starter on a car, or whatever the hell goes bad on cars that have to be recalled. You know what I mean. Clearly, there's something wrong with me if I couldn't even settle down with a nice guy like Greg."

"Your ex was pretty much the textbook nice guy," Delaney says about my former fiancé, a sweet-as-pie coffee shop owner who I brazenly asked out the day I met him after he whipped up a mocha latte for me with a heart drawn in the foam. We dated for seven months and were engaged for two. He was everything I thought I wanted: handsome, kind, sweet, attentive, and always ready with a caffeinated beverage with art on top.

But we were spark-free. He didn't make me weak in the knees, and I'm pretty sure there was no growl in his throat when he saw me naked. Not that I don't look good in my bare skin. I rock the nude look, thank you very much. And it's not because I'm a perfect ten. It's because I like to accessorize every outfit, including nudity, with chin-up confidence. That's my best asset, and it'll last longer than perky boobs.

The thing is, Greg and I were good separately, but together we were toothpaste and orange juice.

Several weeks into our engagement, the lovely little diamond slipped off my finger in the shower, courtesy of my Vanilla Spice body wash. The ring slipped into the drain and hasn't been seen since. For all I know, it's been swept into the great sewers of Manhattan, and a rat is wearing it as a tiara. I was devastated at first, but then decided fate was giving me a sign. I didn't want to marry a man who didn't make me swoon, and so I called it off. Greg married someone else a year later and invited me to the wedding. He and his wife appear outrageously happy, so it worked out for all of us, not just the rat.

Since then, I've had some memorable dates and some not-so-memorable ones. I even went out with a guy from the local dog park who owned a Papillion and a Great Dane, a combination I found utterly delightful, so I stayed with him for four months. The problem is the dogs were so damn cute together that it took me three months and three weeks longer than it should have to realize the guy didn't give me butterfly flutters—it was the pups causing the swoops and dives.

Like I said, the love portion of me is defective. I just don't feel it. I do, however, feel gobs for my friends, my Ruby, my amazing mom, my pain-in-the-butt brother, and every single one of my callers and readers. That's why I can do my show from a place of conviction.

As we round a bend, I say, "I'm just one of those girls who is better off going it alone. Maybe I'm too picky. Maybe I'm a hard-ass. Maybe I'm simply too cynical about love."

"Ironic that the dating guru is a cynic," Delaney says, clucking her tongue.

"I do believe in love," I say, correcting her. "I'm just not entirely sure I believe it's ever going to happen for me. And that's okay. I'm fine with my single lot in life."

See? I'm already in the acceptance phase of the five stages of I'll-never-fall-in-love grief.

"It will happen in its own due time," Penny says, waggling her own engagement ring as a gaggle of geese splashes in the water. "There's a goose out there for you. Geese mate for life," Penny adds, in case I've somehow forgotten Penny often looks to the animal kingdom for dating analogies.

"Perhaps I need to spend more time looking in lakes, then, for Mr. Right," I quip as Ruby yanks gently toward a squirrel scampering up a tree. A quick tug from me reminds her to stay on track. Ruby raises her face, meeting my eyes with a look that says, *See, Mom, I listened to you.*

"Good girl," I tell her.

Delaney inhales deeply as we prepare to run up a steep hill. "In all seriousness, though, why do you think it won't happen to you?"

She asks a good question, and since my job is to zero in on matters of the heart and the bedroom, I've applied the same rigorous examination to myself. I have the answer handy. "Here's why. I believe that writing about dating and love and sexual fetishes has made me immune to love. It's the nature of the beast. The more time I spend breaking down habits and strategies, the more I become resistant to them. I'm like a doctor who can be exposed to all sorts of viruses but won't catch them."

Penny quirks her eyebrow. "So, love is a virus?"

"Absolutely. And it seems I've got more antibodies to it than I expected," I say as a mom crests the hill pushing a three-wheeled jogging stroller in the other direction. My heart skips a beat. My eyes snap to the sweetest little bundle of joy in the stroller—a baby girl, decked out in a cute, pink onesie. A blond angel I just want to smother in kisses, and I don't even know her. Butterflies launch a full-scale fiesta in my chest. Trumpets blare.

"Oh my God, your little girl is so adorable," I call out with a bright smile.

The young mom returns my grin, her ponytail swishing as she jogs. "Thank you."

"How old?"

"Six and a half months."

"She's a little princess."

"She is, indeed," the mom says. "Thank you for the sweet words."

I sigh happily as I jog, and twenty feet later it occurs to me that I'm alone. I stop and bounce in place, looking around for my girls. Penny and Nicole are frozen in their spots, jaws languishing on the running path, eyes the size of fried eggs.

"Why are you looking at me like I've sprouted wings?" I ask as I stop moving.

Delaney goes first, flapping her arms in the direction of the mom. "Yes!"

I furrow my brow and jog back to them. "Yes, what?"

"It all makes sense," Delaney says, jerking her gaze to Penny. "It all makes perfect sense, right, Penny?"

My dark-haired friend nods then gestures to me. "You always comment on how cute babies are. You always talk to the moms in the dog park. At the dog shelter events, you're the one who's interacting with the kids who've come along."

My grin turns to a full-scale beam of the highest wattage. "I love kids. I've always wanted my own."

Penny smacks her forehead. "My God. It's so obvious now. Like at the bookstore a few weeks ago, picking up baby shower gifts for one of your clients," Penny says, pointing to Delaney, and I can remember the day perfectly. A cute little four- or five-year-old was sounding out the words to *Brown Bear, Brown Bear*, and I helped him with the ones he struggled with. It was just second nature to me.

Delaney jumps in. "I knew you wanted to have a family someday, but I guess I always thought you'd want to do it as part of a couple. But you don't need to. You can do this on your own."

My heart bursts full and bright in my chest. I love that they *get* it. That they understand this is part of who I am.

Maybe my path to parenthood is unconventional, but the end result is part and parcel of my very makeup.

"And how adorable was that little girl we just passed?" I turn to Ruby and talk to my dog. "She's so totally cute, and soon we're going to have one of our own." I bend closer to my pooch, tousling her silky, russet coat. "Do you want to be an aunt?" With my hands on her snout, I make her nod yes. "You do. Oh, you do want to be an aunt. You'd be such a good auntie dog."

Ruby wags her tail faster and paws at me. "I know, I know. We'll get you a little niece or nephew very soon." I rise and meet the gawking gazes of my best friends. If I shocked them when I started this conversation, I might have completely rendered them speechless now. I flash a smile and pat Ruby's head. My dog leans against my thigh. "We're going to be like elephants. Ruby and I. Raising our young in a little matriarchal society."

"Yoo-hoo," Penny says, waving dramatically and pointing at her and Delaney.

"Are we chopped liver?" Delaney asks.

"You're in, too?"

Penny rolls her eyes. "If you're doing this, we're all in."

Delaney laughs. "We're going to be part of your elephant matriarchy, you crazy woman."

For the rest of the run, I debrief my best friends on all the research I've conducted so far on Project Bun in the Oven, detailing obstacles and opportunities, pros and cons.

By the time we're done, I've told them I intend to approach this like I do one of my columns—with a Top Five Reasons Why list and a firm deadline.

The clock is ticking.

Chapter Four

Ryder

The next day, as I work on a column on third-date etiquette and expectations—let's be real: the only thing a guy wants to know is if he'll get the third night's lucky charm—Cal Tomkin calls me into his office.

My overlord is a lot like Peter Parker's boss, J. Jonah Jameson, in the *Spiderman* movies. He speaks as if he's firing bullets, and he's made of geometric shapes. His head is a rectangle. His chest is a trapezoid. His lips are an oval.

"Come in, Ryder. Have a seat."

Words you never want to hear from the man who signs your checks. *Have a seat* translates into "I'm so unhappy with your work I'm molting, and you're one step away from getting fired."

I park myself in the blue upholstered seat across from his desk, prepared for the onslaught of angry feathers.

Words don't come, nor do feathers. Instead, Cal stands and strides to his bookshelf. Ah, so this will be a long, drawn-out kind of reprimand. *Great*.

Drumming his fingers over the spine of one title, Cal appears deep in consideration. Like I don't know what book he's about to pick up. "Now, what is it I'm looking for?" he muses, as he taps a chubby, cylindrical finger against his chin.

"Gee, I'm not really sure," I say.

"Hmm. I could have sworn I had a signed first edition from the author himself."

He hunts, dragging his fingers across the shelf in a dramatic show. I wonder, wonder, wonder if he'll find it.

"Aha," he declares and plucks a yellow tome from the shelves. He spins around, a *gotcha* look on his blocky face, and brandishes an incriminating photo of me on the back jacket. A smiling, happily married me.

Tomkin taps the book. "*Got Your Back* by Ryder Lockhart. Number-one bestseller. Translated into ten languages. Sold half a million copies." He inhales deeply, as if he's pleased. "The bible," he says, venerating the book. "Men called this *the bible*."

I chuckle lightly as if humbly deflecting praise. "Well, I suppose you might find a passage or two in there about how to help a woman call to the saints, cry out plaintively to our maker, and say the Lord's name over and over again, and it definitely wouldn't be in vain."

Cal's mouth forms a ruler-straight line. His eyes lock onto mine. I'm the target in his crosshairs. "Yeah, that's the problem," he barks. "You're supposed to be the Consummate Wingman, but lately you're the dickhead in the locker room."

I scoff like a pro. The textbook definition of scoffing because *what the fuck?* I actually utter a shocked "*whoa*" as I hold up my hands, warding off his attack. "That is not my shtick on the show whatsoever."

He calls my bluff. "Cut the surprised act. You and I both know that's the role you've been playing." His tone brooks no argument.

I swallow dryly, shifting in my seat. "It's not my intention to come across that way."

"It's not? You sure?" He flips open the book and settles on my bio on the back page. I brace myself, even though all my old football instincts tell me to tackle him and strip the ball because that shit in my bio needs to stay locked up. "Ryder Lockhart is happily married to a talented and lovely pastry chef, after a whirlwind courtship in Manhattan. They have a dog named Romeo, and they like to cook, hike, and go to the movies. With a degree in psychology, as well as having spent his younger years being raised by the happiest mom and dad around, Lockhart knows what it takes to have the confidence to talk to a woman with the intent of forging a lasting relationship with that special someone."

Cal slaps the book onto his desk. It lands with a loud thud. He reaches for his coffee, takes a thirsty gulp, and sets the mug down on the book.

I point to the book, so he knows his faux pas. "Excuse me, you just put—"

"I know. It was my *intention*. Because that's about all this book is good for these days. It's a coaster, Ryder. A goddamn coaster." He sets his palms on his thighs. "Where is the persona I hired? Is he hidden away in these pages?"

Where is Ryder Lockhart? Ask Maggie. She killed him. Maggie took her cooking knife, sharpened the blade, and plunged it into my chest.

Seven times.

I clench my teeth and suck in a breath. "I'm right here."

Cal arches an eyebrow skeptically—his triangle move. "Then perhaps you'd like to focus more on what the show sponsors want. Be a little less Ten Ways to Screw the Hot Chick, and shift to Ten Tried and True Methods to Win the Love of Your Life."

The love of your life? The love of my life is Romeo. That's loyalty. That's true love.

But the book isn't selling how it used to, the classes are drying up, and surprise, I'm not in such fucking demand as a relationship consultant on account of my picture-book marriage going up in flames with the white picket fence as the kindling.

Turns out that life coaches do better when they walk the walk and talk the talk.

Whodda thunk it?

"I can pull back on the sex talk on my show," I offer, since I don't have a lot of cards to play here at Hanky Panky Love. If the advertisers are getting cold feet, I'll have to do something.

Cal shakes his head, a beleaguered look on his face. "There's nothing wrong with sex. Sex is great. We all love it. We're all trying to have more of it. I'm not silencing you from talking about sex. We built this division of this media business on a willingness to write frankly, honestly, and humorously about sex. But it is always with the underlying goal of *love*. That's why we're named Hanky Panky Love.

But lately, you're all about the hanky panky, and not about the love. I'm asking you to find a way to tie your show and your column back to the mission: *intimacy*."

I shudder at that word.

"Take Nicole Powers," Cal continues, and the second he mentions her name, his expression shifts. He beams as if she's the golden child, while I'm the bastard offspring. "She can talk about orgasms till the cows come home, but everything is tied back to finding *the one*. The one true love."

"Nicole does a great job," I say, and maybe I'm a tiny bit jealous of his praise, but mostly I'm happy for her because that chick is the definition of cool. Who knew the woman could discover so many interesting ways to fit an eight-inch vibrator into the bedroom? I read that in her column a few months ago, and I was damn impressed with how she suggested a squeeze-play action so the rabbit could join in woman-on-top.

Plus, she kills it as a Ping-Pong partner. She's hungry and ferocious and loves to win. So do I, and don't let anyone tell you that that little table sport isn't a wonderful way to work out aggression over your ex.

"One true love," I say, the words acrid on my tongue. But I don't have the luxury of ignoring his request, so I gobble up a big dose of bitter, humble pie. "I can do that, Cal. I can absolutely refocus to finding the one true love."

"Thank you. I know you can, and I'm confident you will. I am sorry your marital fortune changed, but you still have a job to do, and when I hear comments on the show about getting laid, coupled with your remarks at the seminar last night, they concern me."

I tilt my head, a suspicious curiosity zipping through me. "I didn't see you at the seminar."

"Of course not. I sent my son to attend."

I groan as I remember the goateed man feverishly taking notes. "You had a plant there to spy on me, Mr. Tomkin?"

"I don't consider it spying. I see it as conducting due diligence on the investment I made in your brand."

"I told those guys at the class to treat women well," I say, defending my closing act in the session.

His eyebrows shoot into his hairline. "By giving them a huff and puff orgasm?"

I stand and park my hands on my hips. "Is that not part of treating a woman well?"

"It absolutely is, and I make sure Mrs. Tomkin is showered in gifts in that department," he says, and I immediately hit the erase button on the last ten seconds.

I focus on what I have to do next. I need to convince him I can be the guy I once was. I thread my fingers together, showing the union of my hands. "The bond between love and intimacy is a beautiful thing. That's why I aim to give men the confidence to talk to the women of their dreams."

His pale eyes glitter. "Exactly. That's the Ryder I want."

I heap on another spoonful of sugar. "I hear you, sir. I understand what you're saying. You need me to focus less on getting laid, and more on getting her heart," I say, bringing my fist to my sternum and tapping so hard you can hear it.

"Yes. Keep it bawdy. Keep it fun. But don't lose sight of the end game. You've got their backs. You're helping the men of the world connect with their soul mates. Do that, and you're golden."

I need to polish my rough edges. That's all this is. I'll refocus my show, clean up my seminar act, and I'll be good to go. No one needs to know I don't believe the bullshit I'm selling anymore. All I need to do is sell it. "I can do that."

He pats the edge of his desk, which he does whenever he's about to say something sympathetic. "I know it can't be easy, and I know things have changed with Maggie out of the picture," he says, and cold dread runs through my body. It's a knee-jerk reaction to the mention of her name. I'd rather not have the sympathy.

"I'm fine. Romeo and I have moved on."

"Good. I have a new assignment for you. It's a big project." He spreads his arms wide as if showing the scope of the work. "We have an advertiser behind it, and I think we can turn it into a book deal if it works out."

My ears prick. Book deals that work out are like little money machines that spit up cash in the form of royalties every month.

"I want you to produce *The Consummate Guide to Ten Wonderful Dates That Can Lead to Love.*"

"You do?"

"We'll run it as a series of columns. I think it can be wildly successful across all our mediums. You can use it as the fodder for your show as well."

"Isn't that like that movie *How to Lose a Guy in Ten Days*?" I ask, cringing inside because Maggie loved that movie.

Cal scoffs, shaking his head. "Dear Lord, no. That was based on a bet. McConaughey was trying to win an advertising account and if he could make any woman fall for him in ten days, he'd land the deal. This isn't about that sort of romantic swagger. This is a roadmap to the *possibility* of true, authentic love. The point of this assignment is to provide the recipe to help men along in their romantic quests. I want you to outline the dates, the topics of conversation, the stages of getting to know each other, and the expectations."

"A dating guide?" I say, since this is a little different than some of my most popular columns in the last year, like "Ten Post-Sex Pitfalls to Avoid." It's a little squishier than "Five Positions Guaranteed to Bring Your Woman Toe-Curling Pleasure." It's a little tougher than "How to Spice Up Your Sex Life with a Long-Term Lover."

Cal nods enthusiastically, his face now oblong. "I want this to be the definitive handbook on where to take her, how to romance her, and how to win a woman's heart."

And once you do, she'll stick her fist into your chest, hunt around for that damn organ, and rip it out, holding it like a bloodied trophy above her head in the arena.

"That sounds simply fantastic," I say with a grin so roomy you could pack a bunk bed in it. "So you want me to write about how to woo a woman in ten dates?"

This is like being given the directive to build a bomb.

He nods.

"And talk about it on air?"

Another nod.

"And outline ideas for dates to take her on?"

He strokes his chin, taking a beat. "Ideally, I'd love for you to *actually* go on some of these dates."

"With the goal of getting a woman to fall in love with me?" I ask.

He laughs. "Well, we can't really guarantee that'll happen. Love is a fickle and precious thing. But it would be helpful if you can find a woman willing to, say, take a trapeze lesson with you. Think of it as field reporting. You're actually going to roll up your sleeves, get out there on the ground, and let us know what works."

And when the green wire touches the red wire, the bomb explodes in your face, kids.

Cal rises and slaps me on the back. He walks me to the door, stops, and wraps his hand on the knob. "And if you don't turn this ship around, your show is canceled."

That just makes this bomb-making assignment a real winner, now doesn't it?

Chapter Five

Nicole

"Ooh, look! A new one just was added to the database," Penny coos in excitement as she points to the screen.

We're gathered around my iPad at Speakeasy, our favorite Midtown haunt, perusing the latest offerings on a bank I've been in touch with in Manhattan.

"He's five-foot-nine. College educated. Plays the violin. And he has red hair," Delaney reads, then runs her fingers over the ends of my hair. "Do you want little redheaded babies?"

I laugh. "I think I'd like the *choice* whether they should have red hair or not, and clearly I'm only bringing recessive genes to the equation."

Penny swipes left dramatically as if the new donor is a Tinder *no*. "Anyone else? And are we ever going to see what they look like besides when they were five years old?"

I shake my head. "In most cases, only childhood photos of donors are posted. Every now and then you hear of a woman who's seen adult photos of her donor, but that's highly unusual, and only allowed at a few, select banks. It's actually quite rare to even see high school or college photos, since a lot of donors only do it because it's anonymous."

Penny points to the screen, reading another donor's profile in frustration. "Look. This guy is six feet, has blue eyes, played hockey in high school, went to UCLA, and works in tech. But what does he look like?"

"Unfortunately, we're just going to have to imagine," Delaney says, with a heavy sigh.

Penny reaches for her red wine. "That makes me so sad I need a drink."

"And let's be honest, looks do matter," Delaney adds.

I nod vigorously. "They do. That doesn't make me vain, right?"

My girls shake their heads in unison, defending my stance. "We all want a cute elephant baby for our matriarchy," Penny says, patting my hand.

I laugh. "But seriously. You think it's reasonable to want a handsome donor, right? In addition to all the other things that are obviously critical. Not a serial killer. No criminal record. College degree. Height, etcetera, etcetera."

"Absolutely," Penny says, setting her wineglass down with a resounding smack. "How are you possibly supposed to say a green-eyed, five-foot-ten, college-educated man with no murder convictions is enough?"

"It's like online shopping without seeing what you're buying," Delaney adds. "Who buys anything on the Internet without seeing a photo? You don't shop for shoes just by the size, color, and style. You need to see them. Try them on."

"I don't think trying on is an option." I wink.

Delaney sticks out her tongue. "But you need to *see* the goods. You can't fly blind."

I reach for my water. No more chardonnay or mojitos for this mama-to-be. I've had all my health screenings, too, and my doctor sees no reason why I can't get pregnant. All I need is the other half. "I just wish I knew more about these men."

Penny peers at the site's latest offerings once more. "This is crazy. You can select whether someone has skills in auto mechanics, plumbing, or kickboxing. You can choose if your donor has detached earlobes, a particular kind of eye spacing, and his favorite subject in school. You can even opt for someone who's a good cook. But you can't see if his jawline is actually square, if his lips are truly full, or if he's as handsome as you've dreamed."

I scrunch my forehead and imagine my dream candidate. Briefly, my mind is blank, but then an image pops into my head. "I just wish I knew the guy was going to be a Ryder Lockhart level of hot," I say, matter-of-factly.

"Oh, he is a hottie," Penny says, and Delaney nods her agreement. They've both met him at my work events and the occasional group happy hour.

"He's gorgeous. Just the other day I found myself cataloging his features. He really does have it going on. Plus, he's smart and funny and good to animals."

Penny hums mournfully. "Too bad he's not a donor."

"Ha. Yeah, it's a bummer he hasn't made a deposit at this sperm bank." I tap the screen. "I'd order up one serving ASAP. Get that turkey baster inside me *stat*," I bark as if I'd be saying that to the nurses while I tell them to shoot me up with Ryder Lockhart's DNA.

Wait.

Ryder Lockhart's DNA.

The clouds part. The sun rises. The bells ring. Never have three words sounded more like a perfect solution to a problem.

I straighten my shoulders. A zip of electricity buzzes through me. "Girls," I say in a hushed voice, motioning for them to come closer. They scoot in, eyes eager.

"He has everything I could want in a donor. Should I . . .?" I trail off, leaving the unasked question hanging between us.

"Should you ask him?" Delaney supplies, like she wants to be 100 percent certain of my meaning.

I fiddle with my napkin. "Should I ask him to be my donor?" It comes out like a croak.

"You're seriously considering him?" Penny asks, taking a deep breath.

"Am I?" But I know the answer. I am. I really am, and now my stomach is parachuting and loop-de-looping with some wild combination of nerves and possibility. "Yes. I literally didn't even think about it until this very second. But now that the idea is in my head, it sounds like the perfect solution. Is that the craziest thing I've ever said?"

Normally, Delaney and Penny would tease me about all the crazy things I've said about dating, or the ultimate deal-breakers in dating profiles (submissive men need not apply at the house of Nicole), unexpected uses for oranges (guess . . .), and what number of battery-operated friends is too many (for the record, there is no such thing as too many).

But my question isn't in the same camp. It's vastly different, and we all know it.

A hush falls over the table.

"If you're asking if he has good DNA, I'd have to say yes," Delaney says, taking her time with each word.

"He's certainly handsome," Penny says.

"He's clearly smart," Delaney adds.

"He's a perfect gentleman," Penny points out. "At your office Christmas party last year, he offered you his coat. Remember how cold you were?"

"Frozen," I answer quickly. I'd dressed for fashion, not for weather, and the sleek red sweater felt like it was made of cobwebs that wintry night. When we all left the party together and the arctic tundra air slapped my face, Ryder gave me his jacket until the girls and I could hail a taxi. Confession: I wanted to keep that coat. It smelled like him. Like cedar and sexiness and total class. Its warmth and weight made me feel like I was enveloped in his arms.

I wonder if those sorts of traits are passed on genetically – chivalry. In this case, I bet nurture won out over nature, since manners are usually taught, but why not give a man points for chivalry when it comes to rating his DNA, even though there's no chromosome for it.

And he earns lots of points for DNA. A flash of images pops before my eyes: framed photos I've seen on his desk of his niece, the times he's helped his brother with his kid.

"He's a family man, too," I say, penciling more tally marks in his column of pros. "He has a brother and a sister, and he helps his brother with his little girl. He's picked her up after school a few times, and they've gone on little adventures around the city." He has frequently updated me the next day in the break room about excursions to their favorite bakery, jaunts to gymnastics classes, or trips to the art supply store for the budding little painter.

"Those are definitely attributes you won't find in a sperm bank scorecard, but they've got to rate high," Penny says.

I nod, taking in the full scope of his potential, adding up all the little moments I've experienced with him as a friend and colleague in the year since he joined the company. Everything I know about him affirms that he's both a good guy and a deeply good-looking guy. Sure, his show has taken on a sexier slant lately, but since my kid will have a dating guru as a mom, I'm not bothered that the rest of the DNA would come from another sexpert, too.

Silence spreads as we all stare at each other, a tableau of three best friends deep in thought. Here we are considering something that has the potential to be amazing, but also incredibly complicated. I'll need to have paperwork drawn up outlining expectations (just a small cup, please), as well as involvement (no need to send a birthday card), as well as compensation (how exactly do you put a price tag on that kind of prized DNA?).

What would it be like for my friend and colleague to be the fa—

But I don't bring myself to say the F-word, even in my head. Because this isn't a choice about how a baby makes three. Ryder and I aren't a one and two, and that's just fine. This is a choice I'm making to be a single mother, and I don't need a father for my child.

I just need the other half of the baking mix.

As co-workers, the situation might be awkward. As human beings, it might simply be odd, too.

But life is a string of uncomfortable moments, and our job as adults is to navigate through them with the least harm and most love. Asking him to donate sperm is awkward as hell, but it's also precisely the sort of thing that professionals like us, skilled at discussing the ins and outs of the most bizarre requests men and women make to each other, could manage.

That is if he says yes.

Another nosedive.

Oh God, I hope he says yes.

He might say no.

He'll probably say no.

But I'll never know if I don't ask.

"Soooooo," Delaney says, her eyes wide.

"Soooooo," I repeat. "I should ask him?"

They wait for me to answer my own question.

"I should?" It comes out tentative at first. I say it again, stronger this time. "I should." It sounds right. I absolutely should ask him to be my donor.

Penny and Delaney look at each other, then me. They say in unison, "You should."

"It's so much better to know the donor," Penny adds.

"He's the total package," Delaney reiterates.

"He really is," I say, and it feels crazy, but incredibly right, too. It makes me nervous, but it excites me. I set my hand on my stomach, quelling the nerves. I look at the time on my phone. "There's no time like the present. I'll ask him tonight."

After all, this potential donor is as handsome as a girl can dream up and more. He's got a little bit of everything a girl could want, and he has that extra something special that I especially need.

He won't want to be involved beyond the deposit.

Chapter Six

Ryder

I slam the white plastic ball across the table, imagining it's Cal, it's Maggie, it's the institution of marriage.

What it is, though, is a perfect shot.

However, our opponents are tough as nails, even with Steve's crazy-ass swing.

It's down to the final serve. Do or die. The wiry guy is a determined mofo. He extends his left arm so far to the middle of the table that his teammate actually jumps out of the line of fire, like a frog skittering away from the street. But Steve's backhand is so vicious he grunts as he returns the ball with astonishing power, sending it screaming in Nicole's direction.

Tension threads through me. No way can she get this. No way anyone can dive the way she needs to. But somehow, the woman stretches across the corner of the table and saves the ball before it rattles to the floor. In a split second, she hits it with a perfect return.

Perfect because Steve's teammate misses, since he's still scrambling to get back into position.

I thrust my arms in the air. Nicole hoots.

"We are the champions," she says, and that calls for scooping her up. I lift her in my arms. "We absolutely are."

Buoyed by the thrill of victory, I squeeze her tight, and for a second her breasts are pressed flush to my pecs. Naturally, I have no choice but to swing my eyes downward, and *hot damn*. They are highly bitable. But then, this isn't the first time I've noticed Nicole's rocking body. She's lush. Curvy hips, a delicious ass, lean legs. On top of that, she has that long red hair, those fantastic lips, and these light blue eyes that make you do a double take and wonder if they're contacts, because how can anyone have eyes that shade of blue? I even asked her once, and she got in my face, opened her eyes wide, and said, "See anything less than real?"

"Nothing but blue skies ahead," I'd said.

Also, it should be mentioned her ass is something I'd like to worship. I've checked out her backside pretty much every time she's ever bent down to pick up a Ping-Pong ball from the floor. If I ever strip her to nothing, I'll spend ample time nibbling it, no doubt. Then I remind myself to stop objectifying her. Besides, I need her advice and input. I've got to sell her on helping me with Cal's do-or-die project. She's the perfect companion to test these dates with me, and I need to find the right moment tonight to ask for her help.

"Hey, superstar, want to get a glass of champagne and toast to our victory?" I say as we break the embrace.

"I would love nothing more," she says brightly, since the bar that hosts our games—the Lucky Spot—is known for its champagne and Ping-Pong nights.

We shake hands with Wide Swing Steve as well as his teammate, congratulating them on a game well played.

"Good job, guys," I say.

"You, too." Steve shakes his head in frustration. "You two are a tough team to beat."

"Why, thank you," Nicole says. "So are you."

When we reach the counter, I ask the bartender for the bubbly special—since, when in Rome—but Nicole declines and says she'll have an iced tea instead.

I arch a brow. She's not a lush by any means, but we've had plenty of happy hours and Ping-Pong tournaments where we've toasted with wine, beer, or cocktails. A mojito is usually her poison. I'm about to ask why she's going virgin, when she says, "What's the strangest thing someone has ever asked you to do?"

I blink but quickly find the answer. "A girl once asked me to meow till she came."

Nicole laughs. "I didn't actually mean in bed."

"Ah, my misunderstanding. I took that as a natural baseline with you when you asked for *strange*." I flash her my trademark grin. "Pillow talk and all."

She shrugs in a way that says *natural mistake*. "But did you turn on the pussycat charm?"

"I'm all for making the woman happy. If she'd asked me to purr I'd have done that, too," I say, as the bartender sets our drinks on the counter.

Nicole strokes my hair. "Good, kitty-boy."

I reward her with a purr. Because her hand in my hair is purr-worthy.

Her blue eyes sparkle in excitement. She lowers her hand to my ear, dragging her fingertip over the earlobe. Damn, this woman. One peek at the swell of her breasts, and I'm thinking of her sexually. "Can I scratch your ears, too?" she asks in a sexy, smoky voice.

I lean into her touch, pretending to be a cat rubbing up against her, then laugh. "You're right. This is getting strange."

She laughs, too. "Oh, sweetheart. I don't think we've even skirted the surface of weird." She reaches for her iced tea. After she takes a drink, she raises her chin and clears her throat. "What I meant is what's the strangest thing someone's asked you to do outside of the bedroom?"

Her voice is different, more serious than usual.

I stare at the ceiling for a moment. "I suppose it would be the time one of my clients wanted me to help him find a double-jointed woman."

Her eyes pop. "Did you?"

"Nope. I wasn't a matchmaker. I was always the lubricant," I say, as music from the bar's sound system switches to a pop tune.

"*Was* being the operative word?"

We don't talk much about my fall from grace, but it's no secret. "Was indeed. I suppose my days as romance K-Y are behind me," I say curtly, then finish the champagne and set it down. "All right. Time to switch to something stronger."

I signal the bartender and order a Jack Daniels. When he leaves, I meet Nicole's gaze. "It's my turn now."

"Ooh, are you going to ask me a weirdest-thing type question?"

"Not entirely. Mine is simpler," I say, using this as a chance to feel her out about my ten-dates-to-love mission. "Would you be happy if a man took you on a trapeze-lesson date?"

She smiles widely. "If I liked him, yes. I actually think it's a great idea for a date. It's fun, and it's different. It's daring, and it's challenging."

"What else?"

Her brows knit. "My ideal dates?"

"Yes. What would float your boat after a trapeze lesson? A night at the museum? A boat ride around the city? A tour of cupcake shops?" I ask as the bartender returns with my glass of whiskey. I swallow some of it.

"Tell me yours, and then I'll tell you mine."

"Fair enough. I'd like to go to a Knicks game. Maybe a barbecue on a rooftop. She could hijack me and take me to a hotel."

She mimes writing in a notebook. "Taking this all down for posterity. Also, major points for hotel hijacking. That's awesome."

"Your turn now."

"I do love cupcakes. Being female and all." She taps her chin then snaps her fingers. "Geocaching," she says, her eyes lighting up as she mentions the GPS-led outdoor treasure hunts. "I love big old scavenger hunts. I'm quite good at finding things, too."

I hold up a hand and count off on my fingers. "We have trapeze lessons, cupcake tasting, and a scavenger hunt. What else do you think a man could do to facilitate a woman falling in love with him?"

"Besides not being boring? Not being an asshole? Not sticking his dick elsewhere? And not being totally focused on himself, but instead making her the center of his world because she drives him as wild as he drives her, leaving her weak in the knees from his kisses and vice versa?"

I whistle, impressed. "Damn, woman. You just laid it all out."

She takes a deep breath and straightens her spine. "Speaking of laying it out, there's something I would like to ask you. And this might qualify as the new strangest thing you've heard."

Her tone is stripped free of teasing and flirting. It's earnest and honest, as if she's about to ask me something serious, not something of the *can you make me meow* variety.

"Hit me up," I say.

She glances around. Her voice is thin and nervous. "Mind if we go someplace quieter?"

I've never heard Nicole speak with anything but brass-balls confidence. The sound concerns me, makes me want to ensure she's okay. "Sure thing," I say, as I set a hand on her lower back and guide her through the crowds at the Lucky Spot. "And wouldn't you know, I've got something to ask you, too."

"You do?"

"I sure do."

We leave the bar and head to the diner around the corner. She slides into a booth. "Do you want to go first?"

I shake my head as I sit across from her. "Ladies first."

"You're such a gentleman." She places her shaking hands on the table.

Before she can speak the waitress arrives. I order a burger and fries, and expect her to do the same, but Nicole opts for a salad and water.

"Salad, water, iced tea?" I point at her, making a circle with my index finger. "Are you on a diet? Because you don't need to be. You know that, right? Your body is spectacular."

She blushes then shakes her head. "Thank you," she says, and I've never known her to be shy about a compliment. But then, I suppose I've never blurted out precisely what I think of her physical appearance. For a second, I hope I haven't said something inappropriate. But then, this is Nicole. I told her the meow tale. We've long since done away with pretenses.

"But I'm not on a diet."

"Good. Because the burgers want you to eat them, and you'd look sexy eating a burger," I add, since evidently I've become a fire hose of compliments now that I've unleashed the *spectacular body* one.

She tells me she's trying to eat healthier. When she tells me why, I freeze.

Chapter Seven

Nicole

I was raised by a single mother.

Amanda Powers is absolutely kick-ass amazing.

After my father died when I was young, she didn't remarry, but in the last few years she's met a widower named James who romanced her like I suppose only a silver fox can do—dancing, dinners at expensive restaurants, nights out at the ballet.

When I've asked if she plans to marry him, she simply laughs and in her husky Faye Dunaway voice says, "I prefer to have a gentleman caller."

But she loves her gentleman caller, and he loves her, too.

Her grief over my father was intense but not debilitating. A police officer, Robert Powers died a quarter century ago in the line of duty. One night when my father responded to an armed robbery, he didn't come home.

My mother was devastated. My brother and I were, too.

But I don't remember how much or for how long. That's the thing about being five. My dad died when I was too young to have memories of him. My mother's told me stories of my father, too, her high school sweetheart, a brave, honest, and handsome man.

Faced with raising two kids alone, my mother remade herself. She took real estate classes, learned the ins and outs, and started selling apartments in New York City to support her family.

After several years, she became one of the top brokers in this town, and she still is. That's what she focused on as we grew up—mastering her trade and raising her kids. She did it with grace, confidence, and an unwavering faith in her ability to soldier on after the love of her life was killed.

That's why my plan seems perfectly reasonable.

I don't need to wait for Mr. Right when I have a model from my childhood for how to be Mrs. and Mr. Mom, all in one.

But lest anyone think it's easy-peasy lemon squeezy to ask a man to whack off in a small room for your future mommy dreams, it is most assuredly not.

I am a cyclone of emotions right now. They storm and bluster inside me, nerves and fear and excitement all at once. But I batten down the hatches and march on. We Powers ladies know how to get shit done.

I square my shoulders, take a steadying breath, and confess.

"Here's the thing. I'm suffering from a case of baby fever," I say, and holy shit, my voice sounds borderline normal.

Ryder furrows his brow. "Say that again?"

"Baby fever. You know this thing women get sometimes?" I say, going for humor. That's our shared language, Ryder and me. We joke, we tease, we play. "Apparently, I have a very serious case of wanting to have a baby, and it can only be cured by getting knocked up."

He blinks, and yup, I've won.

I've now officially become the person who's asked him the strangest thing ever.

And I'm messing it up.

That was the wrong approach. I grab the controls and try to steer the plane out of this impending crash. I wave my hands in front of my face, the universal sign for *I need a do-over on account of being a ding-dong*. I drag my fingers through my hair and breathe. Breathe again. Holy shit, when did inhaling air become so hard? Oh, right. When I had the harebrained idea to ask my coworker for a cup of baby batter.

When I raise my face and meet his eyes, I see the same confusion etched in them as a few seconds ago. But there's kindness and patience, too, in his sky-blue irises. He's waiting for me to keep going. He gives an easy nod that says *it's okay, I'm listening, even if I don't get it yet*.

"What I'm trying to say is that I want to have a baby. I've been thinking about it for a long time now, and I'm ready to become a mom. A single mom." Once I've said those last two words, I feel emboldened. Bravado surges through me. This is my calling in life. The heart knows what the heart wants, and mine craves the pitter-patter of little feet. "I've been researching all the options, from adoption to sperm donation, and this might seem crazy, but I hope it sounds like the compliment I absolutely mean it to be." I clasp my hand to my heart as the balding man in the booth behind Ryder raises a bottle of ketchup to pour some on his plate. "Would you help me?"

Ryder freezes.

The bald man does, too.

The bottle of the red condiment hovers behind Ryder's handsome head.

I've shocked even the patrons surrounding us at Wendy's Diner.

The enormity of the question I've asked expands between us. It is a balloon being filled with air. With each passing second, it grows larger.

Ryder doesn't move. He stares at me with a quizzical gaze. His hands are in his lap. He's a statue.

I let the air out of the balloon, releasing it abruptly. "What I mean is, would you be my donor?"

The balloon races across the diner, squealing and squeaking, landing splat on the table, the rubber a limp, pathetic mess.

Ryder's brows knit together. He makes a sound. I'm not sure what noise it is. I've rendered him speechless. He swallows. Opens his lips. Tries to talk. He drags his hand over his jaw. His square jaw that I want for my baby. His genes are so fine, and now I'm wantonly coveting the DNA that made his face.

"Nicole."

I try to read his tone, but it's impossible. For several interminable seconds, I'm sure I've ruined our friendship and our working relationship.

I need words. I need to talk my way back to normal. I adopt a bright, cheery smile. "Hey, don't worry about it. We can totally pretend I never said that. Let's bring on the milkshakes and talk about Steve's insane swing."

His lips twitch, and he lifts his arm, stretches it across the table. He sets his hand on my right hand. "Nicole," he says again, and this time his voice is strong, reassuring. "You caught me off guard. I never in a million years expected to be asked that."

"It's not exactly an everyday request," I whisper.

He shakes his head. "It's not."

"More like something from a sitcom, huh?" I say with a little *we're all good* shrug.

"I don't think it's a sitcom," he says, and I want to thank him a thousand times over for not bantering back with me. He seems to realize that now's not the time for jokes. "Let's talk about what you have in mind."

My lungs inflate with oxygen again. I recalibrate, since I was sure he wasn't going to be open to it, based on his initial reaction. But as I regard his kind eyes and his palm on mine, my pulse settles. His hand is warm, and it calms my nerves. It gives me the courage to begin.

"I looked into adoption, and while I think it's amazing, I want to try first to have and carry a baby. I'm completely ready to do it on my own, so I've been looking into sperm banks." I stop to roll my eyes in a self-deprecating way. "Believe me, I know it's the height of irony that the gal who usually has open browser tabs full of the latest and greatest in vibrators and sexual positions now spends more time perusing the offerings at sperm banks."

He smiles, and that's another feature I can add to the list. The man has a great smile. It's warm and exhilarating at the same time. "Some women are checking out Plenty of Fish. You're checking out plenty of tadpoles," he says, then makes a keep-talking gesture with his free hand. "Go on."

"And the reality is pretty stark."

"You mean the pickings are slim? Or there's no one you want to bring home to mama?"

"Let me tell you all about sperm banks."

A soft flurry of laughter falls from his lips. "Words I never thought I'd hear tonight. Or any night," he says, and oddly enough, this conversation is going better than I expected.

Chapter Eight

Ryder

Before she can utter a word, the waitress returns with Nicole's chopped salad and my burger. We say thank you, then I eye the lettuce, tomatoes, and carrots in Nicole's dish with suspicion. "You sure about the burger thing?" I lift the top bun on mine. "Eat me. I taste soooo good," I say in a cartoon character voice.

She laughs and shakes her head. "Thank you for the offer. But I'm cutting back on food that talks."

"Tell me everything I ever wanted to know about sperm banks. But wait. First, can we just agree that the word *sperm* is up there with *moist*, *pucker*, and *slacks*?"

"It so is. We should call it cupcakes instead of sperm," she says, and I'm glad we're keeping it as light as we can, because this is such a serious topic. I meant it when I said never in a million years did I expect her to hit me up for some of my swimmers. I figured she had a crazy column in mind, too, or that she'd also been slapped with a new assignment from Cal—*we've heard from a sexual researcher in*

Indonesia about five newly discovered sexual positions. Can you test them out and report back on their pleasure potential, please?

But this? She's given me a bona fide, certified case of complete flabbergastedness.

I've no intention of becoming a dad, considering I don't have a wife nor do I want one, since wives—in my experience—have a habit of spreading their legs when you're not home.

Mine did at least.

With several men.

Yeah, that's Maggie for you. The sweet little pastry chef had quite a secret life.

The woman who stood next to me in a church and took a vow before God and all our friends and family to be faithful wasn't loyal at all. To top it off, she was unfaithful in spectacular fashion. That's how she did everything. With panache. With exclamation marks. When Maggie made a decision, she was all-in. She didn't just cheat. She cheated seven times. With seven men.

But she was sorry. She was so very sorry. She didn't realize she had a problem. She didn't know she was addicted. Would I please stand by her while she sought treatment for sex addiction? Because she wanted nothing more than to conquer her addictive behavior, change, and remain my wife.

As if that was ever going to happen.

Look, I'm sympathetic to addiction. I have a cousin who has battled the demons of alcoholism. I *get* that addiction is a beast, and it can wrap a person in its clutches. I understand the painful toll it can inflict on a family.

But as a man, I couldn't bring myself to look beyond what Maggie did to *us*. She admitted everything one evening in our living room after I'd just finished a report for a client.

"Honey, I need to tell you something."

She kneeled beside my chair, clasped my hand, and then spewed forth her confession like vomit as she came clean and begged for forgiveness.

I was shocked. I was hurt, and I was, frankly, disgusted. "Whatever forgiveness you seek, you'll need to find it with God. It's not coming from your soon-to-be ex-husband," I told her, and then I kicked her out.

Two years of marriage, nine months of engagement, three months of courtship. That's 1095 days of my life flushed down the drain.

All of them a lie.

In retrospect, the signs of her extracurricular activities were there all along. Too much time on her phone, too many unexplained hours away, too many distracted moments. I'd chosen to look the other way because I'd loved her. But it's amazing how quickly you can fall out of love with someone when they smash the vows of marriage and fidelity, stomping on them with steel-toed boots.

It didn't take long to get over her. The ending of our marriage was like a crash course in how to un-love someone. I don't have any feelings left for her except perhaps . . . mild pity. I'm also so damn grateful she chose to cheat early on—*before* we had kids.

But Nicole's not asking to have kids *with me*. Her proposition is a horse of an entirely different color. It's also one I understand to some degree. My brother Devon and his partner couldn't have kids the old-fashioned way. They chose to adopt, and my niece Simone is the cutest creature alive.

And so, as I lift the burger, I give Nicole my best Salt-N-Pepa imitation, singing, "Let's talk about cupcakes, baby."

"I thought you'd never ask." She holds up her fork to punctuate her statement. "Turns out I've become an expert in sperm. Or cupcakes, as some say," she says with a smile. I wink back. "And the reality is this—there are probably many amazing donors with wonderful traits. But no matter how much testing and interviewing and screening they do, I'd still be getting a sample from a complete stranger. And on top of that, the more I think about it, the more I'd like to know who the"—she pauses as if she's rerouting words—"the donor is for my baby."

As I bite into the burger, I note that she didn't say *father*. There's deliberateness to her word choice, and I suppose that's understandable. I love Simone in a way that makes my heart feel as if it's squeezing in my chest, but I also love that she's *my brother's* kid. Not mine. I'm not ready to have one of my own.

"That makes a lot of sense. You want a better idea of what you're getting into. You want to take some of the guessing out of the equation," I say, as I pick off the onions since I forgot to ask the waitress to hold them.

"Yes. I do," Nicole says, taking a drink of her water. "And, please forgive me for being so clinical, but you really have everything I'd want in a donor."

A burst of pride spreads through me. "Yeah? Tell me what that is. Besides a distaste for onions and an astonishingly good backhand at Ping-Pong."

Her nose crinkles slightly as she smiles, drawing my attention to the small spray of freckles there, like a little constellation. "Those are absolutely at the top of my list," she says, then she picks up her fork and takes a bite of her salad.

I eye her bowl. "Nicole. You miss the meat, don't you?"

She laughs loudly. "Oh yeah, I do miss the meat. And yes, I walked right into that one. But that right there is one reason. You're easygoing. You're charming. You're kind. You're funny. You're smart. You're ridiculously handsome."

"Oh really? Ridiculously?"

"Insanely good-looking."

"Do continue."

"You're amazingly gorgeous. You're out-of-this-world beautiful."

I'm not often called beautiful. It's a word reserved more for women or works of art. Oddly enough, I don't mind it. Maybe because it came with a litany of praise, or perhaps it's the way she says each word with a particular flare. Whatever the reason, I can't help but give some back to her when I say, "And your child will have a beautiful mother."

"And that," she says, gesturing to me. "That right there. You're just . . ." She lets her voice trail off. "You're good, Ryder. You're good."

I raise an eyebrow skeptically. "Is that like nice? As in *he's a nice guy*? Because nice guys finish last." I'm sure Maggie thought I was a nice guy. A perfectly nice fellow she could cheat on.

Nicole shakes her head. "I didn't say *nice*. I said good because you're one of the good ones."

I don't see myself that way. I also don't see myself as donor material. Given how my business nosedived post-divorce, it's hard to see myself as anything but the man with the ultimate black mark on his record.

Ryder Lockhart, Manhattan's so-called *love doctor*. He could help any man score any woman for life.

Except himself.

Hiring me as a dating coach nowadays is akin to hiring a junk-food-scarfing personal trainer to trim down. You just didn't do it. "I don't know about that, but I appreciate the thought."

"You are a good guy," she says, emphatically. "You have a good heart. I understand this isn't a small request. But I hope you'll consider it because I know I'll be a good mother, and I want to give my child the best genes possible. I think that's you."

Nicole is showering me with praise. I'm not entirely sure how to receive it, especially since this is a new side I'm seeing of her. She's always been the cool chick, the bright and bold co-worker. Quick with a quip, but thoughtful and caring, too. I'm reminded of a day last year when Maggie blindsided me with a phone call at work, one of her attempts to win me back. The call didn't last long, but it unnerved me, got under my skin. I didn't get into the details with anyone, but Nicole sensed I wasn't having the best day, so she nudged me with her elbow after my show and said, "Guess what? Two-for-one beers at the Lucky Spot tonight. On me."

A simple solution, but it had done the trick.

"How does it work?" I ask. "The whole donation process."

She stabs a carrot slice, chews, and swallows. "Well, there's this thing guys do when they're horny. It's called"—she glances furtively from side to side—"jacking off."

"I'm well aware of how the protein shake is made. What I mean is, are we talking about one of those little rooms you go into?" I ask, since what man doesn't have an image of a jerk-off chamber? "With magazines or porn or whatnot?"

"Yes, they schedule the donors for forty-minute sessions in them."

"I'm more efficient than that, but that's good to know." I take another bite and chew. I set down the burger. "So, a nurse or orderly would escort me to a special room, and then I'd need to drop my drawers and whack off. Into a cup, right?"

"A plastic sample cup. With a top," she says, and I'm kind of amazed that she's answering every question like a champ. No blushing, no stammering.

"What do they provide for entertainment? Laptops? Computers? Or is it old school with *Playboy*?"

"They provide pornographic material in printed form as well as video on a TV screen."

"Awesome. So I just choke the chicken in a room with a ton of other dudes going at it in their own rooms, too. Hand a cup to the nurse. She seals up the goods. Then, what's next?"

"They do tests on your swimmers."

"They'll pass. Then you come in, maybe the same day, maybe a few days later?"

"Same day. We'd have to time everything to my cycle and when I'm ovulating."

"Fine, so they undress you, prop you up on an exam table, and stick a turkey baster into you?"

"You paint a lovely picture of the process."

I hold up a hand, waving her off. "Wait. I'm not done. You're in nothing but a hospital gown. The doc tells you to put your cute little feet in stirrups, and they stick that baster up inside what I am sure is an absolutely gorgeous and heavenly home," I say, because if she can compliment my tadpoles, I can say something nice about the paradise between her legs. She mouths a *thank you*. "After the boys make the upstream trip, they send you home." I mime patting her on the rear and then sending her out the door.

"I think you've got the basic idea."

"And after that?"

"That's all," she says. "That's all I'd want you to do. I don't expect or want any involvement. I'd have all the paperwork drawn up in advance saying there are no legal rights, responsibilities, or expectations of parenting, and no financial commitments required."

I'm almost ashamed to admit it, but that's the clincher for me—the lack of involvement. If I'm ever going to raise a child, I'm damn well going to do it right. The whole nine yards, two parents, just like my mom and dad raised my brother, my sister, and me.

Nicole isn't asking me to sign up for daddy duty, though. She doesn't want me to help with diaper detail or midnight feedings.

She's a friend asking for the help she needs so she can then do those things on her own.

And helping a friend seems like something I should consider.

Fine, she's asking for a hell of a lot more than a dude to put together an IKEA TV stand, and those things are beyond *Da Vinci Code*-level cryptic. I'd like to see Robert

Langdon decipher some IKEA assembly instructions. Good luck with that, Harvard symbologist.

I like Nicole. I respect the dickens out of this woman. I want to take her request as seriously as she's asking it. "Can I have a few days to think about it?"

"Of course. Take all the time you need," she says, then glances at an imaginary watch on her wrist. "It's only my biological clock ticking."

I laugh, and she adds, "I'm just teasing. And if the answer is no, I'll still be your Ping-Pong partner."

"We'll always have Ping-Pong." I pick up my burger and take another bite.

She digs back into her salad then stops. "I almost forgot you had something you wanted to ask me, too."

I laugh and slouch back in the booth, giving her the lowdown on Cal's assignment. Admittedly, it sounds like such a simple favor by contrast, but I still need to ask. "I was hoping you'd be willing to take a trapeze lesson with me. As well as go on a few other dates. For the column, that is," I say, because I don't want her to think I'm hitting on her. "I would be grateful if you could help me out."

Nicole is the perfect woman for this project. She has no interest in the part of me that causes pain—my heart, that damn organ I've locked up in a steel cage.

"I'm asking you for DNA, and you're asking me to go on ten test dates?" she says, laughing. "The answer, obviously, is yes."

Chapter Nine

Nicole

Ruby is shameless.

The second she lays her big brown eyes on Lorenzo, she wags her tail, drops to the downward dog pose, and begs him to play with her.

The Italian Greyhound rescue pup is above it all. With his snout held high, my mother's skinny beast proceeds to inspect my apartment, sniffing every corner, nook, and cranny.

"He's like a Niffler," I say to my mom, referring to the Harry Potter fantastical creature that sniffed out shiny things. She read the first few books out loud to my brother and me when we were in middle school. Naturally, I picked them up on my own and finished the series in high school and college.

"Perhaps he's found buried treasure under your couch," she says, pointing to her dog, who's now stuffed his whole head underneath the couch.

I remember something that's gone missing—my ten-speed purple vibrator with the dual-action butterfly.

Uh-oh.

My face flushes beet red, and I call off the dog. "C'mon, boy. There's nothing under there," I say as cheerily as possible. What if he locates the missing purple butterfly? My mom is cool, but I do not want her lover-dog turning my missing personal pleasure device into a chew toy.

Lorenzo burrows further. His bottom half sticks out. He is all butt and legs and tail now. Ruby barks, cheering him on. Traitor.

"Maybe he's finally found your lost diamond." She winks. "Or a slice of pizza."

I force out a laugh. Pizza, a precious gem, or a pleasure perpetrator. "Let's hope it's the ring."

Then again, that purple tool was a damn good vibrator, and I miss it fiercely. Would it be such a bad thing if Lorenzo found it?

Honestly, I'm not embarrassed that my mother knows I engage in ménage à moi. She does read my columns and listen to my radio show. "Love, I have to agree," she'd said after a recent bit on deal-breakers. "I would draw the line, too, on men who want to wear my panties. La Perla is not meant to be shared."

When Lorenzo emerges, he's victorious. He brandishes my red and white polka dot umbrella between his teeth and wags his tail proudly. "That's been missing forever!" I march up to the boy. "Give it to me."

He obeys and drops the umbrella into my open palm. This is the perfect umbrella—it fits in a purse but can withstand a strong downpour. I suppose all things being equal,

I'm grateful he located a device for keeping dry, not getting wetter.

I set the umbrella on my coffee table.

"Ready for Project Closet Metamorphosis?" I ask my mom, who is perfectly coiffed, as always. Her shoulder-length hair is blown straight and pristinely styled. Not an auburn strand is out of place. She wears blue jeans and a light zip-up vest over a long-sleeved shirt. The ever-present Bluetooth dangles on her ear like a wedding band.

She pats the tape measure in her palm. "Let's see what we can do."

We head to my bedroom, which adjoins one of the most wonderful closets in all of Manhattan, thanks to my mom. She hunted down this place in the East 80s for me. It was a total steal, and I'm a lucky gal to call it my own. As she surveys my closet, she yanks the metal ribbon and begins measuring.

"You do know I could have done that," I point out.

She laughs, a throaty sound. "You are many things, my love. But good at measuring is not one of them. Besides, we need to make absolutely sure there's enough space to turn this into a nursery."

When she says those words, my heart flutters with hope, even though I'm still in limbo. It's been fifty-six hours since I presented Ryder with my request. Each passing second is endless, and I've become a pathetic clock-watcher, like a high school student staring at the ticking hand on the wall, desperate to escape the purgatory of class. Every time my phone makes a sound, a charge zips through my bloodstream in case it's him with a yes. I've even brought my phone with me to the shower. Well, I leave it on the vanity. I'm not *that* pathetic.

Yet.

I'm prepared for his no, though. A girl needs a backup plan, so in case he turns me down, I've prepped my list of second choices—a few other tall, smart, and hopefully handsome strangers with deposits at the cupcake bank. Just in case.

I've been working out of the office the last two days, so I can't even stalk him at work and try to read his expressions, body language, or secret notes.

Just kidding. I'd never do that.

I mean, not unless he left me no choice.

My mother yanks and measures, then records the intel in her phone. "There. I'll give my handyman the numbers, but I think you should be able to make it work. But I don't think we should schedule the project till you've got a baby in there."

"Sounds reasonable."

"And that means we just need to get you in the family way," she says, patting my belly. She bounces on her toes and shrieks.

I arch an eyebrow. "You've turned into a screech owl, Mommy dearest."

"I'm just so excited that you're doing this. I know there are no guarantees, but you literally have no idea how much I want to be a grandmother."

I adopt a serious look. "Judging from your howl, I have a pretty good idea. I'd say you want it as much as you wanted that bottle of Cabernet you bid on at auction a few weeks ago."

"Shame on you. I wanted that wine more." She winks and hugs me. "Just kidding. I want this for you, and I want it more than anything. But you know, no pressure."

"Right. None at all," I say, drily.

"You'll be knocked up like this," Mom says, then snaps her fingers. "You do know I got pregnant the first time your father and I tried, with both you and your brother?"

"That's because you and Dad only had sex twice, right?"

"Ha. Yes, of course. We were so chaste otherwise."

"Also, how do you know it happened the first time you tried to get pregnant?"

"A woman just knows these things," she says as we breeze out of the closet.

"I hope I'll know, too, since I've found the donor I want."

"Is that so?" She lifts a curious eyebrow. "Tell me more about Donor 4621." We've taken up the habit of assigning random numbers to potentials.

As we leash up our dogs and head out into the crisp fall afternoon, I give my mom the lowdown on Donor 4621. Lorenzo walks by my mom's side while Ruby gamely tries to engage him in dog conversation the entire way. His snout is fixed sternly forward as my girl lolls her tongue and paws at his chest.

"Hmm," Mom says when I finish and we reach Fifth Avenue. Buses grunt and groan, and horns honk from cabs.

"What is the *hmm* for? Just tell me."

She tilts her head as we wait for the light to change. "*Hmm* means that seems like a potentially complicated situation."

"I can handle this. He's a colleague, he's a friend, and he's a Ping-Pong partner. He's a dating expert, too. He's precisely the type of man to ask."

"Maybe," my mom says, not buying it.

"Elaborate."

"What I mean is—it's complicated. Please just make sure he signs on the dotted line. Contracts are critical."

"He's *not* going to suddenly want daddy duty. He's not that type of guy. That's yet another reason he's perfect. He doesn't want a relationship. He's been burned. He's not interested in any type of commitment. I'm sure he's allergic to commitment, in fact."

The light changes and we cross.

"That's all well and good, but the thing I *like* with anonymous donors is they can't get anything from you even if they change their mind," she says as we walk along the edge of the park. "This almost feels like the type of thing you'd write a column about. 'Top Five Reasons Not to Ask a Coworker to Donate His Happy Juice.'" She raises her right index finger, displaying a perfectly manicured, plum-colored nail as she counts off. "One, you see him nearly every day. Two, what will you tell the kid? Three, how incredibly awkward will it be when you bring your child to a work event? Four, will your friendship be tested? Five, what if he changes his mind about wanting to be involved?"

Holy shit. She has my job down to a science. I'm ridiculously impressed, but I also must dispute her. "For starters, what work events am I taking a kid to? Even if I wasn't a sex and love columnist, do you honestly think I'd drag along a toddler or grade schooler to the office Christmas party?" I tighten my grip on Ruby's leash. I adore my mother, but she's still a mother. Sometimes she can't help being a giant buttinski.

"It's not implausible. You might pick up the baby from day care, realize you left something at the office, and scurry back, the baby in your arms," she says, and I clench my teeth because she's fucking right.

But I could handle that. Ryder would be fine with it, too. That's simply not the sort of scenario that would trip us up. He's sophisticated and savvy about social situations. Plus, he knows the score. "Perhaps the column should be 'Reasons Why It's Wise to Snag Your Friend's Baby Batter,'" I suggest, a smart little clip to my voice.

"Do share."

But before I can reel off my five reasons—I have them handy—my phone chirps.

My pulse skyrockets while my stomach flips. I grab my cell from my pocket. His name flashes across my screen in a text, and it feels like my whole future hangs in the balance.

"It's him," I whisper reverently.

My mom's hazel eyes sparkle, and she claps in excitement. Any annoyance I felt is erased by her reaction. She's in this with me, and I won't be able to do it without her.

With nervous fingers, I click on the message.

Are you free tonight?

Chapter Ten

Ryder

Simone drops my hand and scurries toward a table strewn with paint jars, brushes, and mini easels. Her class starts in two minutes. The nine-year-old skids, pivots, and rushes back to me. She throws her arms around my waist. "Thank you for taking me. I'll make a Picasso now."

I ruffle her hair. "Of course you will. His blue period was the best."

"Do you want a painting of a blue horse for your kitchen, then?"

She's obsessed with horses and with painting. "Let me tell you a secret," I whisper. "I've been hoping for a blue horse for a long, long time."

A huge smile spreads across her face. A front tooth is missing. "Then you should have a blue horse. You should always get what you want."

"Isn't that the opposite of what they teach you in school? You get what you get, and you don't have a fit?"

"I think *you* should get what you want. I should get what I want, too. And I would love for us to have an ice cream sundae after class. If I paint you a blue horse, can I have an ice cream sundae? I mean, can *we* split one?"

"Ah," I say, stroking my chin. "Now that I understand you're only thinking of my ice cream needs, I'll consider it. But do you really think your daddy will be okay with that?"

"Which daddy?" She points at me. "If it's your brother, my daddy, no. But if it's my other dad, yes."

"Too bad it's my brother, your daddy, who's picking you up when he finishes his workout." Devon's partner is working all weekend on a big case, so Devon's single parenting today.

"Uncle Ryder," she says, grabbing my arm. "You have to convince him. What if we skipped class so we can get ice cream?" She lowers her voice to a conspiratorial whisper, knowing my brother is a health nut.

"We would be in so much trouble."

"You can't get in trouble with your own brother."

"Have you met your father? He would be furious. Plus, you love class. Go paint. I'm going to think deep thoughts somewhere in this store."

She laughs and spins around, her silky hair like a dark flag trailing behind her as she runs the final few feet to the table and plops herself in a chair.

Her class is only thirty minutes, and even though I'm not artsy, there's something irresistible about perusing the shelves at this shop. The hip notebooks. The freshly sharpened pencils. The soft bristles of paintbrushes. They whisper of creativity and ideas. I amble through the aisles then stop at the recycled paper notebooks when I spot a collection with cats and dogs in spacesuits on the front covers. The images are familiar. I furrow my brow, then I remember.

Nicole's notebook that she carries around at work has astronaut dogs on it. The woman hasn't been far from my mind over the last few days. I pick up the notebook and flip through the blank pages as if I'll find the answer to her question in there. I've thought of little else since she asked me. I promised myself I'd make a decision today, so I texted her an hour ago to ask if she's free tonight. Whether I'm in or out, I want to give her the courtesy of a decision sooner than later.

The question remains, though—am I in?

I swing my gaze to the art class in the corner, staring at Simone, her long brown hair spilling down her back. The tips of her hair are blue. She asked Devon and Paul if she could dye it. They said if she learned the names of the most famous artists and their most famous works, they'd take her to a salon for a proper blue-ing.

That girl is such a source of joy in their life. She's sunshine. She's happiness. And she came from a choice—a choice to open their home to a child who needed one.

I have the power to make that choice for Nicole. I rest my hand against a shelf and stare at the back of Simone's head till my niece is a blur, and my gaze is elsewhere. It's on the future. The weight of the request.

It's awesome and scary. What if I make the wrong choice like I did by marrying Maggie? That decision to mingle my life with Maggie's seemed so right at the time. What if I choose badly again, even if the decision feels like the right one now?

I set down the notebook and noodle on all the possibilities until my brother texts, asking if I mind if he stays another thirty minutes to lift weights.

Ryder: You need it, you scrawny bastard. No problem.

He responds with a raised middle finger emoticon.

When class ends, I inform Simone she's getting her wish for ice cream. She beams and tells me my wish for a blue horse has come true, and she'll finish the painting in the next class.

After a chocolate-sauce-drenched sundae, we meet up with my brother outside his building. His dark hair is sweat slicked, and he's a few inches shorter than me, but still a handsome devil. He's also ridiculously fit and muscular. Simone gives him a big hug.

"Hey, honey bun, can you head inside? Daddy will meet you upstairs."

She nods and runs into the building.

Devon lifts his chin. "Have you decided?"

Nothing like an older brother to cut to the chase. I sought out his advice the other day, but this is the kind of issue that bears repeating, so I ask again, "What do you think I should do, Dev?"

"You know what I think," he says, his tone as no-nonsense as the rest of him. "I want to know what *you* think."

I lean against the side of the building. "I think . . . what if. What if I do this and something goes wrong? What if something happens and it all goes belly up?" I've tried to develop a rhino's thick skin since Maggie, but I've got some tender spots still. "I don't want to get blindsided again."

"I hear you, man." He claps my shoulder. "But that's why you sign papers. You seal it airtight. No one is going to get blindsided when you lay out the terms. This isn't a relationship. It's a business deal."

I laugh. He works on Wall Street, so deal-making is his bread and butter.

"I signed a marriage license, too, and then my whole life was a lie. What if this is the next one?" I ask, since I'm a persistent bastard, too.

"This isn't the same thing. Besides," he says, nodding toward his daughter, who's waiting for the elevator, "look at my girl. I wouldn't have her if someone else—some scared fifteen-year-old girl from North Dakota—didn't give her up. She knew her girl would have a better life elsewhere, and she made that happen. Nicole's not asking you to pledge your life to her like Maggie did. What Nicole is asking is, honestly, a lot simpler. It has a beginning and an end. If you think about it, she's asking you to give her the same gift someone gave Paul and me."

And my heart threatens to melt. "You little shit," I tell him with a sneer. "When you say stuff like that, you make it almost impossible to say no."

"Maybe you don't want to say no."

I go home, and after I walk Romeo, toss balls to him in the park, and feed him the most delicious kibble in the universe, so rich in nutrients it makes his handsome brown-and-white Border Collie coat glow, I flop on my bed.

Romeo hops up and scoots besides me. I rub his head as I think about Nicole. I've known her since I started at Hanky Panky Love. She's always been my sexy co-worker, a fun woman. Now I'm seeing another side of her, one that's daring in a whole new way. To embark down this path, and to woman up enough to ask me to man up, is bold.

It's fucking hot, in fact. It takes guts to do what she did. It takes bravery. That's so damn sexy.

I drag a hand through my hair.

Jesus Christ, this woman has always been gorgeous, and now, she's even hotter. How is that possible? How the hell does asking me to jack off in a cup make her even sexier? But it does. Judging from my dick's imitation of an iron spike right now, I evidently find this new side of Nicole intensely hot.

Why the hell am I so goddamn turned on thinking about masturbating?

"What the fuck is wrong with me?" I mutter. Romeo licks my face. Okay, my hard-on deflates a bit. "Do I want to say no?" I ask my dog.

He rubs his nose against my shoulder.

"What would you do, buddy?"

He pants.

"Good answer."

He jumps off the bed, scampers to a corner where he herds his dog toys, and grabs a floppy giraffe. He vivisected the giraffe a week ago. Now it's a damaged stuffy with a neck and one leg. But he loves it, and holy shit, he loves it a lot. So much that he's jammed it between his legs and he's humping it.

Yup, that's my boy. He's screwing a mutilated giraffe stuffy.

"Get a room," I shout.

But he keeps going, thrusting and pumping.

I know the answer. I've known it since I left the diner. My brother's comments only bolstered what my heart had already decided. I needed the time to make sure I wasn't rushing into this decision.

Nicole is a brave, bold, beautiful woman who's unafraid to carve out a life on her own terms.

I admire the fuck out of that.

And I also want to fuck her.

Chapter Eleven

Nicole

Ever want something so badly it's like a hungry ache in your bones?

Yeah, me neither.

As I leave the subway and walk the few blocks to An Open Book, I try once more to read meaning into Ryder's text message as well as the location. We're meeting at a bookstore on the Upper West Side. What does that tell me? Is his answer a yes, a no, a maybe? Please let it not be maybe. I can't bear this in-between state much longer. I'm a woman who craves answers.

I tug my light blue scarf around my neck. There's a cool breeze in the air. My black boots clack against the sidewalk, the rhythmic sound like a metronome, keeping time with my anticipation. I turn the corner, narrowly avoiding a couple with their arms draped around each other. The sandy-haired man peppers kisses on the cheek of the pixie woman by his side. She seems to swoon, her eyes falling briefly shut. I look away. That kind of love is not in my future, and I'm so incredibly fine with that. But I pray that another form of love will be.

As I near the shop, the warm glow of the An Open Book sign dangling above the purple doorframe feels like an invitation. I look up at the night sky and make a wish. *Inside this little independent bookshop is the man who is going to give me my heart's desire.*

Yanking open the door, I head inside. I stride to the small cafe where Ryder said he'd wait for me.

My chest falls. The man is known for punctuality. I scan the white bakery case and the five round iron tables, but he's not here. When I spin around and survey the bookshelves, my heart nearly leaps from my chest.

He's in the . . .

Oh my fucking God, he's waiting for me in the . . .

I bring my hand to my mouth, and I want to run, to leap into his arms. When he sees me, his blue eyes twinkle with mischief.

I am a teapot about to whistle. I am a dog dancing before dinnertime.

He taps the shelves and holds up a book.

A pregnancy guide.

He's ten feet from me. But I sprint anyway, and I grin like a fool. I stop two inches from him and clamp my hands on his broad shoulders. "Is that a yes?"

"Yes—"

I tackle-hug him before he can say anything more. I knock the breath from him in an *oomph* as I rope my arms around his neck and crash into him.

"But I have one condition," he says, embracing me back.

I'm crying tears of happiness, so I don't care. "Anything. Name it."

"You better hear it before you agree."

The moment screeches to a halt. He's going to want visitation rights. He'll want lots of money. He'll want summers, or weekends, or evenings out.

I unwrap myself from the warmth of his strong chest and swallow. "What's your condition?"

"I thought it would be best to present it in the form of a column."

"A column?"

"Top five list and everything."

I groan inside. He has five conditions? Maybe my mother was right. Maybe asking for baby-mix from someone you know is a big mistake. Anonymous donors request nothing but greenbacks.

I steel myself as he fishes in the back pocket of his jeans. The paper is square, folded in quarters. He hands it to me. "Open it."

I unfold it then read the headline out loud. "'Top Five Positions for Getting a Woman Pregnant'?"

I blink and stare at him. The cogs turn slowly in my brain. I part my lips to speak.

He raises a hand to silence me. "Hear me out. You explained how it worked. The room, the cup, the magazines, the videos. The whacking off in a fucking public place. The cost. But most of all . . . the wait. You'd have to wait for an appointment for me, for the testing, for the jerking off, then for your special date with the turkey baster." He cups my cheek. His hand is big and warm. "What if we did it the old-fashioned way?"

I draw a deep breath, letting the air fill my cells as I process his question. I'm not sure what to make of this change-up. I didn't prep for this option.

Quickly, I weigh the pros and cons of this unexpected offer to take a ride on his baby-making train. On the one hand, I'm asking him to give me a baby. A *person*. The least I can do is make it easier for him, right? A clinical exam room has to be up there on the list of unpleasant places to get off. Surely, I wouldn't want to paddle the pink canoe on a doctor's table.

On the other hand, sleeping with a friend and a coworker is a recipe that calls for just the right mix of ingredients. Add too much of a spice, and it tastes awful. Bake too long and it burns. Would we be able to manage all the complications of working together and screwing at the same time?

My mind latches onto the prospect of . . . *screwing Ryder Lockhart.*

Having sex with the most handsome man I know.

Getting horizontal with this gorgeous, witty, generous man who's willing to give me a piece of himself.

My stomach has the audacity to swoop.

My skin prickles as my mind fills with images. Undressing him. Undoing his zipper. Guiding him inside me. I lick my lips. My nipples tighten.

Oh dear Lord in Heaven.

It sounds dangerous and divine.

Truth be told, it sounds like a faster route from A to B, too.

And it's also eons easier than the other way. This is the

way it's done. He's asking to make my life simpler and to give me my greatest dream.

All I have to do is get naked for him and spread my legs.

Why on earth am I weighing pros and cons? This is all pro.

"You think we could pull this off?" I ask. "Working together and taking baby-making to the next level?"

He scoffs as if it's incredulous that we *couldn't* do that. "You and me—we're pros. Who else can approach sex from such a practical angle?"

"And this is the practical way to achieve a goal?"

He shrugs playfully. "Practical and more pleasurable. Besides, we're mature adults, and this is a quicker and better solution." He takes a beat and pins my gaze. "Unless you don't think we'd have fun in bed . . ."

I swallow and quickly dispel that notion. "Oh no. That's not a worry at all. I'm sure it would be fun."

He lifts a hand and fingers the end of my hair. "What do you think? Still think I'm a good guy?"

The swoop revisits my belly when he touches me. I nibble on the corner of my lip and fiddle with his collar. "Want to know what I'm thinking?" I ask, coy and flirty.

"That I now win the weirdest thing someone has asked you?"

"Would it be weird? Sex with you?"

"Do you like it weird?"

"I like it hard. I like it good. And I like it a lot."

A groan echoes in his throat.

I tap-dance my fingers down his chest. "And I think I'm going to find out if you're as good in bed as I've always thought you might be."

"You've thought about me in bed?" he asks in that deep sexy voice, and oh, how this moment has shifted from baby planning to something dirty and delicious. Something I didn't expect to happen tonight. But my body likes his plan, since it's getting hot and bothered.

"I might have let my mind wander from time to time," I admit.

Dropping a hand to my hip, he yanks me close. "What do you say we test out how it's going to be with a kiss?"

"We get to kiss, too?" I tease.

"Woman, I'm not just going to fuck you. There's going to be kissing and fucking. Fucking and kissing. And coming."

That swoop in my chest settles between my legs now, like a pulse beating.

He bends his face to mine, and he dusts his lips to my forehead.

I shiver.

He presses a soft kiss to one eyelid then the other.

I tremble.

Then he rains kisses down my face, my cheeks, my jaw. Kisses that make me feel as if we're under a streetlamp, the roads slick from an earlier rain.

My lips part, and he seals his mouth to mine.

It's like that kiss on the silver screen when time stops. His lips are all I know. The world is this slow and gentle slide. The wet delicious taste. The feel of this man's mouth pressed to mine for the first time.

Strangely, or perhaps not so strangely at all, I'm barely thinking of babies.

I'm thinking of bodies. Of my own, and how it reacts to being so close to his.

The hair on my arms stands on end as he kisses me with more softness than I ever expected. He's tender and gentle —this is how you take a woman into your arms after you've told her you'll help her dreams come true. You give her a kiss that makes her feel like starlight.

I sigh, sinking into it, savoring every wondrous second of his lips on mine. I'm not sure I've been kissed like this in ages. This kiss is a luxury. We are living in a slow torch song.

Lips glide. Tongues touch. Breath mingles.

He tastes like spearmint, clean and sexy, and I absolutely love that combination in a man.

He groans against my mouth. That sound, carnal and masculine, lights me up.

He slides his hand up the back of my neck, and I wobble the slightest bit. He steadies me with a hand on my hip. His fingers resume their path, climbing upward. He ropes his hands in my hair, and he tastes me more deeply. More insistent.

I let out a little moan when he nips my lips, and then our slow, deep, wet kiss shifts. It becomes a little harder, a bit faster, a lot closer. I might be panting when we stop.

He is, too. "Did I pass the kiss test?"

I blink, trying to reconnect my brain to my mouth. Fortunately, that's one of my talents. So is remembering my half of this deal, which seems like small potatoes. But he needs those potatoes, and I'm going to serve them up however he wants. Mashed, fried, roasted, grilled. "You passed with flying colors. We're going to work through your list of top ten dates, and I'm going to make damn sure you have the best time of your life. Because it's anywhere, anytime, and any position with me."

His smile is wide and wicked. "You're going to make this the best work project ever."

"I think I'm going to like this project, too." I shift gears, my organizational side taking over and kicking into full gear. "Speaking of, I should be entering the ovulation zone in a few more days. I've been charting so I have a good idea of when it should be. Want to get started on a plan for those top five positions and the ten dates?

"How long does ovulation last?"

"They say it can be right in the middle of your cycle. Personally, I don't want to miss a shot, so I think it's best if we try for the five days on either side."

"Ten days in a row." He smirks. "I believe I'm amenable to that."

We grab a seat in the café, and I open my calendar app. We pick a day to start, and I pencil in a few dates for him. I point to a week at the end of the month when I'll be out of town, doing my show on the road. "But at least I'll be at the end of my cycle then," I say, then I meet his eyes. "Will that work out for your dating guide, though, if we miss a week?"

Ryder nods. "Cal sees this as a project that'll last several weeks, so that sounds good to me."

When we leave, I'm still giddy, and something occurs to me.

That wasn't a regular wobble a little while ago when he kissed me. He made me weak in the knees.

But surely that's because he's going to give me a baby. I'm only swooning for the baby.

Chapter Twelve

Ryder

We fly through the air with the greatest of ease.

Nicole might have been a bird in a past life because she takes to the trapeze as if she has wings, or circus performer blood in her.

She's strapped in with a harness contraption and swinging upside down, her knees hooked over the bar.

A September breeze zips through the air at Hudson River Park in lower Manhattan, home of Trapeze School New York. In the quest to find ever more interesting activities for dates and life, the city is home to trapeze lessons, rock climbing, indoor golf, trampolining, and more. God forbid we ever be bored in Manhattan. Rest assured I'm not.

When Nicole finishes her swing, the instructor helps her regain her footing on the platform. The look on her face is pure exhilaration. She's breathless, her cheeks are flushed crimson, and her red hair is wild.

"Oh my God, that was amazing!" She swats my arm. "I want to see you do that upside down."

I scoff. "Piece of cake."

She rolls her eyes. "Oh yeah?"

"I used to cover scary-as-hell wide receivers."

She laughs. "I love that you're actually trying to equate college football with flying like a squirrel."

"Squirrels are pretty amazing. So are strapping safeties."

She shakes her head, amused.

Callie, the pipsqueak instructor with the high blond ponytail, chimes in, talking to Nicole. "You're very natural on the trapeze. I can't believe you've never done anything like this."

"I'm naturally daring," Nicole says with a wink.

Truer words.

"That is the best trait," Callie says, then she regards me. "Do you want to try catching her? I hear you were some kind of superstar safety."

Nicole's mouth turns to an *O*. "Whoa. She's calling you out."

"I was on defense. We didn't catch that often."

"Surely you caught interceptions?" Nicole asks, lifting her chin, challenging me.

I scrub a hand over my jaw, gesture widely to the acrobatic setup, then back at my pseudo date. "So you're daring me to catch you?"

She gives me a tough-girl bring-it-on look, going gangster with her hands. "You're afraid to catch me?"

I toss my head back and laugh. "Woman, you have no idea." I cup her cheek and give her my best smolder. "I'm going to catch you so fucking good."

Her laughter ceases, and she drops her voice. "How the hell did you just turn that into some kind of come-on line?"

Callie is fixated on her sneakers.

"It's my special talent." I bring my mouth to her ear. "Plus, I think you might have nothing but sex on the brain."

She gasps. "How could you say such a thing?" Her voice drips with mock shock.

"Admit it. All you're thinking about is stripping me down to nothing."

Callie shuffles farther away from us. Smart girl.

"Why would you ever think that all I want is your . . ." Nicole pauses, slides her lips up my neck, and whispers, "*cock*."

One word from her red lips and my dick responds as it fucking should. I yank her closer so she knows. "I have no idea where I got the idea that you were into me for my body only," I tease.

A murmur falls from her lips when she presses against my erection. "I'm into your body for so many reasons, Ryder."

I nip on her earlobe. "My date is counting down the hours till she can get me naked."

"By my estimates, I think that in about sixty minutes, I can get these pesky pants off you," she says, running a hand down the fabric of my workout pants. That's what the trapeze lessons call for—exercise clothes.

I sigh heavily as if I'm dejected. "I'm nothing but a sex object to you."

A throat clears.

"Oops," Nicole whispers to me. "Guess we're too dirty." She raises her voice. "Sorry, Callie. He's going to try to knock me up later tonight. We might be a little frisky sometimes."

Callie's expression morphs instantly from embarrassed annoyance to sheer joy. "That's so exciting! I love babies. You two are going to have such beautiful babies." Then worry seems to strike her. She steps closer to Nicole and clasps a hand around her arm. "Is there a chance you're pregnant now? Because you shouldn't be flying."

Nicole waves off the concern. We planned the trapeze date for our first one for just that reason. Get all the bouncing, flying, falling, and jumping out of the way before Nicole might be in the family way.

"Nope," Nicole says to the instructor. "We're starting tonight. This is our foreplay. Can you tell?"

Callie sighs with relief. "The last minute might have been a tip-off." She gestures to the swings. "Are you ready?"

"We're ready to behave now," I say, my tone deadly serious.

I climb down the ladder and walk to the other side of the net. God bless the huge net. The only way newbies like us could fly through the air is with the cushiest, safest, biggest net below us. As well as waivers. Lots and lots of waivers. And tons of harnesses. You can't really get hurt here unless you try hard.

As I reach the top of the opposite platform, Callie's counterpart on this side gives me a quick hello. His name is Mitch, and he has a camp-counselor brightness to him. Once I'm attached to the harness, I chalk up my hands.

"Are you having a good time?" Mitch asks with a big smile.

"A great time."

"Best date ever?"

Briefly, I think of Maggie and our dates. My ex was outdoorsy, but not daring. She liked to head out of the city and hike in the woods. Since we loved movies, we spent many nights at the cinema. But trapeze was never in the cards, nor trampoline, nor rock climbing. I haven't taken anyone here since my divorce, either. Honestly, I haven't dated much since the split, and I wouldn't be here if Cal hadn't said my ass was on the line.

I swing my gaze to Nicole, more than a hundred feet away. "Definitely a great first date," I tell Mitch.

He gives me a toothy grin. "All right. You'll need to hop on then go upside down."

Once I grab hold of the bar, Mitch barks, "Safe to go."

I step off the platform and whoosh. I'm fucking flying. It's as thrilling as it was the first time I did it tonight.

"Feet up," he calls out as the swing arcs. I lift my feet up and hook them over the bar, and then Mitch calls out, "Arms free."

I drop my arms below me, hanging on with my legs. This is like the loop on a whip-fast rollercoaster. Everything is a fast rush as the world flips into a topsy-turvy blur.

Callie shouts instructions at Nicole, who swings at me.

"Let her build up speed," Mitch yells.

I give a thumbs-up as I arc closer.

From my vantage point, speeding upside down, I don't take my eyes off my date. Nicole moves like a monkey, and in mere seconds, she's switching from hanging by her hands on the bar to holding steady with her feet hooked over it.

"Hands catch," the instructors shout in their shorthand as Nicole soars to me, her red hair in a long ponytail below her, her arms reaching for me. I stretch out my arms, hands ready. Closer, closer, and here she is.

For a brief moment, nerves spike inside me. But I shove aside hair-raising images of what could go wrong, and do what I have to do. I grab hold of her hands, and she takes mine.

Her neon laughter lights up the sky as she calls out, "Yes, oh my God!"

I've caught her, and I'm the only thing between her and the net. I grip her tight as she swings once beneath me, then she lets go, dropping to the net, the harness giving her a bouncy, soft landing.

It's not the first time tonight I hope to hear her say *oh my God*.

* * *

"A-may-zing," she says as we pile into our waiting Lyft ride outside the trapeze school.

"I'm sure Cal will be pleased that his first idea for this crazy assignment turned out to be a good time."

"I didn't just have a good time," she says, shaking her head as I pull the door shut.

I arch a brow, curious. "No?"

"I had the *best* time," she corrects. "And you can take that to the bank. Let all your listeners and readers know that trapeze lessons are a big win."

Maybe I won't get canned. I breathe a sigh of relief as the driver heads uptown. "Tell me why you liked it so much. What makes it a great date for the woman?"

She tilts her head, considering. "It's different from the usual, you know?" Her eyes are serious. "And different is good. It gets you out of your comfort zone."

"Out of the coffee, dinner, dates, this-is-so-fucking-boring-sometimes zone?"

"Exactly. You have to trust someone to do something like this. Sure, we have harnesses, but going for a trapeze lesson says the man is willing to put himself in an unusual position. After all, you were upside down."

"It was definitely a new vantage point."

Her eyes grow more animated. "And see, I think that helps two people connect. It helps for the woman to see the man can be strong but vulnerable."

I nod as I take in her assessment. It makes a hell of a lot of sense. "Damn, you're brilliant. That's exactly what Cal wants me to talk about in my"—I stop to sketch air quotes to show what I think of Cal's plans—"*dating guide*."

But Nicole doesn't let it go. Her eyes pin me with an intense look. "But did *you* feel that way, Ryder? I loved it, and it felt freeing. Did you feel like it would be a good first date for a man trying to romance a woman?"

Romance. I shudder at that word and all its implications. I romanced Maggie like I was a fucking hero in a novel, pulling out all the stops, sending her not only the lilies she adored, but her favorite artisanal butter for the pastries she made. We kissed at the fountain at Lincoln Center after a ballet she wanted to see; we strolled through the farmers' market in Union Square hand in hand as she shopped. I rolled out the red carpet for her, and she loved it all, and that's why it was so fun to treat her that way.

In return, she treated me like gum on the bottom of her shoe.

I could answer Nicole with starkness and say, *I don't really care anymore about romancing a woman.*

But she deserves more than that. "For most men, yes, I suspect it would be a great start to romance. And for me, I had a hell of a good time with you."

Nicole doesn't balk at my honest assessment. Instead, she nudges me with her elbow. "Good thing we can be so scientific about this, right?"

I laugh, relieved that we don't have to tread more seriously on this topic. I adopt my radio announcer voice. "Gentlemen, tonight we conducted a highly scientific study of dates in New York City, and we've concluded that the flying trapeze is an excellent jumpstart to romance."

Nicole jumps in. "If you play your cards right, by the end of the evening her heart will be topsy-turvy for you. You might even land a first kiss." She winks at me and whispers, "But I'm pretty confident you're a sure thing."

That's because the sex is guaranteed in ink. It's sex with a contract, outlined in legalese. The last week has been consumed by paperwork for our arrangement. First, I showed her my health records—a clean bill of health and no STDs. Same for her. Then, the more formal agreement. My lawyer checked the contract for me. It's everything Nicole proposed. Sex for the sole purpose of procreation. If she conceives, I owe her nothing. That's the bottom line. No expectations. No future payments. In return, I won't ask for anything, either. No parental rights. Nothing at all.

Fine with me.

At its heart, it's a beautiful sort of deal, one that says neither party expects a damn thing. I run a hand through her hair. "Fuck that romance shit. I want you in bed, woman."

Her eyes blaze with heat. "And that's exactly where I want to be."

I love that she's down to fuck. And I fucking love that we're not playing games. There's something incredibly freeing about this kind of relationship. Maybe this is the way it should be—clear and easy.

But once we reach her place in the East 80s, all that easy, breezy, sexy confidence slips away.

Chapter Thirteen

Nicole

Dogs are a woman's best friend.

They're also buzz killers since I need to tend to my doggy before we get into doggy-style.

Ruby jumps up and down when I unlock the door. She whimpers her excitement at seeing her mistress. She swings her gaze at Ryder and unleashes an accusatory bark at the unknown man.

Who the hell are you?

"Shh. He's a friend," I tell her and instantly she settles down.

"Hey girl," he says, in that sweet but firm voice that dog people know how to use. "You're gorgeous."

My heart goes pitter-patter over the compliment.

"She says thank you," I translate, though it's readily apparent Ruby likes the praise, seeing as how she's waggling her butt. "She's shameless. She falls lickety split."

Ryder shrugs. "Not a bad trait." He quickly adds, like he needs to correct himself, "In a dog."

He rubs her chin, and Ruby's sold. For a second, it hits me how odd it is that they haven't met yet. Despite our work companionship, there's never been a need for him to be here.

Now there is, and it's business time.

But first, I need to take Ruby for a quick walk around the block so she can attend to her business. Ryder joins me, grabbing a dog bag from the stash I keep in an open jar by my door. Dog people get dog people.

"Where's your boy right now? Waiting patiently by the door for you?"

"Romeo's at the neighbor's," he tells me as we head down the stairs and out to my quiet block. "There's a sweet lady who lives upstairs from me. She's been in my building forever, and I mean forever. Rent-controlled and all that jazz. Her niece lives with her and walks dogs, so they have Romeo right now. I booked her because I wasn't sure how long we'd be tonight."

"Hopefully we will . . ." But then I'm not sure what to say. Are we hoping it'll be long or short? Does he want to get in and out with three Hail Marys so he can get home and walk the dog? We've been out for a few hours already. Furtively, I check the time. He probably needs to do the deed quickly.

I'll think dirty thoughts as soon as we finish the dog walk, so I can make it easy for him. I should be a fertile myrtle right now, so hopefully this whole shebang isn't too much of a time-suck for either of us. Women get knocked up on the first try all the time. My mother did. Why not me?

Soon, we return to my building and head to my floor. As I turn the key in the lock, a voice calls out to me. "Hey, Nicole!"

My shoulders tense as I hear my neighbor Frederick. I'm not entirely sure what he does for a living. All I know is he dresses like a hipster and is completely incapable of, well, anything. Last month, he asked to borrow Drano. A few months ago, he begged for baking soda and vinegar. Honestly, I don't want to know what he does in his place.

"Hi, Frederick."

"Hey there," Ryder says, with a quick lift of his chin.

"Hey, buddy," Frederick replies. Yeah, he's one of those guys. Everyone is *buddy*. Frederick strokes his beard and peers at us curiously over the edge of his glasses. He seems to remember something when he snaps his fingers. "Nicole. Any chance you have a plunger I can borrow?"

Oh Jesus.

"Did you ask the super?" I suggest.

"He's not around tonight."

This is when I wish I lived in a doorman building. "Sure. I'll get one for you," I say, thinking how incredibly unsexy this is.

"I'll get it," Ryder offers.

I shoot him the most deadly stare in the history of stares. Seriously. Because there is no way I am letting this sexy-assin man touch a plunger before he gets his hands on me. And it's not like the bathroom plunger has gotten action in ages. "I'll do it. You will not touch my plunger."

He presses his lips together to stifle a laugh, and I realize how weirdly dirty that sounded. "Your plunger," he says with a chuckle.

I open the door, unleash Ruby, scurry to the bathroom, grab the plunger, and take it to Frederick.

"You're a godsend," he tells me, holding up the plunger with the stick end as if I've handed him the Olympic torch. "I'll get this back to you in a jiffy."

I scoff and wag a finger. "No. No, you will not. You will not knock on my door tonight to return a plunger. What you will do is buy me a new one tomorrow. Good night."

I open my door, and Ryder follows me in, laughing. "That was fucking beautiful. Also, what kind of man doesn't have his own plunger?"

I point a thumb in my neighbor's direction. "That kind of man," I say, shaking my head as I head to the kitchen to wash my hands. For a full minute. I give them a surgeon-level scrub.

When I'm done, I turn to see the most gorgeous man leaning in the doorway of my kitchen.

Dear Lord, he's beautiful, and I'm so not in the mood.

From the dog to the neighbor to the plunger. But I need to get it up, so to speak.

"Hey there," he says, softly. Maybe he senses the shift. Duh. Of course he does. He's not stupid.

"Do you want a beer?" I ask.

"A beer sounds great."

I open the fridge and grab one for him. I spin around to yank open the drawer with the bottle opener and I whack my elbow on the edge of the counter. "Ouch."

It stings.

It radiates though my entire body. Gingerly, I cup my elbow with my other hand. In no time at all Ryder slides past me, opens the freezer, and finds an ice pack.

"It's not that bad," I say, like the tough girl I am. "I swear."

But he doesn't listen. He shushes me and presses the ice to my elbow. Great. Now I'm cold, annoyed, hurting, and still not turned on. Fuck my life. I lower my eyes because I just can't even stand myself right now.

"My elbow's fine now. Thanks."

He sets the ice pack on the counter, tucks a finger under my chin, and raises my face. I meet his blue-eyed gaze. His eyes are so kind and so sexy at the same time. How is it possible? I'm going to need to gather all the scientists of the world to study this man. He drips sex appeal and goodness simultaneously. But then, there's a distance to him, too. His armor never seems far away.

"You okay?"

I nod.

He runs a hand over my hair. His touch is gentle. He looks back into my living room. It's lush and pretty with a cranberry-red couch strewn with gold and silver pillows. Framed photos line the end tables. On the wall is a photograph of a rain-slicked street in Paris. Candles adorn the coffee table. I even have mood music ready to go on my playlist.

"I wanted tonight to be sexy," I say, gesturing hopelessly to the living room. "I had a whole playlist of Sade songs on my phone."

His lips quirk in a grin. "We don't need that to be sexy."

His words should send a spark through me.

But they don't.

My heart beats too fast. It's a nervous rhythm. "I don't feel sexy. I feel clinical and weird," I admit.

He nods. "It's okay to feel a little awkward."

A new fear digs in. "Do you, too? I mean, it's fine for me to feel weird. My pleasure doesn't matter. I need you to feel good."

"I didn't mean it like that. I meant I understand. This whole thing is . . . unusual," he says.

"I don't want you to feel weird. I want you to enjoy yourself."

"Funny," he says, running the backs of his fingers over my cheek, a soft, but wholly possessive move. "Because I want you to enjoy yourself just as much."

He grabs his beer, takes my hand, and leads me to the living room. Ruby trots by his side and plops down on the carpet as we sink into the red couch. He takes a drink of his beer. I take off my light jacket.

It all feels so formal.

"Ugh," I say, then drop my face to my hands.

I should punch myself for how I'm behaving. I'm a take-charge woman. For fuck's sake, I asked this man to knock me up, and he's willing to do it. I don't get to behave like a brat.

In an instant, I know what to do.

I lean into him, inhaling his cedar scent as I dust a sexy kiss against his neck, since I've already learned this spot drives him crazy. I'm rewarded with a rush of air from his lips. Straddling him, I plant my hands on his shoulders.

He wiggles his eyebrows. "So this is how it's going to be?"

"Yes, this is how it's going to be." I tell myself to erase the last awkward minutes, and I crush his lips to mine. He groans against my mouth, a low, dirty rumble of desire.

I'm going to kiss my way out of the weirdness. I'm going to devour his gorgeous lips and rub my cheeks all over that sandpaper stubble. I'm going to trace the outlines of his sculpted cheekbones, and I'll grind against his lap until he's hot and bothered.

I kiss him hard, turning the volume to high. I slide my fingers into hair that's so damn soft, and I curl my hands around his head.

I crush his lips.

I own this kiss.

I want this man turned on.

I want him hard.

I want him ready.

And I need his swimmers to be in a good mood.

Judging from the heavy press of his erection against my thigh, his dick is whistling a happy tune. But that's not enough. I want his mind blown, and his cock nearly there, too.

I scoot off him.

"What are you doing?" he asks, his breath uneven from our kiss.

"I'm doing this." I get down on my knees and tug at his workout pants. "I want these off. I want to kiss your cock."

"Fuck," he groans as he drags a hand down his face and lifts his hips. "You dirty girl."

I tug down his pants, then his boxer briefs, and then I die. I die a million wonderful deaths. His dick is beautiful. It's so fucking gorgeous my mouth waters. It's long and thick and curved a tiny bit to the right. It's veiny and proud, and I must taste him.

I bend my face to him and lick the head.

"Fuck me," he mutters.

He slouches back into the couch, his long legs spread open. I draw him into my mouth. He's a little salty and so fucking manly. Maybe that sounds obvious. He should taste like a man. But he does, and it drives me wild.

I wrap a hand around the base and stroke him as I draw him deeper.

"Jesus, that's good," he groans.

I glance up at him, and his eyes are closed. He breathes out hard, and the look on his face is gorgeous. In seconds, I've changed the mood from sober to completely intoxicating, and the turnabout is working on me, too. As I suck, I get lost in the rhythm, in the taste, in the feel.

His hands find their way into my hair. He threads them through my strands and guides my head. "You're killing me," he mutters as I relax my throat and let him fill me all the way.

I slink a hand between his legs, cupping his balls, and his whole body jerks. I'm ready, so ready for him. And that's not just because we timed this first date to the middle of my cycle. I'm so turned on I nearly forget I can't finish him off like this.

"One more suck, baby, and then you need to stop," he says, his voice a warning.

I make it count. I swirl my tongue over the head, then I lick him as I take him all the way in once more. A drop of liquid from the tip slips over my lips, and I nearly lose my mind.

He yanks me off him, pulls me up by my face, and stares at me hungrily. His blue eyes darken. He looks like he wants to devour me.

Chapter Fourteen

Ryder

Clothes fly to the floor.

As she sends the dog to her dog bed in the corner, Nicole yanks off my shirt, her hands traveling over my pecs. I tug off her black V-neck shirt. I'm ready to rip the rest of her clothes to shreds, but when I see the black lacy bra, my mind tunnels to complete one-track-ness.

Must get her tits in my mouth.

Nicole is a busty woman.

It's hard not to notice. I've noticed, and now I get to play. I unhook her bra and let it fall to the floor, and then I breathe out an appreciative groan over these fucking marvelous tits.

"I could spend the night here," I tell her, cupping them. Each one fills a palm, and I have big hands. Though I'd have been content with small ones, I can't help but want to get well acquainted with these full-size beauties.

I pinch her nipples, and she lets out a sexy yelp. I flip her onto her back on the couch, yanking her so she's lying flat. I climb over her, straddle her, and bring my mouth to one delicious breast. I flick my tongue over her nipple, feeling it go hard in my mouth.

"Oh God," she mutters.

Somewhere in the back of my mind, I'm vaguely aware that there's no awkwardness. It's vanished. This is pure lust. This is fire. Whatever weirdness existed a few moments ago has left the house. I want her and she wants me. I don't have the interest to dissect whether it's because she wants my cock buried deep inside her so I can give her my DNA, or if it's just because she wants my cock buried deep inside her.

Right now, they feel like one and the same.

I reach for her yoga pants and shove them off. My hand slides between her thighs and somehow my dick grows even harder when I touch her panties.

She's soaked.

I pull off her last stitch of clothing, and I groan when I see the auburn landing strip.

"So fucking beautiful," I say, then slide a finger down the hair and across her dampness.

She moans something incoherent as I play with her sweet pussy. She arches into my fingers. I want to toy with her, to make her moan and groan and savor every second. I spread her legs and start to make my way downtown. I'm dying to taste her. But the second my head goes below her waist she grapples at my shoulders.

"Ryder," she pleads.

I look up. Her blue eyes are desperate.

"Please fuck me," she begs.

With a wicked smile, I drop my face to the paradise between her legs and kiss her softly. At that first touch, she cries out so loudly that I know, I fucking know, I will have a field day eating her out.

She tries to push me away at the same time as she rocks her hips against my mouth. She's all slick and hot, and wetter than anything.

"Please. I'm begging you," she says, trying again while she thrusts against my lips.

The sexy woman wants my lips and she wants my cock. I flick my tongue against her hard clit, and she keens. It's like a howl, and her dog gets up and heads over.

"Shh, Ruby. Back to your bed."

Obedient girl. She does as she's told.

I lick Nicole again, and I could spend the night here, my face between her sexy thighs, her sweetness all over my jaw. But when I kiss her again, she grabs my hair, pulls me close for one more luxurious devouring of her wetness, then pushes me away. She stares at me, her mouth open, panting. "Please. I don't care if I'm begging. I need you inside me."

I'm not so cruel that I can deny her any longer. I'm also so turned on that what she wants is precisely what my dick wants, too.

"Reporting for duty," I say, rising to my knees. My cock is pointing in her direction, and a sexy smile spreads on her face.

She stares greedily at my shaft. "You're more than ready."

"Get on your hands and knees, then. You want a baby, Nicole? You need it deep, and that's how you're going to get it." I flip her over, raise up her lovely ass, and run my palms over the soft flesh. "I want to bite this ass. I want to bite it and spank it, and do unspeakable things to your ass."

She lifts that fine ass higher.

"Guess you like that idea," I tell her as I swat my palm against her backside, giving her a small teaser.

She yelps, and I spank her once more then drag my finger through her pussy. She's even wetter.

And I get to feel all this slickness on my dick. I get to fuck her bare. That's one of the best parts of this deal. "Have I mentioned how great it is not to wear a condom?" I notch the head of my cock between her legs and admire the long, gorgeous line of her back, the way her red hair spills down her spine, and how she's ready. So fucking ready, in the number-one position for getting the job done that I've been asked to do.

I bury myself inside her.

"Oh fuck," I mutter as I fill her easily. I take a second or two to breathe in hard and savor the way we fit. Her pussy grips my cock, and it's electric. My entire body vibrates with lust. I pull back then slide all the way inside again. She moans.

"You like it, baby? It feels good?"

She nods, her head sinking lower into a gold pillow at the edge of her couch. "Soooo good."

"I want it good for you. This isn't just about me coming, you know that?"

She mumbles something unintelligible. Maybe it's a yes. I can't tell. But whether she wants to come or not, I won't fire without her. Sex is a two-person operation, and I would never send a woman home unsatisfied. There's no way on earth I'm going to be the only one getting off, even if that's the end game.

I grip her hip hard in one hand and slide my other to her belly then down between her thighs.

She murmurs a sexy, drawn-out *oh*.

This woman. She's going to be so fun to play like a violin. Her body is soft and supple, and she's so goddamn aroused. I tease at the delicious rise of her clit as I rock into her. In the back of my mind I'm aware that I've got a job to do, that in fact I have *one fucking job*, but I want this for exactly what it is.

I want to be fucking her.

I want to be buried deep inside her.

I want to be right where I am.

I swivel my hips and punch into her. Her hands curl into fists in the pillows. I rub her clit faster as I shove deep inside. The sounds she makes tell me she'll be blasting off soon.

Pressing a palm on her back, I slope her further. "Nice and deep, baby."

When I fill her like that, she cries out. I fucking love that she's so far gone. Her pleasure matters to me. I want it as much as I want to give her mine.

A bead of sweat slicks down my chest. I ease out so only the tip is in, and I pause there as if I'm holding her in suspended animation while I work her lovely, hungry, eager clit with my finger. She trembles under me. The shudder moves through her body, and I'm as sure as I've ever been of anything that she's galloping to the edge.

"Want to feel you come on my cock," I rasp out as I sink all the way into her, and she shatters. Her knuckles go white as she grips the pillow, and her voice hits some kind of high note that I'm certain her dickhead neighbor can hear, but I don't care because she's coming all over me, and it's fucking glorious.

It's the earthquake.

In seconds, I've got both hands on her hips, and I fuck her hard and furiously as my own orgasm rattles free, rocketing through my body. "Coming so fucking hard."

And the sound she makes then, I swear it's like a shout of joy.

But I can barely tell because my pulse thunders and pleasure consumes every molecule of my body as I climax inside her.

Where she wants.

I'm sweating, she's sweating, and now her dog is howling, too, crying out in unison with the two of us.

And I crack up. She's got one of those. An orgasm chorus dog.

After I pull out, my first instinct is to look for the condom and toss it. I chuckle when I realize—no shit—I'm bareback and supposed to be.

Nicole is still on her stomach. Her face is pressed to the side. Her eyes are glossy and her cheeks are flushed. I've killed her with her orgasm.

"Hey," I say gently, nudging her shoulder. "You need to get on your back and lie flat for a few minutes, okay?"

She smiles woozily. "That's the second position from your top five."

"It is. It'll help give you a better chance." I roll her over and the look on her face is such dreamy happiness that it does something funny to me. It makes me bend down and kiss her tenderly on her forehead. "I hope it worked."

"Me, too."

"Do you know it increases the chances a little bit more since you came?"

"I think I read that somewhere, too."

"I did a little reading myself this week. Supposedly, it helps the swimmers reach their destination. That's all well and good, but I'm just a big fan of you coming."

She offers another sexy smile.

I adjust her, slide a pillow under her ass, elevating her. I hand her a tissue, and I head in the direction of her bathroom to clean up.

When I return, I join her on the couch, because I don't want to leave just yet.

But soon enough, I know there won't be a reason to stay.

My job for tonight is done.

Chapter Fifteen

Top Five Signs You're Ridiculously Attracted to Someone You Work With

By Nicole Powers

1. You admire his ass when you see him in the hall.

2. His sexy, flirty smile sends tingles all over you.

3. You look for excuses to walk past his office.

4. You linger in the break room when he's there.

5. You ask him to bang you in any position, anytime, anywhere.

All clear?

Fine, I'll elaborate, if you insist. Ever been in a situation where you have a super handsome co-worker? We're talking Clark Kent cheekbones, see-inside-my-soul blue eyes, and a world-class athletic body. Maybe he's also bursting with charm, wit, and sex appeal. We are talking the real deal, the full enchilada, the whole shebang.

Somehow, you've worked with this level of handsomeness without turning into a swoony puddle every day. That's because you're a grown-ass woman and you're able to separate your admiration of his attributes from attraction. After all, you can admire a Monet and not want to bang it.

But then, all of a sudden, you want to hump *Water Lilies*. How did this shift occur? Allow me to walk you through the turning points on the path to full-blown attraction.

1. It starts with a new way of seeing someone.

Perhaps you've played together on a co-ed softball team. Maybe you have regular lunches at your favorite deli, the one with the amazing Chinese chicken salad. Or you've simply exchanged banter in the elevator. Then, one day, you ask him for a favor. Could be big. Could be small. You might need him to move furniture for you, lift a vase onto the highest shelf, or deal with the spider on your wall. Possibly, the favor is much bigger. Regardless of whether you ask him to hand you a ream of paper or to give you a kidney, the dynamic shifts. You see him in a new way.

2. Your mind opens to possibilities.

You notice things you never saw before. You give yourself permission to imagine. What would it be like if he touches me here? If he kisses me there? If he strips me to nothing and has his wicked way with me? The possibilities of those *what ifs* parade before you in your daydreams. Soon, all that wondering changes the state of play.

3. The first kiss lights up the night.

Well, duh.

I have no patience for boring kisses. Merely adequate lip-locks can suck it. Kissing should be starlight and fireworks. A first kiss should be butterflies in your belly, wobbles in your knees.

You should feel it everywhere. In your bones. In your eyelashes. In your fingertips.

Yes, I'll admit that some kisses are like wine and improve with age. But no kiss has ever gone from dull to bowl-me-over. Don't settle for ordinary kisses.

Kisses are the sustenance of love. They will feed you.

4. When you take it to the next level, and you are hot to trot.

The kisses rocket from a slow slide of lips to an absolute devouring. Your libido takes the wheel. When you do the deed, you get so lost in the moment that you're telling him how turned on you are, how good it is, how much you want that brass ring.

When he gives it to you, you don't care that the neighbors can surely hear your cries, and you don't care if the people in the apartment across the street hear, too.

Briefly, you wonder how it got to this point. How you went from an admiring glance in the hallway to getting on your hands and knees and begging him. Then, you stop wondering because . . .

5. You do it again and again and again, and it gets better.

Whoever this lucky bitch is, I'm jealous of her. But we can all be her. Be bold. Ask for what you want. You never know —you just might get it.

You might get it really good.

Chapter Sixteen

Ryder

"I can't believe it's that easy. All you have to do is catch her, and then you drop her into the net?"

That's today's question from one of the callers to my show. As per Cal's request, the dating guide is getting the full treatment—columns as well as lots of radio time. "You got it, man. That's what you do. And let me tell you, she'll be wearing a big, happy smile," I say into the mic, picturing Nicole's face after our acrobatics, painted in pure exhilaration.

"Awesome," the caller says in a surfer-dude voice. I'm expecting him to say *I'm stoked* next. "And will this help her want to go to bed with me?"

"There are never any guarantees of that," I tell him. *Unless you sign a deal to knock up a woman.* I keep that tidbit to myself.

He huffs. "But that's what I want most. That's why I listen to your show. I want the best tips to get a woman into my bed, and I don't want to put out the dough for a trapeze lesson if there's no shot."

Mayday, mayday.

A geometric vision appears in front of me. Cal stalks the hallway, staring with beady, judgy eyes through the studio window. I make a wrap-it-up motion with my index finger to my producer, Jason, signaling to end this call. I'd end it regardless, but Cal makes me extra antsy. The leash he has on me is so short I can feel it choking already.

"You might want to find another show, then," I say to the surfer guy. "I can't promise you a woman will want to go home with you because of a trapeze lesson. What I can promise the listeners is if you take your time, plan a fun evening, and don't miss when you have to catch her, then you can have a great time with your woman. And doesn't that increase the chances that everyone has a happy ending to the date?"

Jason gives me a thumbs-up for that save, and I feel damn good about it, too.

The second the show ends, Cal shoves in the door. It smacks the wall. Today he is a beaker, bubbling over. "Do I need to remind you this is not a hookup show? More love. Less *get laid*."

I drag a hand through my hair and step away from the booth and into the hallway. The golden rule of broadcasting is this—don't say anything in a room full of mics that you wouldn't say on air. Doesn't matter if they're on or off.

"I turned the comment around to focus on the connection you can make with your date," I say like a badgered witness.

Jason pops his head into the doorway, pushing his glasses higher up the bridge of his nose. "I screened the call. The caller wasn't like that before the show, so it's on me."

Cal ignores Jason. The buck stops with me. Cal points at my face. "Then redirect him. That's your job."

"I did," I say, exasperated, then wave off Jason, sending him back to the studio. This is my battle to fight. "What more do you want me to do? The second the caller went down Randy Road, I sent him on his way and refocused the answer."

Cal sighs heavily as if acknowledging my point is a burden. "Yes, admittedly, you did." He claps his hand on my shoulder. It's not a friendly clap. "But this is the issue, Ryder. You're attracting this type of listener in the first place thanks to the attitude you've had for the last several months. The advertisers aren't marketing body spray. This is a show about love and intimacy. That is the company mission. We aren't trying to provide hookup tips, and our advertisers don't want to be associated with that sort of content. We have higher-end advertisers who want a show that reflects classier content."

"And I'm working on changing it," I say, trying to keep my cool.

"Work harder. Work faster."

"I said the trapeze was fun." I clench my fists tight at my sides. The more he breathes fire at me, the more I miss the olden days as the Consummate Wingman, when I set my own hours, focused on the clients, and worked on my own terms. I delivered the goods and didn't have to convince a boxed-in boss that I had his sponsors' best interests at heart.

"Yes, you did mention the fun," Cal concedes, then straightens his pastel pink tie. "But why not talk about how the trapeze and the catch and the acrobatics helped you and the woman connect? That's what our advertisers are backing; that's the content they want to support. Talk about the romance. Talk about how you got to know her better." He arches one salt-and-pepper brow. "Did you get to know her better?"

The question is pointed, inquisitive, and none of his fucking business.

And yet, it's precisely *his* business.

Literally, because I charged the trapeze lessons to my corporate card, and figuratively, because the success of these dates is the only thing between me and keeping my fucking job.

Images snap before my eyes—a half-empty exercise room, my book in the bargain bin at the bookstore, a phone that doesn't ring with client inquiries anymore. Good thing I socked plenty of royalties and fat paydays away in the bank, untouched by Maggie. Still, the cushion is thinning.

"Did you?" he asks again, waiting.

I rub my hand over the back of my neck, remembering the way Nicole flirted on the platform, how she announced to Callie I was going to knock her up, how she so willingly took on each challenge on the swing. But I learned, too, that she's not balls-to-the-wall all the time. The neighbor nearly killed her drive. But even when she was embarrassed that night, she was unafraid to speak her mind.

And once she let go, boy, did she ever let go.

The woman is everything you'd think a dating and sex columnist would be—uninhibited. Goddamn, it was hot. It was hot on Monday, Tuesday, and Wednesday night, too.

Yes, we've been practicing baby-making every night. It's not a tough job, and hell, am I glad I get to do it.

"Yes, I got to know her," I tell Cal.

"And did you like her?"

Now he's really getting personal. "We had a great time."

He beams and drops a hand on my shoulder, squeezing in a paternal way. "Now, talk more about that next time. You set the agenda for the show. The callers will follow your lead. I have faith you'll get there."

He turns and walks the other way, and I briefly contemplate finding the nearest boxing gym and signing up for lessons right the fuck now. I blow out a long, frustrated stream of air that does nothing to release the coiled tension in my body.

When I spin around to head to my office, Nicole is walking toward me. She looks good enough to eat in her tight jeans and a pink sweater that hugs her breasts deliciously. My eyes shamelessly tour her body—her curvy hips, her long legs, her gorgeous face.

The tension in me unwinds, and I breathe again.

But it's short-lived when an unpleasant notion touches down. I hope to God Nicole didn't hear that exchange. I don't want her to know exactly how short a leash I'm on. It doesn't exactly cast me in the best light.

"Hey," she says, her blue eyes soft. "You okay?"

I try to school my expression, to erase any residue of annoyance. "Definitely."

She shoots me a skeptical look. "Are you sure?"

I'm not going to air my dirty laundry with her. She didn't ask me to knock her up so she could hear about my shitty encounters with my boss. I change the subject. I let my gaze drift purposefully down her body. "Have we got a date with your uterus tonight?" I ask in my best dirty tone, even though there's nothing sensual about the word *uterus*. "If memory serves, we were going to try position number three, so we don't get addicted to position one."

"Ooh," she says with a naughty edge to her voice. "But position one is so good." She inches closer. "I love getting on my hands and knees for you."

A groan rumbles up my chest, and my dick springs to attention. "And now you've made it virtually impossible for me to work the rest of the day."

She wiggles an eyebrow. "But before we try position three, I think we should tackle something from your list."

"Cupcake tasting?" Cal will like that. I'll talk about cupcakes on air like a goddamn boy scout.

"I have something else in mind. Can you be ready by seven?"

Color me intrigued.

I say yes.

* * *

I lunge to the right, skidding across the court as I reach for the racquetball, slamming it to the wall. The blue orb screams back at Flynn. He grunts as he attacks it with a ferocity that sends it spiraling to the wall once more.

I huff and scramble for it.

We keep up a relentless pace, serving and slamming, slamming and serving, until finally, fucking finally, my friend misses.

"At last," I say, breathing hard as I reach out to clasp his hand.

"Damn it." Flynn stares daggers at me through his racquetball goggles. He's wildly competitive, which is all the more amusing because he was never a high school athlete, nor a college one.

Flynn is a former nerd.

Actually, he's still a nerd, and like many of them, he's a rich one. If you believe the magazines, he's a rich, hot, available nerd, making him one of New York's most eligible bachelors or something, thanks to the lady-killer grin, black glasses, stubble beard, athletic build and fat bank account.

He's a member at this racquetball club, and I'm his guest. Rich, hot, available, and *generous*. I don't mind that I'm the recipient of his guest pass largesse.

Flynn points the racquet at me. "One more game?" The man is intense, determined, and pretty much addicted to both exercise and competition.

I shake my head as I grab my gym bag from the corner of the court, pulling off the goggles. "I need to call it a night, man. I've got a date."

That piques his interest as he takes off his goggles. "Who's the lady?"

"Someone from work. She's my Ping-Pong partner."

"That sounds vaguely dirty. Does she play with your—"

I slice a hand through the air. "Nope. Cutting you off. Don't go there."

He sighs in frustration. "Seriously? I can't make a ball joke?"

I clap his shoulder. "Love you, man. But I've told you a million times. We need to send you back to humor school."

"You don't want to hear my new knock-knock joke?" he asks as I push open the door and we head into the hall.

"What have I told you about knock-knock jokes?"

"But I think you're wrong. Just try this one. Knock, knock."

I groan as the tread of our sneakers echoes in the hallway. "Did you try it on Dylan first?"

Flynn scoffs at the mention of his brother, who's the co-founder of the company they run. "No way. This is solid gold knock-knock shit. I'm not wasting it on my twin brother."

"Fine. I'll bite. Who's there?" I ask reluctantly.

"A pencil."

"A pencil who?"

"Never mind. It's pointless."

His delivery is one hundred percent dry. When his joke fully registers, I laugh lightly. "That's your first *not* terrible joke."

He pumps a fist. "Progress. See? I can learn." He clears his throat as we head down the steps. "Listen, I need to ask you for advice."

"Sure. My advice is if you're going to be addicted to knock-knock jokes, find more of *that* kind."

"I have a date tonight, and since you're the dating king . . ." He scratches his jaw as we near the first floor of the club. "Listen, I'm going to sound like a gigantic douche for this."

"You'd have to try pretty hard to sound like a gigantic douche with me. Trust me—you've no idea the level of douchery I've heard in my job."

He smiles faintly. "Here's the deal. I don't know how to tell if a woman is into me for my huge dick or my huge wallet."

I nod. "Ah, the dilemma of the twenty-seven-year-old tech millionaire."

He shrugs. "Told you. It sounds douchey. Except the dick part. That's just true."

I laugh as we stop at the door. "I don't want to talk about your dick. But the rest is fair game, and I get it. You want to know if a woman likes you for you and not because your company is the hottest shit around."

"Yeah," he says, vulnerability etched in his green eyes. "It's not like I have a problem meeting ladies or scoring dates. But once I sit down with a woman and she finds out what I do, her interest shoots up exponentially. And I don't know if it's me or my money. Dylan has the same issue, so he's going to use a matchmaker. But that's not my bag."

"You've got a date tonight, you said?"

He nods.

I clap his shoulder. "You're good at assessing risk and opportunity in business, right?"

He nods, giving me a *duh* look. He didn't get to where he is now without being fucking awesome at it. "I rock at that."

"Think of her like some new tech app or algorithm."

He blinks, confused. "A woman is like an algorithm?"

I nod. "I honestly have no idea what an algorithm truly is. No one does except tech geniuses like you. The rest of us use *algorithm* as this catch-all term to refer to something behind-the-scenes that makes the Internet do its magic." I pretend to type numbers into a keypad as I make beeping sounds. "The point is," I say, rapping my knuckles on his forehead, "use *that* portion of your head. Try to analyze her interest in you like it's a business problem someone brought to you. If one of your engineers came to you and said, 'Boss, does this algorithm make my app run faster?' you could tell, right?"

"Of course."

"Tonight, when the woman says, 'That's so interesting that you graduated summa cum laude from Yale,' or 'So you say you live in a brownstone in the Village?' as she bats her eyes, ask yourself if those questions make the algorithm work better, or if they tell you a Trojan horse virus is trying to fry the whole fucking system."

Flynn laughs. "Now you're talking my language."

"And if all else fails, just take it slow."

"Because if she wants my money then she also wants to ride my ride?" he asks, pretending to grab his crotch, as he does a dirty grind.

I shake my head. "No. What I'm saying is if you take it slow, then you can make sure she likes you for you. I know that might sound contrary to every piece of advice given to men these days. But for you, since you want to make sure the woman wants your heart," I say, tapping his chest, "you take it nice and easy."

"Nice and easy," he repeats, as if he's hearing the words for the first time. "I can do that. Riding my ride can wait."

"Exactly. Romance her. Get to know her. Let her get to know you. Think of it more like a courtship." Funny, Cal would be proud of me, since I gave advice that's love-related. And I actually enjoyed it, too. I didn't feel quite the same bitter aftertaste I experienced at the session with the Tinder-loving dickheads a few weeks ago. More than that, the advice feels spot-on for my friend.

"What about you?" Flynn asks, raising his chin. "You taking it slow tonight?"

I scoff. "Not in the motherfucking least. But my situation is completely different."

"Because you're not looking to settle down?"

I tap my nose. "Bingo."

It's close enough to the truth, I reason, as I head home to shower before I see Nicole. I've got to smell nice so she'll want to ride this ride tonight, even if I'm a sure thing.

Chapter Seventeen

Nicole

Ryder grabs his hair. He's so worked up I'm surprised he doesn't yank it out.

"Are you crazy? That was totally a foul!" he barks into the sea of screaming fans as he reprimands the refs. Along with nearly twenty thousand others doing the same at this preseason game.

Ryder is one of those obsessive sports guys who get riled up, and I can completely relate.

"Are you kidding me?" I shout down to the court. "That was so foul it should be in the garbage."

He snaps his gaze to me and raises his eyebrows approvingly. "Excellent trash talk. I had no idea you had it in you."

I suppose that's the point of dating—to learn these things. Or, in our case, let's call it practical dating. He parks himself in his seat, and I plop down next to him as the game resumes with an ear-splitting whistle.

"That was highway robbery," he says over the stomping of feet in the stands as the Knicks run up the court.

"It was a bald-faced crime."

"Theft, I tell you." He holds up a hand and we high-five. "By the way, when you said something on my list, I thought you meant the list of dates for the dating guide. But this is way better."

I point at him. "*Your* list of ideal dates. The ones you told me about when you asked for mine."

"And you remembered."

I'd sensed he'd had a shitty day at work. Even if he doesn't want to talk about it, I don't need to be a rocket scientist to know. Our boss is tough as nails, and while I'm Cal's golden child right now, it's because of my show's ratings and the column's popularity. If Cal's riding someone hard, it means he needs more from them to please the sponsors. That's not a fun position to be in, so I called in a favor. Delaney's boyfriend is a big-deal entertainment lawyer with contacts all over the city, and he snagged last-minute tickets for tonight.

Since Ryder's whisking me around Manhattan on my most favorite dates, I can try to do the same for him. Now, I've a happy man by my side, which is exactly how you want the man tasked with knocking you up to feel.

After the Knicks score again, we stand and cheer. Ryder wraps his arms around me and plants a PDA kiss on my lips. "What if the kiss cam caught us?" he whispers.

"How scandalous," I joke.

"If the kiss cam was on, I'd give you one of those kisses where I bend you back and you have to rope your arms around me and hold on tight so you don't fall."

I lick my lips, inviting him.

His eyebrows rise, and he pretends to talk to himself. "And then I said to myself, why am I not doing that now, anyway?"

He loops a hand around my back, dips me as far as he can without bumping the people next to us, and kisses the hell out of me. We're in the midst of thousands of raucous fans, and he kisses me like he knows my body. Like he knows how I like it.

Slow and tender at first. A teasing slide of lips—just enough so I can taste his spearmint breath. Once I'm under his kissing spell, he parts my lips, opens my mouth, and tangles his tongue with mine. Softly, I moan into his mouth. A shudder runs through my body, and everything goes hazy. My brain sends the message to swoon, just swoon.

That's how he kisses me.

But he doesn't stop there. For the second act, he kisses deeper, harder, with a hint of what he'll do to me later. A little rough. A little greedy.

All manly.

My knees go weak.

It's the strangest thing, because I'm in public and the roar of the crowd and the sound of the buzzer should be a turnoff. But *he's* such a turn-on that all I want is to grab his hand, tug him out of the stands, and yank him into the bathroom next to the nacho stand.

And, honestly, I think bathroom sex is way overrated.

Sure, sometimes it works out with *O*s for everyone. But that's mostly in fiction. In the pages of a book, you never hear about the smells in the restroom. Who wants to screw when it stinks like urine? Not this girl.

That's why I break the kiss—so I don't yank him into a public restroom. I breathe out hard, finger the collar of his soft T-shirt, and whisper, "If you kept doing that I was going to tackle you and hump you right here."

He laughs, the sound mingling with the noise of the crowd, the thump of shoes, the jeers and cheers. As we sit, he says, "I probably wouldn't object."

I run my hand up his arm, feeling his bicep. "What the hell do you do to get these guns?"

"Weights."

"No." I pretend to be shocked. "Don't tell me that. You're naturally perfect. You're naturally toned."

"Ha. If only."

I lift my chin haughtily. "I refuse to believe you're anything but a perfect specimen of DNA."

His smile disappears. When it registers what I said, I wince. Have I insulted him by making him think all I want is his perfect DNA?

Well, that kind of is all I want.

Why, then, does it feel as if I've said the wrong thing?

* * *

The Knicks win, and we cheer outrageously for their victory, but something feels off. I know it's what I said earlier about his DNA, except the hustle and bustle of Madison Square Garden is not the time or place to make it right. Even though Ryder isn't a man to hold grudges, I want to clear the air, to let him know I don't just view him in this one-track way. Even though I suppose it would seem like I do.

We reach his building after a short ride, and we head up the steps to his small one-bedroom. As soon as the door shuts, Romeo leaps up and slathers his master in kisses.

"Hey, boy, were you good while I was gone?" The dog answers with a wag and a long sloppy kiss. The master responds with a chin-scratching. There's such affection between them, and I wonder if Ryder was always this sweet with his pup, or if he poured more love into the dog after his marriage ended. Do we have a finite amount of love inside us that we allocate to the people and animals we fall madly for? And if someone breaks our heart, can we simply siphon off that love toward another creature? As the dog rubs his white and brown snout against Ryder's leg, I suspect this creature helped his best friend through heartbreak. I'd like to give the dog a biscuit. I'd like to give him a whole pack as a thank-you.

As Ryder leashes his beast, he looks me up and down, heat in his dark blue eyes. "Do me a favor while I take him around the block." His voice is rough.

"Sure."

"Get in my favorite outfit. Wait in my bedroom. I want you naked and ready when I return."

That sounds damn good to me, too, but even when I strip down to nothing in his bedroom, I can't shrug off the comment from earlier.

Ten minutes later, the door creaks open. There's a clank of the metal end of the leash hitting the hook. The dog slurps water loudly in his bowl. Ryder tells him to go to the couch, then praises him.

And I am the naked redhead waiting on his navy-blue bed.

The naked redhead who should be a cat in heat. But I feel too much weirdness to just flip the switch to sex. When Ryder enters the bedroom, he does that sexy thing men do. He raises his arm over his head and reaches behind him, tugging off his black Henley in one quick move.

His gorgeous chest is on display, and my fingers itch to touch it. But my mind is in charge. Or maybe my heart. I sit up, even as he stalks closer, ready to eat me up.

"You're more than your DNA," I blurt out, meeting his eyes.

His face is hard to read at first, but then a slow smile spreads. It lights up the room. "Yeah? What am I?"

I crawl to the end of the bed and run my fingers up his chest. "I could rattle off a million traits, but I already told you those when I asked for your help. What I'll tell you is this—I care deeply for you. And I believe with my whole heart that dates shouldn't just be about the woman. I could sense you had a crappy day, and I wanted to make you happy again." I brush my fingertips across his cheek. "That's why I took you to the game."

His lips part, and his expression softens further. His lovely blue eyes flash with a vulnerability that is rare for him, but I've seen it more and more. "It was one of my ideal dates," he says as I drop my hand. He catches it, threading his fingers through mine. Sparks fly over my skin. "I love that you remembered."

"I think when it comes to sex and dating, sometimes society focuses too much on the woman and what the man can do to please her and win her." I squeeze his fingers, and he squeezes mine back. "But women should also want to do things to make the men they're with happy. Don't you think?"

He presses a gentle kiss to my forehead. "I was happy tonight."

"Are you happy now?"

He nods. "Yes."

One word. So simple. But it does something to me—his *yes* ignites tingles all over my flesh. "Good. I like it when you're happy."

"I'll be even happier when I'm buried inside you," he says, his voice going low and dirty.

I loop my arms around his neck. "I think this is my last chance this month." That makes me nervous and wildly excited at the same time.

"Then let's make it count."

I turn onto my front because that's the best position, when I'm on my hands and knees, but he grabs my ankle and flips me back over. I arch a brow. He grabs the other ankle, and he tugs my ass to the edge of his bed.

He kneels on the floor and widens my legs.

"Ryder," I say, my voice feathery. A pulse beats between my legs.

He shakes his head. "No protests." He dusts a kiss on the inside of my knee, then travels along my thigh with his lips.

"But I can't get pregnant if you spend all the time going down on me." My protest is, admittedly, half-hearted. I ache for his mouth, even while I crave the long, hard length of him.

"No, you can't. But you can get wet. You can get incredibly wet. And then after I make you come on my lips, you'll be so goddamn ready for me to fuck you. You'll take me deeper than I've been before. And like that, with you so hot and wet, we'll give you what you want."

There's surely no scientific basis for his theory, but I don't need science right now. I need lust. Want. Carnal desire.

His words are a torch. They send flames all through my body, making me ache even more for him. He rewards my ache with his mouth. He licks me up each thigh, and I moan, and I groan, and I quiver. When he presses his delicious lips to me, I tremble.

"Oh God." My pitch climbs an octave as he flicks his tongue up and down my wetness.

I will say this about Ryder Lockhart: he has a world-class tongue. He's a champion with his mouth, and he treats me like dessert. With him, I'm candy, I'm ice cream, I'm all the sugar in the world. His wicked tongue is an instrument of pure, white-hot pleasure.

"You know how I like it, Nicole?"

My cheeks heat as he looks up at me, his lips glistening.

"So hot when you blush," he says, sliding his finger across my center to keep me on edge. "Now, are you going to do what I like?"

I nibble on the corner of my lower lip and nod.

"Good," he growls, as he bites the inside of my thigh. "Fuck my face hard. Grab my head and go to town."

He likes it when he doesn't just lick me, but when I fuck his face, too. He told me the other night he won't stand for it if I just lie there. Now that I've learned how he likes it, I don't intend to take it lying down. The man makes oral sex a two-person sport, and in return I get the best Os I've ever had.

He reaches for my hands and brings them to his hair. He makes me wrap them around his head. Then his mouth is between my legs again, licking and kissing and sucking.

Oh God. I'm on fire. I'm parked on the edge of the mattress, and truly, I'm fucking his face. It feels filthy and freeing at the same time, with him kneeling between my legs, worshipping me with that incredible mouth as I grab and clutch him closer.

"Oh God, it's so good," I cry out.

He murmurs against me, "Want you to come."

The man is obsessed with my pleasure. It's his drug, his addiction, and I want to give him his fix.

I want the fix, too.

I yank him harder between my legs. I'm rewarded with a throaty groan as he buries his face between my thighs, devouring me with his mouth, his tongue, his lips, his long, strong fingers.

Those fingers. They reach a spot inside me that turns me into a shaking, trembling, shattering hot mess.

"I'm coming," I cry out, and then I don't stop saying it. I can't stop. Because I can't stop coming. It hits me in violent waves, a magnificent storm of pleasure that sends me writhing, twisting against his mouth.

Until I'm panting and can't move anymore.

Maybe I can't, but seconds later, he rises, grabs my hips, and flips me. My feet are jelly on the floor. But he's got me, holding me tight. He bends me over the bed, his big hand pressing between my shoulder blades. He flattens my back, turning me into an *L*. He hikes up my hips, raising me, and he pushes inside.

I don't know that I will ever get over how good it feels when he first takes me. When he fills me. When he rocks into me. It's an explosion of pleasure.

My name sounds rough and gritty on his lips as he grunts *Nicole*. "It's so fucking good. Fucking you is so fucking good," he rasps.

I am a rag doll beneath him. My body sizzles. Electric sparks spread over my skin with every thrust, every drive.

"So deep in you," he rasps. "That's what you want, baby?"

"Yes. God, yes." My fingers curl tightly into his sheets, gripping them.

He pulls back then slams into me, and I howl. I'm an animal. I'm wild and hungry. He dips his hand between my legs. His finger slides over my clit, and with one touch I'm about to explode. I'm so damn close to the edge that when he drives into me once more, I shatter.

I break apart into diamonds, into starlight, into the whole damn night sky. I yell his name. God's name. I shout incoherent words.

And I'm not the only one.

His noises. His sounds. His breath. He's so close, and the prospect thrills me. He's groaning and fucking me so hard and so deep that I know, I just know, this has to be it. He shudders, his fingers digging hard into my hips as he comes.

My mind is awash with mad hope. With a crazy faith that his passion tonight did the trick. That he just gave me my heart's desire.

When he pulls out, he tugs me up on his bed and wraps his arms around me. "I think we did it," he murmurs in my ear, and my heart beats harder. I love that he believes the same thing about how we just came together.

I grin as I wriggle back against him. "Me, too." I am a happy, dopey, woozy woman.

"Oh shit," he says, sitting up straight.

"What's wrong?"

He grabs a pillow, pats the bed, and instructs me to lift my butt. I raise my rear, and he slides the pillow under me.

It's the most endearing thing, the way he always remembers. Part of me wants to keep that thought to myself because it feels so couple-y, and I know we shouldn't even pretend we're that. But I want him to know how it makes me feel. "Hey, Ryder," I say, looping a hand in his hair. "You're really sweet about this whole thing."

He narrows his eyes and huffs. "I'm not sweet."

I push his chest. "You're so sweet, and you don't even want to admit it."

"I'm just helpful."

"Hate to break it to you, but being helpful is sweet."

He laughs then levels me with an intense stare. "It's helpful when I put my sperm in you, isn't it?"

"Helpful and so, so sweet," I say, playfully.

I sigh as I run my hand over my belly, imagining. It's an astonishing thought that someday soon I might feel a bump. I want that so badly—to be in my own bed at night, my palm spread over my basketball, feeling the life inside me. I want to know what that's like. So much hope bubbles inside me I have a surplus. I could bottle this hope, sell it, and still have enough. I turn to look at Ryder. He's propped on his side, his head in his hand, his fingers tracing my hip. His firm, strong body is naked and sheened with sweat. He's gorgeous, and I could stare at him all night. "Do you really think it worked?" I ask.

"I do."

"Did you ever think you'd be doing this with your colleague?"

He cracks up. "Hell, no. I thought I'd be . . ."

"You thought you'd still be with . . ." I let my voice trail off, too. For some reason, it makes me sad that he was so connected to someone else.

"Yeah, but that's not something I think about anymore."

"Do you miss her?" I ask, my muscles tightening with the wish for a no.

He shakes his head and drags a hand through his hair. "Nope."

I relax. "Does she ever try to get in touch with you?"

"She did, but not recently."

"Are you glad it ended?"

He draws a deep breath. He's never told me in detail, but I was able to figure out she cheated on him from things he's said. "I'm glad it ended when it did. Before I was in even deeper. Before we had kids."

"Did you want them with her?" I ask, once more holding my breath for a no.

"Eventually," he says, and that's as close to a no as I can ask for. He draws lazy circles along my thigh. "What about you? Did you ever like anyone enough to want to have kids with him?"

I shake my head a little wistfully. "I think that part of me is broken."

"What part?" he asks, his brow knitting in curiosity.

I tap my heart. "I've never been in love. Sure, I felt puppy love for my high school boyfriend. But as a grown woman? I think I've come close, but nothing that feels like mad, passionate love. Unless you count Ruby. I'm definitely in mad love with her. Like you are with Romeo."

When the dog hears his name, he bounds into the room. He plops his butt down and wags his tail. Ryder pats the bed. The dog jumps up and flops next to his master. Just two naked adults, and one naked dog. "And now there's three in the bed," I say with a laugh.

"A *ménage à trois*," he jokes, then his voice turns serious again. "You've really never been in love?" He sounds flummoxed, like he can't quite imagine how I've gone through life without this.

I run a hand through my tangled hair, smoothing it out. "It sort of felt like it once a few years ago, with someone I was with for several months," I say with a shrug. "I thought it was. But looking back, I don't think so."

"Why?"

I stare at the ceiling. "Why?" I repeat. "I've asked myself that question. I liked Greg so much. He was a good guy. But I didn't feel that zing," I say, tapping my breastbone. "That magic here. You must have felt that."

He nods. "Definitely."

My heart plummets, and I'm ashamed that I'd wanted him to say he never felt the zing with his ex. I shouldn't be jealous that the man has fallen in love in the past, especially when I'm not interested in love. I focus on Greg instead. "I didn't feel that zing with my former fiancé, so I called it off."

"Ouch."

I crinkle my nose. "I'm mean. A terribly cruel woman."

He laughs lightly. "No, you're not. Hell, I'm sure it hurt him. Any man would be devastated to lose you," he says, and my heart dares to twirl. It's such a strange little sensation hopping around in my chest. "But better at that time than once you were married."

"That's what I figured. Because I'm pretty sure you're supposed to be certain you're in love. You're supposed to get that feeling when you know it can't be anything but love, right?"

His lips curve into a smile. "Yeah," he says, and his hand slides over my belly, on top of mine. He squeezes my fingers. "The way you'll feel soon."

"Yes." My eyes light up because he gets it. He truly understands me.

"Still," he says, shaking his head in amusement, "it's amazing you can talk about love the way you do, and yet you've never really felt it. You understand on this deep level, but you've never been in love."

I'm an oddity to him. I'm the clock in the antique shop that doesn't tell time. "But see, I don't think romantic love is all that different than the love for your friends, or your family, or a dog. Is it? That kind of love?"

He turns away from me and strokes Romeo's soft fur. "That kind of love is different, but I try not to think about it." He stops then exhales heavily. "Or to let myself feel it."

My chest aches, and sadness tunnels through me. I despise that his ex-wife hurt him so much that he has to turn off his heart. I run my fingers through his hair. He tenses briefly then relaxes. He sighs, and it sounds almost happy, as if he's truly content in this moment here with me. I know the feeling—it matches my own right now. But whether I'm content, whether I want to throat-punch his ex, or whether my traitorous heart spins when he says sweet things, I'm still a practical woman, and I'm well aware of how absolutely critical our arrangement is.

"It's a good thing we know the score, right?" I say, keeping it light before it gets heavy.

"Absolutely. And speaking of score, I'm including the Knicks game in the dating guide, especially because you liked pretending to be on the kiss cam so much."

I smile, remembering how very much I enjoyed his version of the kiss cam. "Loved it. You'll be doing men all over the city a service if they kiss their woman like you kissed me."

He runs a finger along my hipbone. "By the way, thanks a lot for planning to be out of town right when you got me all hyped up on regular sex."

I leave in another day for a trip to California so I can record a few shows with live audiences. Cal likes to do that from time to time when a show is popular, so I'm thrilled to have the chance. "Tell me about it. I'll have to pack some vibrators."

He holds up his right palm and stares sadly at it. "This is all I've got for the next week."

I laugh, then it turns into a sigh, and it occurs to me that even though I desperately want our banging to do the trick, I'm going to miss sleeping with him. I'm going to miss seeing him, too.

And since *we know the score*, I see no reason not to tell him. "Is it weird that I'm kind of bummed about not seeing you while I'm gone?"

"Only if it's weird that I'm kind of bummed, too," he says, then he drops a kiss to my forehead. Tingles spread everywhere—all over my body, to the tips of my toes and the ends of my hair.

"Do that again," I command as the world falls away and all I feel are his lips, his tenderness, and his warmth.

"As you wish." He kisses me, soft and gentle, as I lie on his bed in Chelsea, praying to the goddesses of fertility that a piece of him is mixing with a part of me tonight to make a whole new person.

Chapter Eighteen

Nicole

The leaves crackle beneath my sneakers, and the cool fall air nips at my cheeks. California is lovely, but it's good to be back in New York after eight days away. The city is glorious in early autumn, and Central Park is a carnival of burnished-gold, cranberry-red, and pumpkin-orange leaves. Fall is blazing, bursting with shades of fire on all the branches in the trees—one last cornucopia of color before winter chills the city.

I inhale a crisp lungful of air as we jog on a late Sunday morning in early October. This is the perfect weather for running. This is the perfect weather for learning your life is about to change.

"Are you going to take the test soon?" Delaney asks.

I nod as Ruby tugs on the leash. "Definitely. As long as my period doesn't come today, I'll take the test tomorrow morning."

Penny lets out a little cheer as we round the top of the reservoir. "Can we all join you?"

"Sure. We'll have a pee-pee party at my place tomorrow at six a.m."

"You're going to take it the second you wake up, right?" Delaney says, her tone serious. "First morning pee and all."

"Absolutely." I'm a font of knowledge on all things pregnancy related. I've researched every last detail on when to take the test, and I've bought three kinds from Duane Reade.

"And your periods are regular, right?" Penny asks.

"Twenty-eight days. On the dot. I usually get it in the middle of the night on the twenty-eighth day, and I didn't last night." I cross my fingers. I've got an extra spring in my step from Aunt Flo's apparent lack of appearance.

Penny gasps in excitement.

"That's a good sign, right?" I ask. "That I didn't get it?"

They say yes in unison.

I can't mask my excitement. "Maybe it's crazy, but I felt a little nauseated, too. And don't laugh. But—"

Delaney jumps in. "Your boobs totally look bigger."

I pump a fist and raise my gaze to the sky. "She noticed the girls, Lord. Hallelujah, she noticed the girls."

We jog for another thirty minutes then slow to a walk as we amble to a park exit. "How did it go, though? The sex and all? Tell us everything now that you're back," Penny says. I haven't seen them in nearly two weeks, though I did share text updates.

I wiggle my eyebrows. "It's amazing. He's a god in bed."

Penny happily sighs. "I love good sex."

Delaney raises a fist for bumping. "Good sex rocks."

"Bad sex can suck it," Penny seconds.

I raise a finger to make a point. "Bad sex should be eradicated from the world."

"Let's make an ordinance outlawing it," Delaney suggests.

Penny tuts. "But how would we ever know something is amazing unless we experience the bad stuff? Or even just the completely lame sex?"

I tug Ruby closer as we leave the park. "Good point. You need the lows to savor the highs."

Delaney furrows her brow, considering this. "If all sex was great, would we become numb to it? I'm not sure I would."

"No, but I think to *appreciate* that something is out-of-this-world good, we need to have experienced the bad."

"True. I'm just glad that all the sex I'm having is good," Delaney says. "And I'm glad you're having crazy good sex. Are you guys truly able to manage this whole deal without any weirdness or feelings?"

"Absolutely," I say with a tight nod, flashing back to all my conversations with Ryder about our arrangement, even the one from the other night in his home, right as the window was slamming shut on the fertile time of the month. "Honestly, I'm kind of impressed with us. We were able to treat it completely like a transaction."

Penny does a little dance, gyrating her hips as Shortcake barks at her. My friend smacks her own rear. "It's a transaction, all right."

"He's making a deposit," Delaney says in a singsong voice.

I pat my belly. "In the bank of me."

The three of us laugh, amused at our own bawdy cleverness.

"But seriously." Delaney prods again. "You were able to keep everything separate? Emotions and all?"

I answer her as if I've been asked the question at a job interview, my tone professional and steady. "It wasn't that hard. We're both good at this. He's not looking for anything more, and I'm not looking for anything but his—"

"Deposits," Penny cuts in.

"Let me tell you, when that man goes to the ATM, he goes there," I say. "He gets that money in so deep, so far, and he delivers it all the way to the bank."

High fives abound, and Penny rubs my belly as we stop at a crosswalk. "I'm tempted to kiss your belly for luck, but that's totally weird. Also, I think we need to get in the habit now of patting your belly."

"Pat it. You can feel up my belly as much as you want for the next nine months."

As we say good-bye and I walk the rest of the way home, those words play over and over in my head.

Nine months, nine months, nine months.

I intend to enjoy every single second of every day of them.

By that night, I am still blissfully period-free. I wash my face and loop my hair into a ponytail. I open the closet door all the way and appraise my appearance in front of the full-length mirror. I stand sideways, considering my breasts, my legs, my hips, and most of all, my flat belly. I run my hand over my middle. I swear I can feel something happening. Like my mom said, maybe you just know. I clasp both hands on my stomach, lace my fingers together, and send a wish to the universe to take care of the baby I hope is growing inside me.

I turn off the lights and fall into a deep, dreamless sleep.

When I wake on Monday morning, it's as if I've been shot full of anticipation, and nerves, too. Everything feels different.

When a tongue slobbers up my cheek, I remember that I'm not the only one who has to pee. Ruby licks my face again, and that's my cue to toss off the covers, tug on some sweats, and leash her up. I have to go, too, but I can hold it for five minutes while she does her business. I want to be able to savor the moment when I see those two pink lines. Then, I can spend the rest of my morning calling the whole world. Well, just my mom and my girls and that man who made it possible. I'd tell them, but no one else.

I pull on a fleece, grab a plastic bag, and leave. After a quick trip around the block, I race back up the stairs to my apartment.

When I unhook Ruby's leash, I pat the side of my leg, her cue to follow. My loyal girl trots behind me as I head to the bathroom. My new plunger is parked next to the toilet, nice and pristine. I grab the test box and read the instructions for the twentieth time, even though I've memorized them. But I don't want to mess this up.

I'm ready for the news.

I'm ready to head down the path to motherhood.

I'm ready to go this alone.

I inhale deeply, pull down my panties, and I see blood.

I freeze.

And a whole new emotion washes over me.

Foolishness.

I've never felt like a bigger fool in my life. Tears leak down my face. I can't believe I let myself get so carried away. I can't believe I let myself think it would be easy.

Chapter Nineteen

Ryder

As I round the corner, I check my messages again. Still no word from Nicole, and I know today is the day. I stuff the phone into my back pocket, reasoning that can only mean good news. She's probably caught up in the excitement. I bet she cabbed it to her mom's house already and they're shopping for baby blankets or maternity clothes. Does it make me a complete dick if maternity clothes give me the willies?

Look, I'm not saying pregnant women aren't hot. Some are sexy as fuck, and Nicole would look smoking hot as a pregnant chick with a giant basketball belly and those perfect tits. All I mean is, I'd rather not see her in clothes with a pouch just yet.

"Fuck," I mutter.

I do sound like a dick. Even in my own head.

While I'm at it, I guess I might as well make all my asshole confessions as I weave through the Monday morning crowds on the way to work. God knows, when I get to the office, I'll have to put on my good-boy cap. But here goes. There's a part of me that hopes she's not pregnant.

I drag a hand through my hair as I march up the avenue.

I can't believe I just thought that. But let the wild rumpus of dickhead ideas roam free in my brain. I really enjoyed fucking her, and I wouldn't mind trying to score a touchdown a few more times inside her. The nights with her were everything I could want—amazing evenings with a wonderful woman, the hottest sex of my life, plus some of the best conversations in the post-fornication glow.

Nicole and I *get* each other on an instinctual level. Not just in bed, but out of it, and I will miss that.

I will miss having her.

When I reach the office, I shove those notions aside. Surely Nicole is in the family way, and I'm going to be the most enthusiastic sperm donor ever in the history of sperm donors.

I square my shoulders, take a deep breath, and go inside. I say hello to the receptionist, make idle hallway chitchat with a few co-workers, then check my phone one more time. Still nothing. She's probably not even here. I bet she took the day off to celebrate her good news.

I head to her office and tap on the door. A weak voice says, "I'm busy."

My heart falls, and I know instantly that it didn't work. "Nicole, it's me."

There's a honk as if she's blowing her nose.

She pulls open the door, and her smile is the most plastic thing I've seen. My poor girl. She's so sad, and she's trying so hard to be tough. I close the door behind us, lock it, and gather her into my arms.

"I'm sorry, baby." I stroke her hair, and it occurs to me I've called her *baby* when we're not screwing. In the heat of the moment, I just say it and it feels right. But at this moment, too, it feels surprisingly right.

"It's okay," she mutters, but her voice hitches.

"I know how much you wanted this. I thought it was going to happen," I say softly in her ear. I wish I could take away her sadness.

"Me, too."

She doesn't cry, though. She lets me hold her, and she wraps her arms around me. As much as I wanted to have her again, I'd rather she be happy. I'd rather all her dreams come true.

She raises her face. "Want to know what really sucks?"

"Tell me." I tuck a finger under her chin, meeting her eyes.

"I feel so stupid." Her lips quiver.

"Don't say that. Why would you say that?"

She swipes at her cheek. "I really thought it worked. I was so foolish. I know better, Ryder." She grips my shirt. "I'm supposed to be this smart and rational woman, and instead, I became a fluttery, hopeful fool. I couldn't imagine any other outcome than wonderful beginner's luck."

She rolls her eyes.

"You're not a fool," I say, soothing her as I rub her shoulders. "You're just a normal person who wanted something badly. You stayed positive and believed in the possibilities. That doesn't make you foolish. It makes you human."

"It makes me idiotic. I should have known better. Instead, I practically walked around Manhattan with a hand on my belly, dreaming." She lets out a long, frustrated sigh.

"Stop saying that. There's nothing wrong with *wanting* something. So often we think we need to temper our hope so we're prepared for bad news. Guess what? Bad news hurts whether you're prepared for it or not. There's nothing wrong with hoping for the best."

"Ryder," she whispers, "I feel so dumb."

My heart aches for her. I press a kiss to her forehead. "You're anything but that. It didn't happen the first time. So we try again."

She rests her cheek against my chest and breathes in heavily then sighs against me. All of a sudden, she flinches and looks up. "I didn't even ask if you mind if we keep trying. I just assumed."

I grin. "You know what they say about when you assume."

"You'll make an ass of you and me?"

I shake my head, giving her a naughty look. "No. When you assume, it means I get to bite your ass."

When she smiles what is clearly a please-bite-my-ass yes, it lights me up in a whole new way. Different than before. Not just in a physical way, but inside my chest, like a lightbulb is glowing.

It's such a strange sensation, and I'm not sure what to make of it. "What are you doing tonight?"

"Wallowing in ice cream."

I mime hitting a buzzer. "Wrong. It's date night. I'm taking you cupcake tasting. Call me sexist, but I'm going to presume since it's that time of the month that you don't mind eating sweets."

She runs her hand down my arm. "Let me tell you something, handsome, so you never have to make any assumptions about sweets and me." She pats her stomach. "I've got an equal opportunity belly. Any time of the month you can put sweets in me."

"I've got something I'd like to put in you," I say, because I can't resist.

* * *

I could watch her eat cupcakes all day long. She dips her finger into the pink frosting and sucks it off with a low, sexy moan.

Or maybe that's *why* I could watch her eat cupcakes anytime. Because she's fucking torturing me. Making me think of sucking. And licking. And how far she could take me.

I'm sitting in a white and pink cupcake shop, surrounded by families, little kids squealing over mini chocolate cupcakes, moms and dads scarfing down confetti cupcakes, and I'm aroused. Under the white wood table, I make an adjustment. Good thing we grabbed a spot in the corner, far away from everyone. Pop music plays overhead, and the scent of sugar wafts through the air.

Nicole lifts the pink cupcake and darts her tongue along the frosting. "You're going to need to stop making love to the frosting," I whisper harshly.

She shoots me a naughty little glare. "But it's soooo good," she says, the same, drawn-out way she says it feels soooo good when I fuck her.

I drag a hand over my face as I slump back in the chair. "You're killing me."

"How does tonight rank on your dates list, then?" She winks.

I laugh. "With your cupcake antics, it's pretty damn high. The trouble is, I'm still turned on, so how about we discuss something non-arousing?"

"Basketball? Sweaty gym shoes? Oh, wait. I know." Her eyes light up with a wicked flare. "My neighbor Frederick."

"And his plunger." I raise my index finger and then let it droop. "You have successfully entered the anti-erection zone."

She smiles and reaches a hand across the table, squeezing mine. "And you have successfully lifted my spirits."

I look down at the table then up at her. Her eyes are wide and vulnerable, full of emotion. "I'm glad, Nicole. I don't like it when you're sad."

"Seriously. I'm so grateful. I'm still completely bummed that it didn't work, but you made me feel good tonight." Her voice hooks into me, stirring some emotions best forgotten. Maybe that's because this whole arrangement with her feels so real, so honest. The way she talks, her openness about her heart—it's the complete opposite of my cagey, clandestine ex.

"It's the frosting that's making you happy. Let's give credit where credit's due." I try to make light of things, but she won't have it.

"It's you. It's completely you," she says, leveling me with her intense eyes. "But the frosting is really good, too."

I clear my throat. "When do we start up again?" I don't want to sound too eager, but I could seriously screw her every night.

She looks at an imaginary watch. "Ten days?"

"You have ten-day periods?"

She shudders in mock horror. Or perhaps real horror. "God, no. I'm just thinking that's about when we head into the fertility zone again."

"Right. Got it." I snap my fingers in an *aw shucks* gesture. "I was hoping you'd say ten hours. Wait. Ten minutes."

"You have no idea what I would give for a ten-minute period. I'd give up frosting." After another bite of her cupcake, she pushes the plate aside and her expression shifts. "I want to ask you something."

"You want more than my boys? Want a liver and a side of kidney, too? Sheesh. You're demanding."

She laughs but quickly stifles the sound. "I don't know exactly how to broach this, so I'm going to be blunt."

"Ah, unlike all the other times you've asked me something," I tease, even as my shoulders tense. It's a gut reaction —when people say they need to broach a topic, it's often one you don't want to hear.

She smiles faintly. "I'm not exactly known for beating around the bush. But I realized there's an important item we didn't entirely discuss."

I wait for her to continue.

"I hope you know I'm not sleeping with anyone else," she says.

I flinch. "You better not be."

"Trust me, you wear me out. And I suppose it should be obvious that for the purpose of this arrangement, there's no way in hell I'd sleep with anyone else. It's not something I'd do under any circumstances. Still, since we've been so direct from the start, I thought it best to make it clear that I am not dating, seeing, sleeping with, kissing, or getting involved with anyone else in any way, shape, or form. I don't know if it's reasonable for me to expect you to be exclusive to me when we're in the middle of this project," she says, taking a beat, "but I'm sincerely hoping you're—"

I can't even let her finish. I hold up a hand as a stop sign. "My ex-wife cheated on me seven times. I will *never* touch anyone else while I'm with you."

Her eyebrows shoot into her hairline. She mouths *wow*.

"Pretty shitty, huh?"

A long nod is her answer. "That's pretty much the definition of shitty. And part of me wants to ask how anyone could cheat on you? But that makes the cheating about you when it's about her and the horrible choices she made."

Relief floods me. The times I've told people, I hear how they're sorry, how it sucks, or disbelief that someone could do what Maggie did. But Nicole gets it. Maggie's crime isn't a reflection on me. It's a reflection on Maggie. "She made a lot of bad choices because she's a sex addict. And I don't mean that in an 'Oh, cool, she's a nympho' way. It's not that she wanted to screw constantly. She was addicted to affairs. She craved the chase. She wanted to reel in a new man, over and over. She needed constant affirmation, and she sought it by finding other people."

Nicole sighs heavily, her brow knitting. "Did she seek therapy? Is she trying to change?"

I shrug. "I think so. She tried to convince me to stay while she went to rehab. But I didn't want to be with her. And I had no interest in giving her another chance even when she begged me to."

"I can certainly understand that. I wouldn't have, either."

"The funny thing is, you asked about that zing. About being in love. Obviously, I was in love with her, since I married her. But let me tell you, falling out of love was the easiest thing in the world. She made it a complete piece of cake since I can't love a cheater."

Nicole nods, her tone serious as she says, "Addiction or not, you don't break a vow."

"It's so simple. Fidelity is so goddamn simple. You keep it in your pants. Case closed." I take a beat and stare into her eyes. "You can count on me to be faithful. I don't have any desire to be with anyone else, and I also won't do that."

"You don't miss dating?" she asks like she feels bad for holding me back.

"What is this thing we're on? Chopped liver?"

"You know what I mean. A date that goes somewhere."

For a second, I linger on the *somewhere*. I start to imagine I'm on the path to *somewhere* with Nicole. Somewhere beyond cupcakes and Knicks games. But that's probably just all the frosting and sugar going to my head.

"Our dates go to your bedroom," I say with confidence. "This is about as perfect as dating gets."

"Good." She gives me a sly smile. "By the way, do you know what shark week means?"

"No sex?" I say, adopting the mopiest look ever.

"Let's get out of here, and I'll show you."

* * *

Her hands are the fastest draw in the west when we reach my place. My belt's undone, my jeans are unzipped, and my briefs are down. My cock salutes her. I'm ready. Just fucking ready, and she knows it. She has no need to kiss me all over or drag her nails down my chest.

I wouldn't object to either, but I want her wicked mouth on me. *Stat.* "You toyed with me that first night, Nicole."

She drops to her knees. "I did. I wanted to know how you tasted."

"Now you're going to find out."

"I. Can't. Wait."

She wraps a soft hand around the base of my dick, and I hiss. Her lips part and she flicks her tongue over the head. I groan. She takes me in, sucking on the crown of my cock.

"Jesus Christ," I mutter as I grab her hair, threading my fingers through those red strands as she kisses the tip. She lets go and runs her tongue along the underside. Shocks of pleasure rocket through me. It's so fucking good.

She licks all the way down to my balls, then draws one into her mouth and sucks hard. Electricity shoots through me. "That's so fucking hot."

Her eyes dance with mischief as she sucks, her hand curling into a tight grip as she shuttles her fist up and down my shaft. My thighs shake as I watch her. No way am I closing my eyes. No way am I doing anything but staring at her lush mouth playing with my dick. When she lets go of my balls, she wastes no time. She doesn't tease. She doesn't toy. She opens wide.

I curl my fingers around her skull. "Want to be in all the way."

Her eyes twinkle as if she's saying *in due time*. But due time is now. I'm a horny fucking bastard in general. That's amplified ten times over with this wildly sexual woman. And God bless her, she doesn't make me wait. Her warm mouth becomes a tunnel for my dick. I moan my appreciation, and then she does the sexiest thing ever. She lifts her hands and clamps them over mine on her head. She moves our fingers so I'm thrusting deep into her mouth. She drops hers, giving me control, giving me permission to fuck her mouth.

I shudder as my dick hits the back of her throat. Her eyes water and I pull back. "You okay?"

She nods, and her eyes are blazing. They say *do it again.* I grip her head tighter and pump. She gags a bit, but she grabs my ass, her nails digging into my flesh, urging me on. I give in to all my base desires, and she lets me. She stops to take one quick breath, then she opens wide, offering me full access to her delicious mouth.

My skin sizzles. Sensations speed into overdrive. My body goes haywire. I am nothing but a collection of nerve endings, firing at once, as I fuck her lovely, gorgeous, willing mouth.

"So fucking good," I grunt as I rock into her.

She answers me with a hard grab of her nails, a scratch on my skin. Her touch torches me all over and obliterates any last hold I have on the here and now. Release is imminent. Pleasure thunders across my body, and I groan loudly as I come. My thighs shake, and I breathe so fucking hard as I pull back, let go, and watch my dick fall from her mouth.

"Wow," I say, still seeing stars.

She grins and licks her lips, like a cat finishing his dish of cream. "Guess you like blow jobs."

"I fucking love blow jobs. But I'm *in love* with *your* blow jobs. Madly in love." I offer a hand and tug her up from the floor. Cupping her cheeks, I look into her eyes and murmur, "Thank you."

She laughs. "You don't have to thank me for a blow job."

"I know, but I'm thanking you for trusting me to do it like that. To do it hard."

"Don't you know? I trust you completely."

For a second, I tense when I hear that vicious word. Trust is a farce in my universe. And yet, when I'm with her, I feel it. I trust in what we're doing, in how we treat each other, in the openness of what we have, and the mutual understanding of what we don't want to have. "I'm glad you trust me. It's the same for me."

She presses a soft kiss to my cheek. "And I want everything to feel good for you."

"Oh, it felt more than good."

"Better than frosting?" She arches a brow.

"It felt like the world was ending."

She runs her hand over my abs, then along my happy trail. "Or maybe a week of blow jobs is beginning," she says.

That's how the next several nights go. We tackle a few more dates, including a night at the arcade and an epic game of mini golf. Each night ends with an absolutely spectacular, out-of-this-world blow job.

I hereby rename shark week to my favorite week ever—blow job week.

Chapter Twenty

Top Five Tips to Turn Geocaching into One Hell of An Awesome Date

By Ryder Lockhart

Let's say, for the sake of argument, that you want to impress the woman you're seeing. I know, crazy idea, right? But c'mon, men. It's going to take more than just dinner.

And look, I'm a fan of dinner. A juicy steak, a glass of whiskey, a great restaurant—that rocks. But any guy can do that. Presumably, you like this woman, so you want to stand out from the crowd.

Here's a surefire way: geocaching.

It's not just for the kids. If you aren't familiar with geocaching, it's basically going on a scavenger hunt around the city, tracking down little caches of buried treasure with a

GPS app, and then celebrating when you find them. Simple, right?

It's also a fantastic way to get to know someone. My personal recommendation? You'll need to stock up in advance with a few knick knacks—maybe a snow globe, a matchbox car, a key chain. If you take something from a cache, you need to replace it. Otherwise, you're a douche. And you don't want her, me, or the lamppost to think you're a douche, do ya?

Here's what you need to know.

1. Do your research online in advance and tailor the caches to her interests, even her mood.

Maybe she had a crummy week. Perhaps something didn't quite go her way. Traipsing around the city hunting for treasure is a much better way to get her mind off the shit that didn't work out than dinner is. Searching for a little pouch of treasure tucked away on a shelf in the New York Public Library is guaranteed to improve her mood. Plus, there's just something about libraries. They're catnip for most women. When she finds the red drawstring bag tucked behind *Jane Eyre* with a miniature book inside it, she might even give you a kiss. And that's one more thing to help her out of her funk. If she keeps the miniature book, replace it with a snow globe. A snow globe will get the next man who finds it a kiss, too. Pass it on, bros. Pass it on.

2. Listen to her.

Maybe she's got a thing for the Brooklyn Bridge. Include a cache on the bridge on your hunt. When she tells you the story of how her mother took her and her brother to this bridge to watch the sunset when she was younger, you listen. If she shares a story of how those walks remind her of someone she lost long ago, you pay attention. Look in her eyes, tuck her hair behind her ear, and let her know you care.

3. Have some motherfucking fun.

Include a geocache in Grand Central. (There are hundreds. Look them up.) Track one down and replace the Lego dude you discover inside it with, say, a small model train or a matchbox car. But you're not done. This is a two-part cache, and the second part is a surefire winner.

Head to the Whispering Arch Gallery on the lower floor of the terminal. It's near the Oyster Bar, between the intersection of two walkways. If you press your ear up against the tiles, you can hear someone whispering from the diagonal arch. This acoustic anomaly is a chance to tell her something that you've been keeping secret, holding back, or just weren't quite ready to say before. Maybe you'll say *do you want to go out again*, or maybe you'll tell her how you feel about her. Or maybe you'll admit there's a part of you that's glad things worked out the way they did so you can spend more time with her. She might even whisper back her own sweet nothing that can be heard crystal clear over the din of crowds, but only by you. She might even say *Me, too*.

4. Pick one in a park.

Wander through Central Park searching out a cache hidden behind the Alice in Wonderland statue, as kids clamber all over it and she watches them with a smile and a wish in her eyes. When she asks your favorite memory from when you were a kid, tell her it was the hours you spent in the park with your brother and sister, pretending you were pirates and hunting for treasure, too. Tell her you loved that it was always your job to make sure everyone made it home safely. But, dudes, that's my fucking story. Tell your own.

5. Accept you won't find them all.

Some geocaches will bedevil you. No matter how hard you try to find that one that some website said was absolutely in the 72nd Street subway station or definitely in the lobby of Radio City Music Hall, you'll never track it down.

Remember, you're in this together with your woman, and if you don't find one, try to have the best time possible. Tell her you'll do it again the next month. There's something about those words—try, try again—that might be exactly what she needs to hear.

When she thanks you at the end of the date, you can thank me for being your guide. Because she just might be into you.

Chapter Twenty-One

Nicole

We barbecue on a friend's rooftop, and we screw. We go lingerie shopping, and we do it. One evening, we see a revival of *Private Lives* at the Neil Simon Theater, and Ryder takes me backstage afterward to meet the director, Davis Milo, who happens to be a good friend of his.

"Your work is amazing. I loved *Crash the Moon*," I gush, mentioning a musical he recently won a Tony for. "Almost as much as I loved what you just did with Noel Coward's work."

He nods a thank you. "I'm thrilled to hear you enjoyed both. I had good material to work with."

He's as humble as he is handsome.

"Speaking of good material, I've been enjoying your radio show these days," Davis tells Ryder as the men do their man-hug thing.

"Good to hear. And if you ever want to commission my life story for Broadway, you know where to find me," Ryder says.

Davis laughs. "Indeed. Finding the cocky bastard to play you will be the real challenge."

Ryder laughs. "Just find the most handsome fella around, and you're good."

Davis turns to me with a sly smile. "You agree with his casting strategy?"

I run a hand down Ryder's arm. "I agree wholeheartedly."

When we leave the theater, Ryder has a town car waiting for us—one with a partition. We make excellent use of the private life we temporarily have in the backseat of the sleek, black auto that cruises through Manhattan. I'm not taking any chances. Just like last month, we've been doing it every night in the middle of my cycle. I'm not going to risk missing the window in case it turns out I ovulate early or late. I like to think I'm being thorough.

I'm also just the slightest bit addicted to sex with Ryder.

The next evening, we come up with the genius idea to play spin the bottle with an empty Pinot Grigio from my pre-baby-making days.

Cross-legged on my floor, I spin. It lands on Ruby, and I laugh. "Does that mean I kiss the dog?"

"Do it."

I bend to her and kiss her soft snout. Next, I plant a wet, slobbery kiss on Ryder's lips. He returns my lip-lock with an equally tongue-drenched one. When we break the kiss, he says, "Bet you thought I'm one of those guys who doesn't want to be kissed after you've just kissed a dog."

"The thought actually never occurred to me."

"Let the record reflect, I don't mind at all."

It's his turn to spin, and the amber glass bottle whizzes in four or five speedy rotations. After it slows, it settles on my door. "Is that your subtle way of kicking me out?" He shoots me a skeptical stare.

"Oh yes. I weighted the bottle because I just don't have it in me to send you on your way. I had to have the bottle do it."

He grabs at his crotch. "I'll just take my sperm and go, then."

"No, not the sperm, not the sperm," I tease.

He points to the bottle. "By the way, how the fuck do you play spin the bottle with two people?"

I laugh and shrug. "I don't actually know."

"Shame on you. I'm going to tell Cal there is something you don't know about dating games."

"Ooh. Those are fighting words." I stretch my arm to my coffee table and grab my phone, googling *spin the bottle for couples*. A few Pinterest boards turn up first, and I click on the photos. I zoom in on one from a dating site. It goes with an article called "Date Nights for Couples."

Hmm. That doesn't entirely apply. We're not a couple. Still, I enlarge the photo. It's a pink homemade board. "Ah, here's how you do it. You make a game board of challenges."

"Like what? Like *take off your bra*, or *give me a kiss*?"

I study the board. "Basically. But there are others, like *truth or dare*, or *slow dancing*, or *hold hands during the next turn*, or *coupon for massages*."

He scoffs. "I remember spin the bottle being more fun in middle school."

"I had my first kiss during a spin-the-bottle game."

"Yeah? What was his name? How was it?"

"Peter Lansing. He was this beanpole of a seventh-grade boy. He had braces. I was so terrified of them getting stuck to my lips that I gave him a quick peck and then scurried back to my spot."

Ryder huffs. "Great. Now I'm jealous of Peter Lansing."

I shove his shoulder. "You're jealous of a skinny thirteen-year-old who didn't even get tongue?"

"Evidently," he says, grabbing the bottle and setting it on the coffee table. He tugs me up, and before I know what's happening, he's scooped me into his arms.

"What was that for?" I ask, wondering why he's holding me as if he's going to carry me over the threshold.

"This is my version of spin the bottle," he says, his voice deep and husky. "Every single piece on the board is the same. *Fucking you.*"

Shivers sweep down my arms.

He carries me to my bedroom and sets me on the bed. He strips me, spending extra time on the red, lacy bra I bought when we went lingerie shopping. "That'll cover the taking-off-your-bra piece," he says, as he cups my breasts, making me moan as he kneads them.

"And this will take care of another one," he says as he drops a kiss on my lips. His kiss is hungry and fevered, and my back arches as he consumes my mouth.

He lets go and brings his mouth to my neck, leaving a hot trail of kisses in his wake. My hands dart out, and quickly I undress him, too.

We are naked together once more. He grasps my hips to move me up the bed. "Truth or dare. Do you want me to come inside you now?"

"So badly."

He shakes his head, plants his hands on my knees, and opens my legs. "Wrong answer."

"How was that wrong? That's what I *always* want."

"And you'll get it. But you come first. Always."

He stares at me with such heat in his eyes, such fire in the blue sky of his irises. I've never felt so wanted in my life. It floors me that I asked him to give me something tremendous, and yet here I am with a man who's ravenous for me. He climbs over me, straddling my thighs as he runs a hand up and down his gorgeous cock. I writhe as I watch him.

"You like this, baby?" He grips himself with a tight fist.

"Yes. God, yes."

"You want it, don't you?"

I lift my hips in answer. He stares down at the wetness between my legs. His throat rumbles. "So fucking pretty."

"Please," I moan, begging.

His hand slides up and down his hard-on. "In my game, we've just landed on *make her come*."

Chapter Twenty-Two

Ryder

Her eyes give her away.

She wants me to make her scream in pleasure.

She always does. I've learned in this short time with her that she's as addicted to orgasms as I'm hooked on giving them to her.

I've got her pinned like this, her attention solely on my dick. "I want you so fucking wet. So fucking crazy." I stroke from the base to the head, and her back arches.

"Ryder, please."

"Please what?"

"Please give it to me."

I shake my head. I grip harder and tighter, rocking my fist up and down my cock.

Her breath comes in fast, erratic pants. I want to tease her so badly. I want her wild with desire. "Don't let me do this alone," I say.

Her brows knit together. "You're not going to jerk off on me, are you?"

I nearly laugh at how worried she seems over the prospect of spilled seed. Coming on her chest would be pointless for her during this "window." I grab her hand, wrapping it around mine. I move our joined hands up and down my shaft. For a brief second, I am damn tempted to finish the job and jack off all over those glorious tits. "You'd look so good wearing my come all over your chest," I tell her with a groan as we stroke my cock together.

"No," she says with a desperate cry.

The image turns me on so much that a drop of liquid beads at the head of my cock. I swipe it with my thumb and bring it to her lips. "Suck it off," I tell her as I push my thumb into her mouth.

She wraps those sexy red lips nice and tight around my thumb and sucks off the first taste of me. My dick grows even thicker. I bring my hand back to my cock and play with myself some more.

"Touch yourself, baby. I want to watch you get yourself off."

Her hand shoots between her legs, and I scoot back, parking myself between her knees. Her legs are a *V* and her fingers fly over her wet clit.

"Oh God," she cries out as she arches into her fingers. It hits me like a flash of light in a darkened room. She's so turned on she's nearly there.

"You're going to come, baby, aren't you?"

She bites her lip and nods. Her face twists in exquisite torture. Her fingers fly over her pussy, and I have a front-row seat to the hottest show in town. I jack harder, faster. This is the sexiest thing I've ever seen.

In seconds, she goes off. She rocks her hips against her hand. "Oh God, I'm coming."

Her beautiful body writhes and twists and bucks, and I can't wait. I move up her, wedging myself between her gorgeous thighs. I bury myself in her and groan. Her wetness envelops me, and it feels so fucking good. "Nicole," I murmur as I lower my chest to her. "You're so sexy when you come."

"So are you."

She's even sexier when she comes twice, and I'm determined to bring her a double. I slow the pace, ease in and out. I swivel my hips, and bring her back up the hill. With each thrust, she pants harder. She moans louder.

"Yes, baby. Give it to me. Come again. I want it so bad."

She digs her nails into my back and pulls me deeper, matching me thrust for thrust. Her hips rise in one long, gorgeous lift, and she falls apart. Her eyes squeeze shut, and she calls my name as she comes again.

Something in me rattles loose.

Pleasure, but also more than that. Something I haven't felt in ages.

Intimacy.

Rather than fight it, I let it pull me under. I let it become part of us tonight. I reach for her hand, thread my fingers through hers, and I sink deep inside her as I climax.

When we both come down from the high, we're still holding hands. I don't want to let go.

"Like spin the bottle," she whispers as she stares at our linked fingers, a reverent look in her eyes.

"Yes. Just like spin the bottle."

We're silent as we lie there, me collapsed on her, but I don't want to move, and she doesn't seem to want me to. Her other hand travels to my hair, and she runs her fingers through it. "Do you want to stay the night?"

"That's not on the spin-the-bottle board," I say with a husky laugh.

"I know."

I raise my face from her shoulder and meet her eyes. I'm not a clueless guy. I'm not a twenty-something playboy who doesn't know what emotions are when they smack him in the face. I'm thirty-two, with a degree in psychology and a career based on a fine understanding of what happens between men and women when they come together.

I am 100 percent aware of what's happening here.

I *get* why my heart is expanding in my chest.

What scares me most is that even though I get it, I still say, "I do want to stay with you."

I call my neighbor, ask her to watch my dog, and then I spoon Nicole all through the night.

Chapter Twenty-Three

Nicole

This time we don't stop.

As we slide into the last week or so of my cycle, we don't quit our horizontal hobby.

I tell myself it's because we have his dates to finish, and it would be silly not to screw. We don't go at it nightly like we did when I might have conceived, but it seems foolish to execute the hotel hijacking date I promised without making full and proper use of the bed.

Because of our dogs, we make the hotel escape during the workday when we take a long lunch. It comes complete with shower sex at a swank Gramercy Park hotel, as well as another round on the bed.

In the post-orgasm haze, he wraps an arm around me and tugs me close. "For the record, I absolutely want you to be pregnant, but this has been the most fun I've ever had, and I'd be lying if I said I won't miss it once you're knocked up."

I smile and snuggle into the crook of his arm. A wistfulness settles over me, but it comes with sadness, too. "I know. Same here."

"It's sort of strange. That this is just going to end," he says in an even tone, as if he's making a scientific observation.

I close my eyes because the reality hurts.

Yes, we will end.

Yes, that's always been the plan.

We were supposed to be practical. A wham, bam, thank-you, ma'am. We weren't supposed to miss the sex, or the closeness, or the cuddling when this ends.

Our relationship has always been finite. It has a beginning, a middle, and a clear and obvious end. Like a rotation of a planet, our relationship starts in one spot and ends there, too, and no one should bat an eye or shed a tear.

Perhaps this makes me foolish, or maybe it just makes me focused on the mission, but I hadn't thought about how I might feel when this is over.

Now, I feel more sadness than I expected, and a longing, too, even as I'm consumed with my own amped-up hope for a baby.

"But we'll stay friends," I say, drawing in a breath that strengthens me. "We'll be friends and colleagues and Ping-Pong partners."

"Yes, we absolutely will."

I wonder if that prospect sounds odd to him, too.

But then I stop thinking when he kisses me once more, because I'll take what I can get for the next few days.

* * *

Three in the morning.

The twenty-eighth day.

The bitch doesn't show. But I don't trust her. She fucked with me once before. She might do it again.

The navy-blue night has draped its blanket over the city as most of Manhattan slumbers. But all over this island, there are pockets of people awake like me. Some with lonely hearts, some with graveyard jobs, some unable to let go of the day.

I lie awake, moonlight slicing through the blinds, casting a silvery glow on my bed. Ruby sprawls next to me, her russet tail twitching, her snout fluttering. She is dreaming of bones, peanut butter, and beef jerky while my wide-awake wishes are for soft breath, angel-wisp hair, and a new life to love.

I flash back to the time Ryder and I talked about how much love one has to give. I imagine when I do finally have a baby, I won't be wondering if I have enough love for everyone in my life. I'll be wondering how I can store so much inside me.

I like to think our ability to love is infinite. I want to feel the limitlessness of love.

But I know better than to blindly believe this time is the charm. I need to be prepared for my monthly bill to ruin my morning with her blood-red appearance.

When I first asked Ryder for his help, I thought he'd give me a cup of batter and I'd send him on his merry way. It would be a true transaction, and then I'd turn to basters and exam tables and appointments. Any disappointments I'd process on my own with friends and family.

Now, no one is more enmeshed than he.

If my test is negative again, do we simply go on? Do we have monthly dates in my bed during the nights when I'm most likely to conceive? Do we go about our separate lives the rest of the time? What if it takes three months, six months, or more?

Ryder's nearly done with his field guide to dating, and it thrills me to see his show and column inch back up in popularity. I gave him what he needed—a dating companion. But my need for him has no end date yet.

How can I expect him to maintain this sort of commitment to making love to me every month until I'm pregnant? How can I ask his commitment-phobic heart to keep practicing fidelity with my body?

But the more nights we spend together, the more it feels like we have some sort of commitment. I feel it in the pounding of my heart, in the calm inside my chest, in the warm glow that comes when he holds me. I see it in him, too, in the way he looks at me, in the tenderness of his touch, in how he sets his hand on my belly as if he's hoping too.

I don't know what to make of any of it, though. I let the thoughts repeat over and over, and in the tangled mess of my mind, I finally find sleep.

In the morning, I'm still blissfully period-free.

She doesn't show during the day, either, and that old friend hope bubbles up again, like a tease. Surely, she'll pull the rug out from under me any second. I tell myself that soon the crushing waves of cramps and disappointment will collide in me, mixing up a new cocktail of sadness.

But hope is a potent drug. It overpowers fear. My wish is stronger than my need to tamp down all this fervent want.

The next morning, I walk my dog in the chilly dawn, the remnants of this week's Halloween still in store windows. After I race back to my apartment, nerves and anticipation jostling inside me like boxers in a ring, I take the stick I never peed on last month, and I pee on it.

I stand in my bathroom, counting the seconds.

Chapter Twenty-Four

Ryder

"Cupcakes. You need cupcakes."

The caller sounds intrigued by my statement, but happy, too. I can hear the smile in his voice as he says, "Cupcakes? Tell me more."

I lean back in my chair, park my hands behind my head, and give him my best advice. "There's just something about cupcakes. They make you happy. When you're tasting cupcakes, you can flirt with your woman, you can get to know her—you can find out what makes her tick and what ticks her off."

The caller laughs. "Cupcakes are like a universal lubricant, then?"

I tense for a second, worried Cal will freak the fuck out if anything is remotely dirty on the show. Across from me, Jason widens his eyes in concern.

But I've learned that *dirty* isn't entirely the problem my boss has with my work. It's the *heartless dirty* he abhors. He doesn't mind a sex joke if it's mingled with a wish for intimacy. "Cupcakes sure do seem to pave the way for good things. I've concluded that it's the frosting, man. Frosting is everything."

"Awesome. I think I'll find a cupcake shop for my date tonight."

Jason shoots me a thumbs-up as we say good-bye to our caller.

It's just me and the mic now as I close out the show. "But the real frosting is this—it's listening to the woman. When she wants to talk, you listen. When she opens her heart, you listen. When she tells you her fears, you listen. Make her feel cherished, and that's how you win a woman, whether with cupcakes, mini golf, geocaching, trapeze, an afternoon hotel hijacking, or a night at the arcade." For the first time in a long time, I don't feel like a fraud when I talk about intimacy and emotions.

That doesn't mean I want those things in my life. I'm just glad I can do my job again without hating it. I've learned through this time with Nicole—maybe because the boundaries are safe and clear-cut—that getting to know someone doesn't mean giving them your heart to drop into a Cuisinart. Nicole hasn't chopped and julienned one of my favorite organs.

I suspect that's because of the nature of our arrangement. The terms and conditions we set in place created a test lab of sorts. A safe zone for dating. In our test lab, we didn't launch the rocket of romance into space, but we learned it can withstand the pressure of the atmosphere.

When we sign off, Jason offers a palm for high fiving. "Great show. Did I ever tell you I took Lizzie geocaching?"

"Oh yeah?" The geocaching column went viral, and we've heard from tons of men and women about their very own treasure hunt dates.

"Best time ever," he says as we leave the studio. "Followed your column to a T, even the Whispering Arch."

"How'd that go?"

Jason shrugs sheepishly. "Told her I loved her there."

"Wow," I say, smiling. "What did she say?"

"Said she loved me, too. I'm a lucky bastard." He points at me. "And you're the master. You know your shit."

"Glad I could help."

As Jason turns the other way, Cal marches down the hall, his long legs eating up the carpet. I draw a deep breath like I can protect myself from his ire. He stops and fixes me with an intense stare. "More. Of. That."

I relax. "Thanks."

He claps my shoulder. "Keep it up." He resumes his pace, and finally, the leash he's had on me loosens.

I turn the corner in the hall, and when I reach my office, I do a double take. A small box is perched on my desk. It's blue with a white bow on top. I furrow my brow, but then the color registers. Blue like the Katherine's jewelry store. Why on earth would someone send me a Katherine's box?

But even as I pose the question, the answer arrives, fully formed in my head. This box can only mean one thing. I fight off that tiny wish in the back of my mind that I'm wrong.

I tug at the ribbon, letting the white fabric fall on my desk, then I park myself in my chair, staring at the box as if it's a moon rock, an artifact from another planet. Or maybe a relic from another time in my life. Because I suspect that this box marks the end of the best two months I've spent with anyone.

I flick my finger against the robin's egg-blue cardboard, reminding myself that it may be an end, but it's the beginning of something else. Something Nicole has always wanted. Her heart's true desire.

That's all that matters. Not that I might miss her.

I remove the top, fish around in the wrapping paper, and pull out a silver key chain.

This is no dime-store key chain. It's not a knick knack you'd leave behind in a geocache. It's silver and real, and I grin wildly as I hold it up, watching the emblem dangle. I let my happiness for her blot out any unexpected, bittersweet emotions.

She's given me a key chain of a tadpole. It's engraved. "*I am eternally grateful for your gift.*"

I swallow past the dry, scratchy feeling in my throat, and let out a quiet whoop of excitement for my girl. I mean, for the woman I knocked up. She's not my girl. She's not my woman. She's not mine.

I pick up the phone and call her. When she answers, she's like a whole new woman. "It worked!" she shouts.

"So I gathered. That's fucking awesome."

"I am so unbelievably happy."

"You are going to be one hot mama."

She giggles. "And you are one sexy . . ." She stops herself from saying *dad*. "Sexy man. Do you want to come join us? I'm with my mom, and we're having lunch."

"I don't want to intrude."

There's a rustling sound, then another voice, older and confident. "Ryder, I hereby command you to meet us for lunch. I'm becoming a grandmother, and I must thank you in person."

Her tone brooks no argument.

* * *

Fifteen minutes later, I walk into a nearby cafe and scan the tables for Nicole. Her back is to me, and she's in a booth, seated across from a handsome older woman who looks like what I suspect Nicole will look like in twenty-five years.

I zoom in on Nicole's mane of red hair—hair I've had my hands tangled in, hair I've pulled and yanked, hair I've stroked when comforting her.

That red hair is *her* signature. She could have a child with that hair color. Or, I think as I drag my hand through my own hair, with mine. The life in her belly, the size of a chickpea or a fingernail or however those things are measured, already has our DNA—my genes twisted with hers to create the blueprint for another human being.

It's staggering.

It floors me.

I grab hold of the hostess desk. A young woman with a sleek ponytail asks how many in my party. I don't answer. My world comes to a standstill. Everything's a blur. I'm not sure how to speak. How to walk. How to talk. The enormity of what we've done slams into me, and this must be what shock feels like.

Like a vibration in your body.

Like your blood slows.

Nicole is going to have a baby, and I'm the father.

But I'm also not the father at all.

Not in the least.

Nicole's mother spots me and says something to her daughter. The woman I've spent so many nights with jerks her gaze around. When she sees me, her eyes dance, even from all the way across the cafe.

She jumps up from the booth.

I snap out of my slow-motion haze as Nicole rushes across the cafe, weaving through the tables. When she reaches me, she ropes her arms around my neck.

"Thank you," she says, breathlessly. "Thank you so much."

I bring her closer, hug her tighter. I can feel the happiness radiating off her in waves. It's a palpable thing. It has its own energy, its own temperature.

When she lets go, she takes my hand and guides me to the table.

"So, this is the man who's making me a grandmother." Her mother greets me as if I'm some kind of conquering hero.

I join them, and it's like I'm me, but I'm also not me. I don't know how I fit into this scenario. My part is over, like a character in a play who was killed off in the first act.

My role in the story of her life has ended.

Chapter Twenty-Five

Nicole

There's a new member of my life.

I've gotten to know her quite well during the last five weeks. Her name is Grace, short for "saving grace." I hug her, resting my cheek against the porcelain bowl.

We're so tight these days that I just shared my dinner with her. Though, to be fair, *dinner* is a rather generous term to describe the meal I had tonight.

An apple and peanut butter.

By my rough estimate, there is about ten percent of it still left inside me. I wait for my Rosemary's Baby to heave it out of me. I picture her or him down in my belly, having a conniption fit, tossing furniture, bureaus, whatever he or she can get her baby claws on.

When I saw my doctor earlier this week, she assured me this level of morning sickness is normal.

I told her we might have different definitions of the word "normal."

She said it was perfectly reasonable to barely keep a thing down, and that my body was producing all the nutrients my Rosemary's Baby needs, even if crackers and bread are the only food items my body will accept. She laughed when I used the name of the spawn-of-Satan baby from a famous horror flick for my unborn child. Obviously, my baby is truly an angel, but sometimes the behavior in my belly is devilish.

I asked my doctor how long morning sickness lasts.

"Till about the twelfth week," Dr. Robinson told me with the cheery smile on her face that never seems to disappear. I surmised she's never been a host for a parasite baby, but then she went on to inform me she had morning sickness for all four of her pregnancies.

"*Four?* You had three other ones after the first?"

She patted my hand. "Just wait till you get to labor, honey."

She sent me on my merry way, and here I am, with three more weeks left of morning, noon, and night sickness. It's the worst at night.

But even as Rosemary's Baby mercifully holds on to the remaining ten percent of my dinner, I wouldn't change a thing. Because the baby is healthy and that's all that matters.

I pull myself up from my new worship zone and pat Grace on the seat. "You did well tonight. We will meet again soon."

In fact, we spend breakfast together the next morning before I leave for work.

When I step into the hallway, my neighbor calls out to me as he walks to the elevator.

"Hey, Nicole! Your plunger is awesome," he says as if he's never experienced anything better than that household device.

"Glad to hear," I say as I lock my door.

"Any chance you could loan me an iron sometime?"

I shoot him a look. "Frederick, I can't loan you an iron. But do you need me to take you shopping for an iron?"

His eyes light up. "You would do that?"

I laugh. This poor guy. He's so helpless. I bet his mother did everything for him. Time for his neighbor to fix that. "I would. Let's go iron shopping soon."

* * *

When I reach the office, my stomach flips, and I bring my hand to my mouth.

Dear God, let me make it to the bathroom.

But then, the sensation fades away, and maybe it's actually nerves, because there's Ryder's office at the end of the hall. I'm not nervous to see him, per se. After all, I've seen him most days in the five weeks since learning I'm pregnant. We've pulled off the slide back into just-friends as seamlessly as we migrated into friends-with-benefits. We've grabbed lunch a few times, we've made a few dirty jokes, and I've done my darnedest to glide into this new phase without a hiccup.

The fact that he's done with his dating guide and I'm done with—well, with needing his sperm—has eased the re-entry. We don't have to spend time together like we did, so keeping our hands off one another has been doable.

But mostly, this new phase has been manageable because my morning sickness had the audacity to appear in week five and send my sex drive to Pluto.

Sometimes, though, the nerves show up when I see him. Perhaps because he's still handsome, and he's still kind, and we still made this Rosemary's Baby together.

I shove aside the nerves and pop in to say hello, as I do every day.

"Hey." I give a faint wave.

He swivels his chair around and smiles, a magnetic smile that nearly sends my stomach flipping once more. Maybe from butterflies this time, but I can't tell anymore. Too much is happening in my body. "Hey. How are you doing today?"

"Fabulous." I mime retching.

He grabs his waste bin and pretends to catch. "I've got barf bags from my last cross-country flight. Need one for the trip to your office?"

I manage a small laugh. "I think I'll make it, but I can't speak for whether I'll need one for this assignment. I have to write a column today on how to tell if the guy you met online is catfishing you. Several readers shared their horror stories with me. I'll probably retch from that."

"I might join you in the yakking. Catfishing curdles my stomach." He lifts his chin with a question. "Does Cal know yet?"

"About the column?"

Shaking his head, he swirls his finger in the direction of my belly.

"Not yet. I'm waiting till the first trimester ends before I share the news."

He nods. "Makes sense. Gotta make it past that point. The doctor still says everything is good?"

I detect a hint of concern in his voice, and it's endearing. So sweet, in fact, that I want to curl up in his lap and mope and whine and cry and then demand he bring me crackers and juice, and stroke my hair. Clearly, this pregnancy has warped my mind. My body is so out of whack that I'm picturing things I shouldn't be picturing.

Instead, I hold my chin high. "I'm the spitting image of health, she tells me."

Ryder smiles, though it doesn't seem to reach his eyes. I wonder if he thinks of me differently now. Maybe that's the reason his smile isn't the same. Perhaps I've been sorted into some other class of woman now. I was once a sexual being; now I land squarely in the miserable pregnant woman section. I still see him the same way, though. When I look at him now, I think about how handsome he is with those jeans and that shirt. Other times, my mind wanders to how devastatingly gorgeous he looks without a stitch of clothing on.

But I can't even hold on to those thoughts in my mind because my body is a rebel. My stomach yanks all dirty images from me and blends them up with toast and crackers.

"Gotta go." I make it to the bathroom, and I've named this room Mercy because some sweet soul designed this building with single bathrooms, instead of stalls. It makes it that much easier to keep my little baby all mine.

When my stomach is empty, I dive into the tales of catfishing, and I want to throat-punch every man who ever did this.

I'm confident Rosemary's Baby agrees.

At the end of the day, Ryder knocks on my office door. He stands in the doorway, looking cool and relaxed. I catalog his clothes this time, since I'm not about to heave. He wears dark jeans that fit him so damn well I bet they gossip to other jeans about how good it feels to hug his legs. The dark blue Henley makes his eyes look even more like the sky, and that damn black leather jacket reminds me how sexy he is. It's such an edgy look for a man who's so goddamn good. I want to stare at his beauty all night. Revel in his hotness. Freeze this moment when I feel good, and I can spend the night staring at him.

That's not weird at all.

"Hey."

"Hey," I say as I zip my bag and toss a scarf around my neck. December has fallen in Manhattan.

"Are you up for Ping-Pong tonight? Match against LGO."

My eyes widen, and that *oh shit I totally forgot* feeling sweeps over me.

"You forgot," he says, his lips twitching as if it's cute I can't remember anything.

I grab my coat from the back of the door. "Baby brain. I can start using that excuse already, right?"

"If you ask me, this is your chance to milk it. Use it for everything. For the next thirty-one weeks, right?"

I stop, with one arm in a sleeve. "You know exactly how far along I am?"

"I counted. Conception was mid-October, so that was two weeks. You were four weeks when you found out you were pregnant on November second. Now it's five weeks later, and you're nine weeks along."

Endearing doesn't cover it anymore.

Ryder steps behind me and finishes the job with the other sleeve, putting my coat on me. He faces me, adjusting the scarf and the collar. "Stay warm."

"Wait! I'll play tonight."

His eyes twinkle. "You will?"

I hold up a hand. "Unless Rosemary attacks me again with another bout of nighttime sickness."

"You named the baby? Are you having a girl?" His voice rises at the end with a touch of excitement.

I wave that off. "No. Rosemary's Baby. Like the movie."

"Ah. Got it. But Rosemary is a cute name for a girl."

"It is." I sling my bag over my shoulder, turn off the light, and lock my door.

We leave together, and before I know it, he's walked me all the way to my home, twenty blocks away. At the entrance to my building, a pang of sadness darts through me. I desperately want to invite him upstairs. But for what? I'm not in the mood for sex, and I can't stomach food, and besides, I'm seeing him in a few hours for Ping-Pong.

Still, I wouldn't mind just hanging out with him, watching one of my favorite flicks. *Gone With the Wind* or *Talladega Nights*.

I part my lips to speak, but I yank the words back in. I might miss him in moments like these, but we had a deal. We had an arrangement. He did his part so damn well. He put the bun in my oven in a mere two months, and now I've got to do my job and bake it without being a psycho emotional pregnant freak who invites the baby donor upstairs for no reason other than she's a weeble-wobble of out-of-control hormones. I remind myself that he was in it for the hot sex with a horny woman trying to get knocked up, and for the companionship on a work project. The work project is done, and now I'm anything but a horny woman.

"I'll see you at eight at the Lucky Spot," I say, bouncing on my toes, trying to muster all the chipperness I possibly can. "And I'll bring my lucky paddle."

"See you then, Nicole," he says, then plants a chaste kiss on my cheek and leaves.

See? He's completely content to be my Ping-Pong partner, and only my Ping-Pong partner. He's not looking for a hormonal co-worker to watch Scarlett O'Hara with.

But he does need someone to help crush the opposition tonight. I can be that person for him. I head upstairs, determined to drag my sorry ass out of my apartment in a few hours' time. I walk my dog, shower, pull on jeans and a pretty red sweater, and eat a few spoonfuls of rice.

I take my time with the rice, hoping to coax the grains to stay down.

But Rosemary has other plans.

Chapter Twenty-Six

Ryder

Sweat drips down my chest, and I breathe hard from the racquetball game as I walk down the hall of the club. Flynn grins like a fool. The bastard.

"You're gloating," I grumble.

"I know. But you have to know I've only beaten you nineteen percent of the time—"

I jerk my head. "Nineteen percent?"

"Dude. Math is my forte. We've played forty-two games, and I've won eight, including tonight's."

"No wonder you're a rich bastard. That brain of yours is an impressive beast."

"That's nothing. You want to talk impressive math? Let's get into irreducible polynomials with integer coefficients."

I whistle in appreciation, and I'm about to hassle him some more when my phone rings. I grab it from the side of my gym bag. Nicole's name flashes. I slide my finger across the screen in a nanosecond. "Hey, how's it going?"

"I don't know how anyone craves pickles in the first trimester." Her voice is beleaguered. "I don't know how any pregnant woman has ever craved anything in the history of being pregnant. I ate rice and I can't even keep that down. I think I have a date with Grace, my toilet bowl."

"You named the toilet bowl, too?"

"We're besties these days."

"Do you need anything? Can I get you anything at all?" I ask, wishing there was something I could do for her.

"No. Just go on without me," she says like a soldier in a war movie telling his platoon to keep fighting.

"Seriously?"

"If I show up tonight, I might dry heave all over the opponents, so while that could be a great strategy for winning by default or scaring the daylights out of them, I should stay home."

I laugh but then quickly correct myself. "I meant *seriously* as in you seriously don't need anything? I'm happy to help."

She scoffs. "Night sickness is best not seen by someone who might have found me attractive at one point."

"He still does," I say as we head into the stairwell.

But she's heaving and coughing, so I doubt she heard me. When she stops, she asks, "Is there anyone else who can be your partner?"

I glance at Flynn. "Yup. I'm looking at him now."

We say good-bye, and I point at Flynn. "You're my new Ping-Pong partner tonight, and I am counting on you to kick unholy ass one hundred percent of the time."

He pumps a fist. "I will, and trust me, I won't make any ball jokes. Or knock-knock ball jokes for that matter."

* * *

Two hours later, we've crushed the competition, and Flynn is a happy motherfucker. Wish I could say the same about myself. While I'm glad we won, I keep thinking about Nicole, alone in her apartment with her no-fun nausea.

But I do my best to enjoy the moment.

We head to the bar to toast our victory, and while we order, a woman in a slinky red dress at the end of the bar stares at Flynn. Out of the corner of my eye, I notice she grabs her cell phone, looks at my buddy, quickly taps on the screen, then looks at him again. Recognition dawns on her face.

As the bartender delivers our drinks, Slinky Dress makes her way to our end of the bar. "Hi," she says, cutting in front of me to chat with him. Her voice drips with honey. "I couldn't help but notice you from the other end of the bar. You have the most gorgeous green eyes."

I arch a skeptical brow. She noticed his eye color from across the bar? Or perhaps she googled Flynn Parker's vitals?

Flynn smiles. "Thank you. Your brown eyes are lovely, too."

He's such a gentleman, and I've got to look out for him.

"I love this place," the woman says. "It's so close to where I live. The vibe here is great."

As she chats up Flynn, I give them some space so I can conduct both research and recon. I google morning sickness treatments while keeping an eye on Slinky Dress. Something is off about her. The woman's dress looks cheap, as if it's from a discount mall, judging from the weird stitching down the side. Meanwhile, she's telling Flynn she works at an advertising agency, planning campaigns for all sorts of high-end consumer products.

Her coat is draped on the empty stool next to her. The corner of a white ticket pokes out of the pocket. Her back is to me as she talks to my buddy. "It's so thrilling being young and living in Manhattan, isn't it?" She drops her chin in her hand, surely batting her eyes at Flynn as I find a site that gives me an idea for something—a small thing—that I can do for Nicole.

"The city's awesome. What part do you live in?" Flynn asks.

"I'm in the Village. I walked here tonight after work."

That's when the alarm bells ring. Holding my phone as if I'm simply trying to get a better signal, I lean closer to her coat and peer at the white paper in the pocket. It's a New Jersey Transit ticket with today's date on it.

I hit send on the online order, toss some bills on the counter, and clear my throat. "Flynn. We need to get out of here."

"That's okay. I'll hang a bit."

I tip my forehead to the door and give him a meaningful stare. "You were going to help me move my TV stand."

"I was?" He blinks, then a second later, it hits him. "Yes, I was."

Once we're outside, he says, "What was that about?"

As the cold snaps my face, I pull up my collar. "Just a little live catfishing. That woman was from Jersey. She doesn't work on Madison Avenue. She watched you from across the bar, looked you up on her phone, figured out who you were, and made her move. I bet she's a gold digger."

His jaw drops. "Shit, man. You are good."

I shrug. "Sometimes the radar works."

He points at me. "That radar of yours is spot on. Like when you told me to assess a woman's interest like an algorithm. I tried that strategy on a date recently, and the woman had Trojan horse written all over her, so I moved on."

"Good. I don't want anyone taking advantage of you."

"I appreciate that," he says as we walk toward Seventh Avenue. He's quiet for a minute. "You know . . . a buddy of mine is recently divorced. He's eager to get back out there. Throw his hat in the ring. I should have him talk to you."

"Always happy to help a brother out."

"I didn't mean for help. I meant as business for you, asshole."

* * *

A little later, as I walk Romeo around the block, my phone rings. Nicole's name flashes on the screen, and it's as if a light flashes in my chest.

I answer it. "All Day Sickness Solutions, at your service."

She laughs. "Grape Gatorade is my favorite. How did you know?"

"Took a wild guess."

"It tastes like heaven. Thank you."

"Is it helping?"

"If tasting good helps, then yes."

"I wish there was something I could do for you." My heart feels like a compass pointing uptown. It aches with the need to go help her.

"Me, too. But seriously. This drink is the bomb."

"I looked up how to treat morning sickness. I figured you had tried most things, but it couldn't hurt to send reinforcements."

"I do feel better now. And I plan to dive into the crackers later. And the ginger ale."

That's all I can ask for. "I'm glad to hear that." I raise my gaze to the sky. "Looks like snow is coming tonight."

"I love snow in Manhattan when it's falling. It's so peaceful," she says as Romeo sniffs a bush by the stoop of a brick building.

"Me, too. It's the one thing that transforms New York entirely. It's like this blanket of white, and the whole city is hushed as it comes down."

"One of my favorite things is waking up in the middle of the night as the snow falls. You look out the window and New York has become an idyllic snow village where everything is soft and white, before the city wakes up." She sighs dreamily.

I crane my gaze heavenward. "I think you'll get that tonight, Nicole."

"I want it tonight, and if I'm allowed to be greedy, I'd like a white Christmas, too. Preferably, one without any Christmas morning, Christmas day, or Christmas night sickness."

I laugh lightly. "I'll ask Santa to bring that to you. Seems you've been a good girl this year, and you deserve it." I turn the corner onto my block. "What are you doing for the holidays?"

"I'll go to my mom's. My brother will be in town, so he'll want to spend most of the holiday making fun of me."

"Why would he do that?"

"He's a big brother. It's in his DNA. Plus, he now gets to make pregnancy jokes nonstop."

For a moment, I wish she'd invite me to join her. Not because I want to hear pregnancy jokes, but because I want to be the guy who gets to defend her and volley back, maybe even say something a little off-color about how I got her that way. I want her family to know the pregnancy jokes are because of me. Yeah, they know I gave her the DNA and all that jazz, but they don't know *me*.

Though, I thought I knew Maggie, but it turned out I didn't know her at all. I might have met her family, might have made jokes with them, but in the end, none of that saved me from the hurt.

I don't bother inviting myself over.

"What about you?" she asks.

"I'm going skiing with Devon, Paul, and Simone, and our sister Claire, who'll be in this neck of the woods for the holidays."

"That sounds like fun."

"We try to go every year."

"Lots of snow bunnies probably," she says, her tone tight, and I detect a note of jealousy in her voice.

"I doubt there will be any snow bunnies."

"I think if we were taking bets, I'd win this one."

I'm about to dispel that notion when she groans. "Are you feeling sick again?"

Ask me over. Ask me to help. I'll do it.

"No. Ruby is pacing. She has to go out. And it's late and cold."

I could offer to walk her dog right now. But she's sixty blocks away, and the dog only needs to whiz. If I offer to haul ass uptown for a five-minute pee break, that'd sound like I didn't pay attention to the contract I signed. *No commitments.*

I don't make the offer. But I offer the grape Gatorade equivalent. "If I were there, I'd walk her for you."

"If you were here, I'd take you up on that."

When we hang up, I'm standing in front of my building, holding my keys with the tadpole charm, wondering what the fuck I'm supposed to do about the whole no expectations part of the arrangement.

Right now, I want expectations.

Chapter Twenty-Seven

Nicole

I don't erase the photos he sent me of the falling snow.

I don't delete the ones he sent me a few days later when it snowed again.

And I don't delete the pics he sent last night when it flurried, because the caption made me laugh. "It's barely a blanket. More like a Saran Wrap of snow. But maybe you'll have your white Christmas. May it be free of barf."

On Christmas morning, my wish comes true.

Snow, and a peaceful belly.

Happy almost-end-of-the-first-trimester to me.

My appetite is back, too, and its timing couldn't be better since my mom made us chocolate chip pancakes. Ruby and Lorenzo wait in the living room like good little Christmas elves as we eat in the kitchen. My mother's gentleman caller, James, will join us shortly.

My brother, Aiden, digs in then points at me with his fork. "No more morning sickness?"

I twist my index and middle fingers together. "Seems that way."

He chews then stares at me with his intense green eyes. He has our father's eyes. "Ever thought about what it would be like if men were the ones who got pregnant?"

Our mom answers right away. "Maternity leave would last for two years with full pay, for one thing." She reaches for her orange juice. No Bluetooth today. Even hard-working brokers take Christmas off.

Christmas music plays from her sound system. "Let it Snow." It's the perfect soundtrack for today. Her home smells of nutmeg and pine, and I want to spend the day savoring the scents that delight me once more.

"And morning sickness would rank as the nation's number-one health problem," Aiden adds. He lifts his chin toward me, switching gears lickety-split. "How's the baby daddy with all this?"

"Aiden," my mother chides with a sharp look.

"What? We don't call him that? Baby daddy?" Aiden is genuinely surprised.

I cut in. "He's fine with everything."

"No, seriously," my brother says, adamant. "What do I call him?"

"He's not here. You don't have to call him anything," I say, irritation starting to bubble up.

"Donor, then?" Aiden presses.

"Donor will be fine," my mother says. "Now, what was your question?"

Aiden puts his fork down. "So, he's good with all this. He's a friend, you said?"

I nod, my shoulders tensing. "He's a friend."

"And he's good with just firing off and . . . boom," Aiden says, thrusting one arm far in front of him as if he's demonstrating what it means to take off.

"They have an agreement, Aiden. Everything is fine," my mom says, her tone crisp and her meaning clear. *Shut the fuck up, son.*

He holds up his hands, such the innocent. "Hey, whatever works. It's the Modern School of Relationship Theory, right?" my brother says, quoting one of my column topics back to me. The theory goes like this—who is anyone on the outside to judge? Maybe a woman has two partners because they're all cool with polyamory. Perhaps a couple decides to be swingers and maintain an open marriage. Or possibly, two lesbians ask their gay best friend to donate sperm for a baby that one of the women will carry. If everyone is happy and consenting, why should anyone on the outside decide what's right or wrong?

"Yes, I suppose it is, and he's completely fine with it," I say, unable to breathe Ryder's name in front of my brother. Maybe because I feel judged, and I feel Ryder is being judged, too. Even though I know in my heart that my brother isn't condemning anyone, I will defend Ryder no matter what.

"Good," Aiden says, stabbing another bite of the pancake. "And you look good. You're . . . what do they say?" He gestures to my face. "You're glowing." He raises an eyebrow. "It's the same kind of glow you'd have if you were getting some regularly."

Getting some. For the first time in ages, the thought of sex is mildly appealing. But not while I'm at the table with my brother.

My mother glares at him again. "Aiden. Not at the table."

"So I can make randy jokes anyplace else? Excellent."

"Ignore him," my mother says to me. "If you feed the wild animal, he'll keep coming back."

Aiden flashes a gleaming grin. "Too late, Mom. You're stuck with me. Also, these pancakes are awesome."

When breakfast is over, Aiden cleans up, telling us to sit by the tree and relax. My mom says she's going to freshen up, so I settle into the couch alone, tucking my feet under me as Ruby rests her snout on a cushion. A nutcracker stares at me from the table, and the music shifts to "Have Yourself a Merry Little Christmas."

Such a melancholy song for the holidays, happy and sad at the same time. As I wait for my family to join me, the words about muddling through somehow echo in my mind, and my eyes land on a photo of my father on the end table. My mom took the shot—my dad is walking down the street, his back to the camera, one hand holding mine, the other one Aiden's.

I must have been three, my brother four. I've seen this image so many times, but this morning, on this holiday, the twenty-fifth without him, I miss him more than I have in a long time.

Absently, my hand slides to my belly. It's softer, and I feel the first sign of a little baby bump.

The lump in my throat turns into a hard, sharp pain. I try to swallow past it, but it stays there because I'm happy and I'm sad at the same time. I'm hopeful for the future, and yet I long for the people I miss so much.

My mom returns to answer the door, letting James in. He wears a Santa hat.

"Ho, ho, ho!" He hangs his coat by the door before he gives me a hug, his blue eyes crinkling at the corners as he smiles and waves to my belly. "You look beautiful."

"Thank you. Good to see you, James."

My mother beams as he compliments me. She chose well with him.

"Time for stockings," she declares, and she unhooks four from the mantel, handing a silver one to James, a red and white one to Aiden, and a cranberry knit one to me.

The stocking with the paw print on it is in her hands. "This one is for the dogs," she says, then stage-whispers, "Ruby and Lorenzo won't mind sharing a stocking, will they?"

"I doubt Ruby minds, but Lorenzo might be mad at you for days," James remarks. My mom's greyhound mix raises a disdainful snout in our direction then huffs as he plops his long nose on his soft, downy dog bed. Ruby, meanwhile, smiles shamelessly.

"Lorenzo is jealous. Be careful, James."

"Oh, I am well aware of his jealousy."

My mom points to my stocking. "Now, I know we'll start working on your closet/nursery redo in the third trimester so you're ready, but I'm not getting anything for the baby until he or she is born." I nod, understanding. She doesn't want to tempt fate. "So this is for you."

I dip my hand inside and grab a wrapped envelope. I slide my thumb under it and take out a homemade gift certificate. I laugh. It's for dog babysitting services. Redeemable anytime.

"I'll practice my babysitting with your dog. Whenever you need a break, you call on me," she says.

"I will."

The lump returns once more as I think about someone else I want to call on.

* * *

That afternoon, I join the crew for a few hours. Delaney and her boyfriend, Tyler, invited me for Christmas cookies, hot chocolate, and hot toddies. Tyler's best buddy, Simon, is hosting the soiree with his wife, Abby, at his swank East Side home.

I've gotten to know them a bit, but I haven't seen them in a few months, so I'm surprised to find Abby has a little belly, too, though she's clearly further along than me. With the amount of time I've spent studying pregnancy, and with Abby's small stature—she's a pipsqueak—I'm guessing she's five and a half months.

I ask her if she is.

"Five months and three weeks." Abby holds up her hot chocolate and clinks mugs to mine. "Very impressive pregnancy radar."

I hold up my thumb and forefinger to show a sliver of space. "I'm only slightly obsessed about pregnancy. I'm eleven weeks." She beams and congratulates me, and I add, "And I can't wait to get out of the first trimester. I finally got my appetite back."

Abby scans the room as if she's making sure no kids are around then says, "That's not the only appetite you get back in the second trimester."

"Oh yeah?"

She runs a hand through her honey-colored curls. "Some days, it's like all you want to do is jump on him and climb him like a tree." She casts a glance at her handsome husband across the room.

I laugh. "Sounds like fun."

"It's like you're walking around in this state of constant arousal. He'll touch your shoulder when you're getting out the pasta to make dinner, and you grab him, and he takes you right then and there. Who cares about the penne?"

"God, that sounds heavenly," I say, and if I wasn't missing Ryder before, I am now. A lot.

"And the orgasms," she says quietly. "Better than any I've ever had before, and it's not like they were mediocre to start with."

I whimper. "I know what I'll be doing tonight. A little online Christmas shopping for some new vibrators."

"Get extra batteries, too. You'll need them."

When I hop on the Internet later, I do just that. I'm like a bear, stocking up for the winter.

A few weeks later, I take Frederick shopping for an iron. Then, I teach him how to use it. Later that night, he sends me a pizza as a thank-you gift. It's delicious.

The next day I get an even better gift. At my thirteen-week appointment, the doctor brandishes an ultrasound wand and squirts some gel on my belly.

"Don't tell me the sex," I warn.

Dr. Robinson laughs. "You've only told me twenty times not to tell you the baby's gender."

"Yes, I'm what's known as a repeater," I say.

I lie on the table, my purple sweater tucked under my breasts, my jeans undone as she travels across my stomach, peering at the ultrasound screen.

She nods as if she's pleased. The look on her face makes me relax even more. There's nothing better than a satisfied doctor when you're the patient. "We're looking good," she says, then she meets my eyes. "Do you want to hear your baby's heartbeat?"

"Yes," I say breathlessly.

As she positions the wand just so, searching for the right spot, I hold my breath, waiting.

I hear galloping horses, thunder across the sky, and I know the meaning of the word *joy*. It floods my entire being as tears streak down my face. "That's amazing," I whisper, as if we're in church.

I feel as if I'm in the presence of something holy. Something greater than I've ever experienced before.

New life.

The smile that spreads across my face is like wings, and I'm soaring with happiness.

"It's beautiful, isn't it?" the doctor asks.

"The best music ever."

We listen for a few more seconds, the heartbeat the only noise in the otherwise quiet exam room. It's the only sound in my entire world.

I wish Ryder were here to share this moment with me.

"You can record the sound on your phone if you want to play it later," she offers.

For a moment, I'm tempted to take her up on it. But I shake my head. I've no idea if Ryder would even want to hear the heartbeat, and for me, I want to just live in this moment, not on my phone.

"That's okay," I say, shaking my head. "I like experiencing it live better."

The doctor continues her travels over my belly, away from the heart, checking everything else one more time.

As I lie here, I think of the man who made this happen—his kindness, his goodness, his humor. I swallow back another round of tears and try to shove away these scary new impulses.

It's wishful thinking to long for him to be a part of this phase. He didn't sign up for this role. He didn't ask to be by my side. He gave me the part of him I needed most.

Just because I might want more right now doesn't mean I can expect it.

Later, when I go home, I let myself linger once more on that wild idea of Ryder sharing this with me. Then I dismiss it, because the sky fills with dark clouds, as if agreeing with me that nothing good can come of it.

Chapter Twenty-Eight

Ryder

I see it from one hundred feet away.

Adrenaline takes over as Simone crashes on the slope, a hot pink blur tumbling around the curve in the run.

Jamming my poles into the packed snow, I ski as quickly as I can to her, stopping abruptly and bending to offer a hand. "You okay, sweetie?"

She winces but nods bravely. "Just a crash. I'm fine."

I breathe a huge sigh of relief. "Are you sure?"

She looks at me, and even with the ski goggles on, I can see her brown eyes twinkle. She laughs. "I fell on my butt, and you're freaking out."

I am.

She's right.

I'm completely freaking out.

I huff and act indignant, going with it. "Oh, that's nice. Make fun of the caring, considerate uncle."

"It's cute. You're sweet," she says and takes my hand as I yank her up. "I'm totally fine. Falling is normal."

"It still worries me when I see you do it, especially since you're my responsibility."

Devon and Paul are racing the black diamonds today, so Simone and I have tackled the easy to medium runs. She's a snowboarder, and I prefer to kick it old-school on skis. This is our ski weekend trip over the Martin Luther King Jr. holiday. We already skied during Christmas and had an absolute blast.

In the last few weeks, I've spent more time with Simone and Devon on the weekends than usual, grabbing any chance I can to join them for ski trips, movies, and dinners out. I was so damn occupied in the fall that if I don't keep busy now, I'll be like one of those lonely lions in a cage at the zoo, pacing back and forth all day long.

Simone pretends to whisper, "Since I'm your responsibility, do you want to sneak off and get a hot chocolate?"

"I love the way you think. But let's make it down the hill first."

She nods, as she readjusts herself on her board. "Race ya."

She pushes off, shushing down the slope with ease, and I follow as I've done the whole day, watching as I go. I don't let her out of my sight. Lately, I've felt even more protective of her. Every time something *might* happen to her, my heart feels as if it's beating outside my body. The other day when I walked her to art class in the city, I kept her even closer to my side when we neared the crosswalk. That's just smart in New York, of course. But I was like a fucking hawk the way I kept my eye on her.

That evening after the day on the slopes, my brother and I hang in the lodge while Paul and Simone get ready for dinner back in the cabin.

Devon lifts his glass of Scotch and takes a drink as we lounge in big wooden chairs by a roaring fire. "I've been meaning to tell you about a woman we chatted with while skiing."

"You chatted with a woman? Has hell frozen over?"

He rolls his eyes. "We shared a fucking chair lift with her, dickhead."

"Oh. For a second I thought you were switching to my team."

"The likelihood of that is about the same as you switching to my team."

"About a ten million below zero chance?"

Devon winks. "You got it. Also, I talk to women all the time, on account of not being a sexist asshole."

I raise my glass. "Good point."

"Anyway, this woman was fun, smart, and I suppose she was pretty, if you like that sort of thing."

"Pretty ladies are definitely my sort of thing," I say, sticking out my tongue and flicking it at him.

He gazes at the ceiling. "Why do I bother to help him?"

I rub my ear. "I'm sorry, did I need help for something?"

"Yes," Devon says adamantly, leveling me with his big brother stare. "Do you want me to invite her to dinner so you can meet her?"

I nearly choke on my whiskey. "Are you setting me up?"

This is so not my brother.

"I'm trying to. It's been more than a year since Maggie, and you and Nicole are done with your project, so it seems like a good time."

"I just never thought you had any matchmaking bones in your body."

Devon waves me off. "Forget I said it."

I lean forward in the chair. "No, seriously. I appreciate it. But . . . I don't know."

He takes a swig of his drink. "You're not ready to date yet?"

I drag a hand across my jaw as I sigh. His assessment is spot on. "That sounds right."

"Maggie, still?"

I don't answer him at first. I take a swallow of the whiskey, letting it burn in my chest while the fire warms my back. There was a time not so long ago when I would have answered quickly with a yes. But my ex-wife isn't front and center in my mind anymore. She might still be my roadblock, my "danger ahead" sign. But she's not preventing me from wanting to go on a date.

Someone else very much is, and she doesn't even know it. She doesn't even know what she's done to me. I barely comprehend it myself. "No. It's not about Maggie."

Devon raises an eyebrow in question. The answer dawns on him. "Because of Nicole?"

I heave a sigh and nod. "Yeah, turns out I kind of like her."

"Well, isn't that a humdinger?"

"You can say that again."

* * *

I get my Ping-Pong partner back, but no greater clarity on my humdinger of a quandary. February flurries into town, bringing with it another epic chill, and a rounder belly to the woman at the epicenter of my thoughts. The month also means Valentine's Day, and Cal tells me my show is going on the road for a few weeks.

"Ratings are improving," he says as he tells me the plan. "Your columns and field guide were a hit. And the crazy thing is, you've got female listeners and readers now, too. We want to do some live shows and talk to the crowds about their ideas of love, relationships, and what it takes to have several great dates. The best part? We've got a brand-new sponsor for it."

Sponsorship means the leash has loosened another few feet. A quick tour might also mean I can rebuild my credibility as a dating coach. Plus, I've nabbed my first consulting client in months in Flynn's buddy.

All in all, I can't complain about work anymore.

Nicole seems happier, too, now that her miserable days are behind her. She's the picture of health and vitality, from the reddish tint in her cheeks, to the spring in her step, to the smile she's been sporting a helluva lot more around the office. She told Cal she's pregnant, and while she hasn't said a word about who the father is, no one has pressed her, even our boss.

"He didn't try to get the nitty-gritty out of you?" I asked over lunch a few weeks ago.

She shook her head. "HR rules. He can't."

Ironic, since he had no problem getting personal with me when it came to bringing up my ex-wife. But I do understand that Nicole's situation is different—seeing as how she's baking a person inside her. A few years ago, a gal in advertising who has a female partner was pregnant. She never breathed a word about where the other half of the DNA came from. I have no doubt our co-workers are whispering and wondering who knocked up Nicole. But this is Manhattan, and everyone seems to know someone who's gone into parenthood in an unconventional way.

As we play tonight against our long-time rivals, I watch her more closely than I have before. Not just because her ass still looks great. It does. Oh yes, does it ever look bitable. But because I understand that worry I felt for Simone much better. It's doubled with Nicole, given what she carries inside her.

Make that tripled, since our opponents are Crazy Swing Steve and his regular partner.

Nicole bounces on the balls of her feet, paddle in hand, determination etched in her eyes. Steve juts his arm out as he slams a ball to me. I stretch for it, smashing it back across the table to his teammate.

The other guy smacks the white ball in a neat diagonal to Nicole, who sends it screeching to the other side.

Steve lunges for it, his teammate leapfrogging out of the way. The ball comes to me, and we volley like that until Steve's swing seems to exhaust his teammate so much that the guy curses loudly as he runs for the ball, swatting it wildly across the table in Nicole's direction.

Ever the competitor, she races to the far corner, slapping the prize with a crisp backhand that sends her reeling. She's all forward momentum, and it topples her, taking her down.

The paddle tumbles from her hand, and she has no place to go but the floor. Her arms shoot out in front of her, and she breaks the fall with a loud smack of her hands.

A rush of harsh breath.

A crack of her knee on the hard surface.

Falls are not uncommon in Ping-Pong. I've hit the floor a number of times. So has Steve. So has Flynn. So has Nicole.

But none of that matters. My stomach plummets and dread ices my bones the instant the pregnant woman I'm crazy for hits the floor.

Chapter Twenty-Nine

Ryder

"I'm okay, I'm okay, I'm okay."

Nicole says those words over and over again, like a mantra.

Or like she wants me to shut up because I can't stop asking if she's okay. With one hand on her shoulder and the other on her lower back, I gently help her to her feet.

"Are you okay?" I ask again. My heart screams in my chest. Nerves skate up the back of my neck. If I was worried when Simone fell on her butt, that was nothing compared to now.

Once she's upright, I set a hand on her belly, feeling the small curve for the first time. I flinch inside, but not because I'm freaked out. My reaction is because she feels so different, of course, than she's ever felt before. Gone is that flat belly. In its place is this blooming roundness that's unexpectedly . . . attractive. But the awareness of what's behind this curve brings an even sharper reminder of the stakes. *A life.* I have no clue what I'm doing with my hands on her stomach. I'm not a doctor. I can't feel if the baby is okay. But I've got to do something.

"I'm fine, Ryder. I swear." She shakes out her wrist, wincing. "But . . ."

"But what?"

She sucks in a breath as if she's in pain. "My wrist really hurts."

"We're going to the ER. Now."

Steve strides over. "You okay?"

"I'm totally fine," she says.

"She's not," I snap. "Her wrist is sprained." I have no clue if that's the case, but it feels true, and I'm taking her to the hospital.

I grab our coats and guide her through the bar, my arm wrapped around her like a shield.

We make it to the doorway, and I slide her coat onto her arms then put my leather jacket on. Once outside, I hail a cab and tell the driver to take us to Mercy Hospital.

All I can think about is her and the baby, and if the baby's going to be okay. But I don't want to say that out loud. I don't want to scare her, don't want her to know my mind is zipping to terrifying conclusions. On the drive to the hospital, I chatter on about Steve and his swing, and I smooth her hair, and I stroke her arm, and I tell her that we're just being cautious by going to the ER.

"You're crazy," she says, meeting my gaze. "You're worried for nothing." She's trying to reassure me, and I will have none of that. It's my job to take care of her.

"You fell on your wrist and can barely move it."

And I'm terrified about our baby.

I catch my breath, inhaling sharply.

Holy fucking shit.

I've never thought of her baby as mine.

Not till now.

But there it is. I've thought it. It's moved from a shapeless, formless concept to the concrete way I see the life growing in her belly. *Ours.* Now that the new possessive pronoun is in my head, it won't exit. It echoes as we reach the hospital.

Our baby.

"Are *you* okay?" she asks when I've gone quiet.

I shake off the new thoughts. "I'm good. Let's get you checked out."

We head inside. We aren't seen quickly, and I suppose I should take that as a sign that she's fine. An hour later, she's called in, and I rise to join her when the curly-haired nurse gives me a steely glare. "Just the patient."

"But she's eighteen weeks pregnant," I say, and those are magic words. The nurse's expression transforms, and even though she surely knows Nicole's knocked up since Nicole disclosed it when we checked in, I bet there's something about hearing the guy with the pregnant woman say it aloud that activates a sympathy bone. The nurse doesn't know I'm the donor. She figures I'm the dad, and that's good enough to give me full-time access to the mom-to-be.

She shoots me a sympathetic smile. "You can come with her. But be quiet."

I mime zipping my lips.

Ten minutes later, the nurse has taken Nicole's blood pressure and vitals, and says an ER doctor will be here any minute. She leaves, and I'm alone with Nicole, who's perched on an exam table, cradling her wrist in her lap.

"You know I'm fine, right?" she asks, gently chiding me.

"That's why we're here. To make sure."

"I'm okay. I told you I'm okay." But she doesn't sound annoyed. She sounds like she wants to reassure me.

"It's not just you, Nicole. It's you and the baby." I gently place my hand on her belly, and touching her bump feels as good as it did the first time. She smiles and presses her hand on top of mine.

"How does it feel?" she asks, her voice soft and gentle, a stark contrast to the harsh lights and sharp noises beyond the curtain.

"Amazing," I whisper.

"I know, right? I'm barely showing, but every day my little bump astonishes me."

"Has the baby kicked yet?" Hope rises in me. The hope that she'll say yes, and that I might feel it.

She shakes her head. "Not yet. Probably another month."

I turn my hand over and thread my fingers through hers. It feels so right to hold her hand.

Another smile is my reward, and so is the swift appearance of a doctor, striding into the room.

"Dr. Summers." He extends a hand. He's young, and his hazel eyes are kind. "Let's see what we've got here."

He wheels a machine closer to the table, grabs an ultrasound wand, and slicks some gel on Nicole's belly. As he roams her stomach like a man trawling the beach for buried treasure, he stares at the screen.

Naturally, I stare at the screen, too, jaw agape.

Holy shit.

Holy fucking baby.

Holy perfect baby. It's all curled up, but I can see the shape of the baby's head. The curve of the back. The knees tucked up.

It is awesome, and I don't mean awesome like the sandwich I had for lunch was awesome. Seeing your baby is awesome in the true sense of the word—I am filled with astonishment.

That astonishment coils into something even more intense when a noise bursts into the room. It sounds like hoofs beating.

I. Can't. Breathe.

I'm listening to our baby's heart, and it's the most incredible sound I've ever heard. I swear it moves through me, stirring up an unexpected kaleidoscope of emotions that's magnified when I meet Nicole's eyes. They're wet, filled with happy tears. It's almost too much for me to take, and I blink, looking away. When I do, I realize it's because my eyes are threatening to fill with tears, too.

My throat catches, and I swallow roughly.

It's as if I've been punched in the gut, but it doesn't hurt. It feels shockingly wonderful, and I want to remember this moment forever. I want to recall every second of my own amazement.

"Sounds like you've got one healthy baby in there," the doctor says with a smile as he wipes the gel off Nicole's stomach. After a quick examination of her hand, he decides it looks like it's sprained, but can be treated with ice, an ACE wrap, and, ideally, no ibuprofen. As he writes up his orders, I meet Nicole's eyes once more. Neither one of us says a word. We just hold each other's gazes, and I'm sure we're thinking the same thing—*our* baby is healthy.

She flashes me a smile, and I return it with a goofy grin of my own.

Holy shit. *Our* baby is healthy.

I want to take a snapshot of this moment. I want to record every second of this strange and joyous connection I feel with her and the life growing inside her.

The doctor leaves us alone, and I bend my face to her belly and press the gentlest kiss to her skin. "Hi, baby," I say, and I know, I fucking know, that I'm already in love with our child.

* * *

I take her home. I ice her wrist then reapply the wrap. I walk her dog around the block. When I return, I ask her if she wants me to spend the night.

"Yes."

Romeo is already at the kennel since I leave on my trip the next day, so I don't need to call the dog-sitter. I drop my keys with the tadpole charm on the living room table next to my phone. I take off my jeans and sweater, but that's all. I'm not going to try anything with Nicole, given her damaged wrist. Besides, I'm not here to make a move on her. I'm here to take care of the mother of my child.

She wears fuzzy pajama bottoms with snowmen on them, and a black tank. Her breasts look bigger. I keep that thought to myself. Now is not the time to compliment those beauties. She slides under the covers, and after I brush my teeth with an extra brush she says I can use, I join her in bed. She yawns, then sighs.

"Hey, you."

"Hey, you," I say.

"Thank you."

"For what?"

"For taking care of me tonight."

"It's the only place I wanted to be."

She yawns again.

"All right, sleepy baby. Let's make sure you get some rest."

She flips to her side, and I move closer, draping an arm over her. "Is this okay? Does it hurt your wrist?"

"No. It feels good."

"Yeah. It feels really good," I echo.

Nighttime shrouds us, and shadows play on the dark walls.

"Did you like hearing the heartbeat?" Her voice is an imprint on the air. It feels like a wish. A hope.

I run my fingers through her hair and answer with my whole heart. "I loved it."

"Me, too." Her voice is feathery. "When I first heard it, I wished you could hear it, too."

"Yeah?" I might be grinning like a fool.

"I did. I wanted you to experience it, too. It's the most wonderful sound I've ever heard."

"It really is magical." I press a kiss to the back of her neck, and before I know it, she's asleep in my arms.

In the morning, it pains me to have to say good-bye. But work calls, and I've got to hit the road for a few weeks, right when I'm starting to feel so much for both of them.

Chapter Thirty

Nicole

Penny plucks the pouch of a pair of maternity jeans, pulling it taut like a slingshot. She fires and the blue cotton bounces. "Oh! Look at the stretchiness! This is such a winner."

I narrow my eyes at her and deliver my absolute best *you've got to be kidding me* stare. "Those. Are. Hideous."

Penny bats her eyelashes. "They're a building block." Her voice is pure innocence. "A stepping stone to mom jeans."

"Did someone say mom jeans?" Delaney rushes to us with a shirt wadded in her hand. "Your mom jeans would go so well with your new peekaboo."

She unfolds it with a ta-da and strikes a pose.

I mime gagging. The shirt has a cutout over the belly. "Why? Tell me. Why on earth does that exist? Who even authorized a cutout maternity T-shirt?"

Delaney cracks up. "If you were a fashion writer, you'd have to do a column on the five worst maternity items."

Penny snaps her fingers. "I know one to include. That Christmas maternity shirt that said 'Santa's Favorite Ho.'"

I laugh. "That is totally going on the list."

Delaney hangs up the holey shirt then adjusts her bright blond ponytail. "Have you found anything you like?"

I shake my head. "Not a single stitch of fabric. Am I just too picky?"

"No way. You can never be too picky with clothes," Penny says, her brown eyes intense. "Let's keep looking."

We wander through the racks in the maternity section of a department store in Brooklyn that we traveled to for this purpose. The chichi maternity boutiques in Manhattan are just too pricey for items I'll wear only a few times. As Penny considers a rack of tent-like shirts, my phone pings.

My Pavlovian response kicks in.

Butterflies descend into my chest.

I grab my cell and slide my finger over the screen.

Ryder: Look. I'm just going to be blunt here. That okay with you?

In the two weeks he's been gone, our texts have veered from gentle concern over my wrist—it's totally fine now—to flirty, so I have a hunch I'll enjoy his bluntness.

Nicole: I like blunt. Especially blunt hardness.

Ryder: Yes, blunt hardness is apt, since I need to tell you that your boobs look spectacular.

Nicole: You were always a big fan of the girls.

Ryder: I'm their number one fan. I had one of those big foam fingers commissioned to say Number One Fan of Your Tits. But it seemed a little too—how shall we say—inappropriate to actually wave around.

Nicole: Appropriateness is overrated.

Ryder: Anyway, I noticed the spectacularness of your chest last time I saw you.

Ryder: Let me amend that. I always notice your breasts. They are always spectacular. And now they're at a whole new level of spectacularity.

Ryder: Fuck, now I'm really fucking turned on, and I have to go on air. Thanks a lot for having such perfect tits.

Nicole: I wish I could say I was sorry that my boobs are distracting you from 2,000 miles away, but I'm not. I'll leave you with this thought—they're even more sensitive now.

Ryder: Did you hear me groan across half the continent? Dear Lord, woman. What are you doing to me?

Nicole: Distracting you, since I'm buying a new lacy bra to hold my bigger boobs in.

Ryder: I demand pictorial evidence.

As I contemplate the best angles for shooting a selfie boob-shot later tonight, I look up from my phone. I flinch when I see Penny tapping her Converse-sneakered toe against the floor. Delaney joins in, beating out a rhythm with her dove-gray boots.

Both stand with arms crossed.

The sharp look in two pairs of eyes reads *busted*.

"I couldn't help but notice Ryder's name pop across your screen." Penny sounds like a cop interrogating a suspect.

"And I couldn't help but notice the ridiculously silly grin on your face," Delaney adds.

"Umm . . ." But I've got no alibi. No excuse. I'm flirting with my baby daddy.

"What's going on?"

I sigh, shrug, and hold out my hands. "I don't know."

"But you're texting, as in sexting him?"

I grip my phone tighter, the words we just sent—words like *boob* and *hard*—flashing as neon signs before my eyes. "I think so."

Delaney gives me a sharp stare. "*Think?* You of all people should *know* what sexting is. Were you or weren't you?"

"We were," I admit.

"Were you going to tell us?"

"That we were sexting?" I furrow my brow. "That hardly seems like something I need to issue a bulletin for."

"Nicole," Delaney says, admonishing, "this isn't flirting with an ex. You're flirting with the guy who knocked you up."

They point in unison at my belly. I'm twenty weeks now. It's no longer flat. My stomach is a crescent moon, and I love it.

Penny rests her arm on the silvery bar of a rack of tunics. "Is something happening between you guys?"

I drop my face to my hands momentarily, hiding behind my utter I-don't-know-what's-going-on-ness. But this isn't my style. I don't run from things. I don't hide. I look up and meet the twin gazes of my best friends. "I like him so much," I say, though that hardly feels like enough. It barely covers the way his kisses make me weak in the knees, how his touch is both reassuring and an absolute turn-on, how my stomach executes backflips when he stares at me like he wants to eat me up. And *like* doesn't even skim the surface of how my heart soared when he took care of me a few weeks ago after my fall, treating me like I was the most precious thing in the universe.

My throat hitches. "He's kind of amazing."

Penny clasps a hand to her chest and sighs dreamily.

Delaney shoots her a look then turns to me. "It's not that simple. Amazing isn't what this is about. You gave me tough love when I was debating whether to give Tyler a second chance. It's your turn to be the recipient."

I back up to the mirror, lean against it, and beckon with a curl of my fingers. *Bring it on.* I can handle it.

Delaney talks into her fist. "He's the father of your child." She drops the imaginary mic.

"You're falling for the father of your baby," Penny says, stating the obvious because, evidently, it needs to be stated.

"I don't know if it's falling in love," I say, trying to approach my feelings like a show topic. "How would I know, after all? I've never felt that before. It might just be pregnancy hormones. You've got to understand, everything feels good right now. In the second trimester, you're like this gigantic walking endorphin. Every single thing is wonderful. I'm all happy hormones and love right now."

"I know, but even so," Delaney says, keeping on point, "what are you going to do?"

I'm a planner. I should have a plan, but I don't. "I honestly don't know."

Delaney tries to provide one for me. "If you guys are spending time together, don't you think that *might* mean he wants to be involved with the kid?"

I flash back to Ryder's reaction to the heartbeat. To the magic I saw in his eyes. To his care and concern for the baby. And it hits me. He's falling for his child.

Talk about endorphins.

I'm made of nothing else right now. I float to the ceiling of the store, and I don't even need a bouquet of balloons to hold on to.

But I drop back down with Penny's next words. "Are you going to amend your agreement?"

Right. We have a contract. We have no expectations. He has no parental rights.

I shrug. "I don't know. I'll see how it goes."

And later that night, it goes like this.

I slide into my new black, lacy bra. It makes my breasts rise even higher. The swells of flesh are visible against the lace. I take aim, snapping a few shots.

I send one to him.

His reply is instantaneous.

Ryder: You're an angel. And I want to bury my face between those beauties.

More replies rain down, rapid fire, ping after ping on my phone.

Ryder: Kiss them, suck them, pinch them.

Ryder: Worship them.

Ryder: Kiss you everywhere.

Ryder: I want my tongue everywhere on you.

Flames lick my body, and I do the next logical thing. He doesn't even ask for it. But I take off the bra. And I snap another photo. No nipples. But plenty of flesh. I hit send.

Ryder: If you don't hear from me, assume I've died and gone to heaven.

And so have I, because minutes later, I'm starfished on my bed, my new vibrator playing his role, as I call out Ryder's name when I come.

Attraction has always been the easy part. I'll figure out the hard stuff some other night.

Chapter Thirty-One

Ryder

Time slows and speeds at once.

The trip is both amazing and frustrating.

I finally feel as if I have my groove back when it comes to work. The show is a blast, and the events Hanky Panky Love has set up in cities around the country energize me. We're not talking Tony Robbins stadium-sized crowds, but a couple-dozen attendees soon turns into fifty, which turns into a cool grand. I do the radio shows live from the stage, taking questions from the audience, and everyone has a blast. Cal even sends an email telling me he's pleased.

That's all he says. *Literally.*

From: Cal Tomkin
To: Ryder Lockhart
Re: Your work

I'm pleased.

Honestly, that's all a man needs from the guy who signs his paychecks. The next thing I know, my lit agent sends an email, too, and tells me sales for my book ticked up, and *Got Your Back* is going into another print run. It's been ages since that's happened. I tell my agent I'm thrilled, but we need to change the bio on the jacket. It takes me forever to write a new one, which is slightly embarrassing since it's so short.

Ryder Lockhart loves his family, his dog, and spending time with good friends and good people.

It's the truth, and it's also true that my life now doesn't hurt like it used to.

One night in San Francisco, after a workout at the hotel gym and a hot shower, I wrap a towel around my waist and stride across the room to grab my buzzing cell phone.

A bead of water slides down my chest as I open a text from Nicole. Nerves tighten my gut. There's this ever-present worry now that any message from her could bring bad news. I'm not a pessimist by nature, but I've accepted this worry.

I want good news from her. She had a doctor's appointment at the end of her day, and I asked her to tell me how it went.

Nicole: Everything is good! The doctor says I'm officially fat.

Ryder: Ha. You're not.

Nicole: No, I am. It's the medical definition. She also said it's totally normal that I ate spicy pumpkin curry, a jar of artichoke hearts, and a whole pineapple for dinner last night.

I laugh as I sink onto the edge of the mattress.

Ryder: Calling your bluff. You did not eat an entire pineapple.

Nicole: But a jar of artichoke hearts is plausible?

Ryder: Fair point. Plus, pineapples are delicious. I'll believe your tropical fruit tales after all.

Nicole: I might also have fruit on the brain. She said the baby is the size of a papaya.

Ryder: How do they come up with this stuff? Anyway, got pics of the papaya?

Nicole: You really want to see them?

I'm smiling as I answer. How can she think I don't want to see them?

Ryder: Yes. Show me the papaya. Please.

My knee bounces as I wait. I'm an addict, craving a hit. A minute later, an image loads in my text messages, and I slide my finger against it, clicking it open. My chest does funny things, like a jig. I stare at the grainy black-and-white image. I can see the shape of a nose, the jut of a chin, and perfect tiny hands with matchstick fingers. That's all I can make out, and it blows my mind that a doctor or ultrasound technician can actually identify the gender, so I decide to tease her.

Ryder: So it's a boy? I see his penis.

Nicole: What??? You cannot tell if the papaya has a penis. No way.

Ryder: So it's a girl papaya?

Nicole: I'm not finding out the sex. I've told you!

Ryder: That's definitely a penis.

Nicole: I'm giving you a side-eye glare right now like you've never had before. You. Can't. Tell. I was in the exam room, studying the machine, and I have stared at the photos for hours. You can't tell the gender unless you're the doctor, and she knows not to tell me.

Ryder: You really don't want to find out?

Nicole: This is one of the last true surprises in life. You don't like surprises?

The word is like a kick in the gut. Surprise! *I fucked seven men.* Surprise! *I'm a sex addict.* Surprise! *Our marriage was a complete sham.*

Ryder: No. I'm not into surprises.

I hold the phone, waiting for a response. But it doesn't come quickly, so I set the cell down and return to the bathroom to rub the towel over my hair. I leave and pull on a pair of boxer briefs. The phone buzzes again.

Nicole: I can find out the sex for you. Do you want me to?

I close my eyes, inhale, and let my breath fill me. She is utterly wonderful. She is so good to me. This woman is everything I want, and everything I don't want to lose again.

Ryder: I want you to have your surprise.

* * *

Ten short and long, miserable and wonderful days later, I'm on a flight back to New York.

I plug in my earbuds, buckle my seatbelt, and toggle through my podcast app. I download the latest episode from Nicole's radio show, hit play, and close my eyes.

"Who wants to talk about the best positions for sex when you're pregnant?" Her bold, pretty voice fills my ears. "Anyone? Oh wait. It's just me. Look, ladies. I know I'm not the only one sporting a belly. With the amount of love-making my listeners are doing with their significant others, I'm surprised the whole lot of you aren't pregnant. But I've heard from enough, and it seems my pregnant ladies want to know the best positions for getting busy when they've already gotten the busiest."

I sit up straight, my interest 100 percent piqued.

She's talking about sex, and this is precisely what our boss wants. Because there's no mention of getting laid. No talk of hookups. It's all about intimacy, all about pleasure, and I'm all about how very much I want to give that to her tonight.

I want her to experience an overdose of pleasure.

Especially when a caller says, "Do you find that you're just constantly horny? The second I walk in the door from work, I pretty much tackle my husband. Oh, and yes, edge of the bed works wonders."

Nicole laughs. "Edge of the bed. Make a note, ladies. And to answer your first question, yes. A big fat yes."

Yes. She's going to be saying that very soon.

Chapter Thirty-Two

Nicole

A text arrives when I know Ryder's flight is landing.

Ryder: Listened to your show. I'll be taking care of that issue for you tonight.

Nicole: What issue would that be?

Ryder: The one involving constant horniness.

I'm aroused from the text. I'm aroused from the thought. I'm aroused from being alive. I don't know if I can wait until he comes over. I try valiantly, knowing how good it'll be. Sex with Ryder was mind-blowing. I flop down on the couch and let my mind return to memories of hot, sweaty sex. His hands all over me. His mouth everywhere. His gorgeous, glorious cock sliding into me.
And that's it.

I can't wait. On the couch, I take matters into my own hands, sliding my fingers up my skirt and inside my panties.

It never takes long these days. I'm on the edge all the time. Four minutes later, I'm there, with his name on my lips and his face in my mind.

Later, my phone rings, letting me know he's here. I buzz him in. When he reaches my door, I'm ready to jump him. To hump him. To mount him for the rest of the night. I don't know how we went from no sex since he knocked me up to the certainty that we're screwing tonight, but it is a fait accompli. I'll think about what it means later. Right now, it means I'm having him again.

When I open the door, Ruby beats me to it, barking and jumping like a jack-in-the-box. "She's happy to see you."

He strokes her head and whispers sweet dog nothings to her, then meets my gaze. "Are you?"

"Happy doesn't even cover it." I step closer, wrap my arms around his neck, bring my lips to his ear, and say *please.*

He groans, drops his bag, kicks the door shut, and heads to the kitchen to wash his hands.

Bless this man.

After he dries them, he scoops me up in his strong arms. As soon as we reach my bedroom, he sets me down on the bed, cups my cheeks, and stares into my eyes. "You need to know I haven't been with anyone since you."

My happiness bucket tips over. "It's been four months." There's wonder in my voice.

He presses his forehead to mine. "Four long, hard months. Wanting you the whole time, too."

I whimper. Please, may he end the drought this second. I'm not above begging. I have no shame when it comes to the bottomless pit of desire I possess for Ryder Lockhart. "I haven't been with anyone, either." I pull back to meet his eyes. "Unless you count my vibrator."

His lips twitch in a grin.

"But that was only, maybe, fifty times."

He arches a brow as he fingers the hem of my skirt. It's loose and flowy. "Fifty isn't too bad."

"That was just this week," I say.

His laugh is deep, and it echoes in my home. It fills my chest. It spreads in me. I want to bottle the sound of his laughter. Play it over and over when I need a pick-me-up. His deep, husky voice is my good drug.

His tongue is, too.

He presses a soft kiss to my lips. As his dust mine, he murmurs, "Missed you. Missed this."

"Me, too," I say against his mouth. "So much."

His kisses are gentle, but full of need. With his hands on my face, his tender touch tells me he's longed for this. His husky groans say I'm the only one he wants to kiss. When his tongue slides between my lips and I open for him, my kiss says *I'm desperate. I need you.*

Kiss me harder, take me soon, drive me to the edge.

I moan against his mouth and try to pull him closer, wanting so much more of him. I'm the one who kicks things up another notch until I'm wriggling, panting, dying. It feels like I might die if he doesn't put his mouth on me everywhere.

"You eager for something, baby?" he asks, toying with my libido in overdrive.

I grab his face, his jaw rough with stubble. "Please. Have mercy on the horny pregnant woman."

"Define what this mercy entails."

"Go. Down. On. Me."

See? I'm not afraid to make demands, either. I'm about to dry hump the air if he doesn't put me out of my misery.

He scoots me up on my bed, and I sink down on the pillows. He places his big hands on the inside of my thighs, and I quiver. I'm easy. God, I'm so easy right now. It's possible my panties are already soaked.

"Are you just worked up, or are you worked up for me?"

"Don't torture me. It's you, Ryder. It's you. I need your mouth on me. I need you to go down on me. I need *you*."

The noise he makes is the sexiest sound I've ever heard. Carnal and dirty, it's a rumble from deep within him. I arch my hips, begging for him to bring his face between my thighs.

He reaches for my panties and removes them in record time. *Seriously.* That's just gone down in the record books as the fastest removal of underwear ever, and then . . .

My world is a blur.

A white-hot neon haze.

His lips are on me. His hands spread my legs. His tongue flicks against me. He moans and groans, and murmurs my name in some kind of dirty prayer of lust. My hands grab his head, my fingers slide into his hair.

And I lose myself.

I lose the world. I lose my mind.

This man. His desire. My need. It all smashes together in one radiant moment of erotic bliss. I rock my hips into his face, I curl my hands around his head, I cry and moan and pant, and I fuck him.

I absolutely fuck his face.

But it feels like more than fucking.

It feels like so much more than mere bodies coming together. It feels like he knows me, like I know him, and together we can let go and give in.

That's what this is.

It's surrender to everything inside my heart.

As I writhe and moan and thrust and grab, I surrender to how much I need him now, and in my life.

He gives me everything. His tongue strokes me, his lips kiss me, his mouth consumes me.

I'm not a difficult one when it comes to coming. Tonight, I'm a piece of cake. I reach zero to sixty in less than three minutes. Everything in me tightens and tightens, and the pleasure coils.

"Oh God," I cry out.

The rest is just sounds. Syllables. Incoherent noises of pleasure as I shatter. I break apart into a thousand, million, infinite diamonds of pleasure. "Oh God, oh God, oh God."

When he stops, I'm still buzzing. Electric pulses sweep over me, the remains of my orgasm. The aftershocks of the earthquake he gave me.

Ryder climbs over me. "I love the way you come. I love making you come. I bet you need another one."

My eyes widen, and I nod. I'm ravenous, and will take anything he has to give.

He kneels between my legs. He drags a finger across me, tracking a slow, torturous line along my wet, soft, aching center, and my hips shoot up. How the hell can I feel this way again? But I do, oh God, I do.

He thrusts a finger inside me, and I see stars.

"Ryder," I moan, and my eyes flutter shut. It's too much. Too good. Too intense. I'm liquid. I am a molten woman as he strokes a long finger inside me, another one rubbing against my clit.

"Baby, I feel terrible," he says with a groan.

"Why?"

"Because you need it so badly. I feel fucking terrible that you were this desperate for so long."

"I did need it. I need you. Oh God, I need you."

I ride his hand to the edge again. I fly off in seconds, coming again, harder, more intense. Deeper. When I open my eyes, he's stripped down to nothing.

My mouth waters, and I push myself up in bed. I'm breathless. "What are you doing to me? I don't even know how I'm alive."

"You're alive and so fucking beautiful," he says, then reaches for the hem of my shirt and tugs it off me.

I'm in my bra and skirt, my belly pushing at the elastic waistband.

I'm not in the least bit sexy. I slide to the edge of the bed, push off my skirt, and unhook my bra.

He's standing. His mouth falls open. His cock twitches, and I swear it grows even harder as he gazes at me.

"Nicole." His voice is nothing but a dry husk.

I'm keenly aware this is the first time he's seen me completely naked since he knocked me up. My body tightens with nerves. I hope he still finds me attractive. I hope my weight gain doesn't change how he sees me.

He touches my breasts first. But he doesn't stay there. He travels down my body, to my belly, to the baby, and he dips his head. He plants the gentlest kiss on my navel. "You're so beautiful."

Whatever tension I felt pours out of me.

"I am?" I can't help myself. I need to ask. I'm not some fertility goddess hippy earth mother. I'm a dating and mating columnist in New York City, land of the free, home of the beautiful skinny women. I'm not skinny, and I don't want to be right now.

But I want to know that he still wants me.

"God," he says, running his hand over my naked stomach. "You're stunning." He grabs my ankles and pulls me to the edge of the bed. "And I have never wanted to fuck you more."

I shiver.

I love that he says fuck. I love that he knows that's what I need to hear, that he can still want me in the same raw, carnal way.

He runs his hand along his hard length, and I shudder.

I get to have him again. This man I'm crazy for.

Chapter Thirty-Three

Ryder

I position her ass at the edge of the bed and open her legs. A groan rattles free as I gaze at the warm paradise I've already visited twice tonight. She's so fucking pretty. So pink, plump, and perfect.

I can't get enough of her.

"Lie back on your elbows," I tell her, because she's not the only one who can research the best positions. She leans back, all breasts and belly and beautiful flesh.

I rub the head of my dick against her, and she stretches her neck and moans to the heavens.

I push in.

She takes me easily. So fucking easily. It's a wet, hot slide into her pussy.

And it's fucking magnificent. I shudder when I'm all the way in. I still myself as my skin sizzles. I've missed this. I've missed her. I've longed to touch her again. And I swear, it's as if she's vibrating with pleasure already. She was wonderfully orgasmic in the first place.

But now?

She's a live wire.

She doesn't hold back. She never has. But tonight, she's a new woman. She rides the edge the entire time. I can see it in the exquisite torture on her face. In the way her mouth falls open. In how her fingers grip the covers as if she's clutching them for dear life.

And I hear it in her noises.

My lovely, gorgeous woman can't shut up, and pride and desire suffuse me in equal measure as she cries out with every goddamn thrust.

Every single touch.

Everything.

My hands grip her hips as I drive into her, her heat enveloping me. She moans my name.

I groan. I try to form words. To tell her something dirty. Something filthy. Something to get her even hotter. But my brain is shot. All I can manage is a simple, "Feels so good, baby."

"I know," she says, panting. A bead of sweat slides between her tits. Lucky sweat.

I run my finger through it, stopping at the top of her bump. I grab her hips again and yank her down even tighter on my cock. I go deeper, and it's fantastic.

"Nicole," I rasp, and that's all I've got. I'm nothing but heat, and sparks, and desire. Pleasure snaps everywhere in me. It bathes my brain. It floods every molecule in my body. I'm where I want to be.

Not just in her.

But *with* her.

This woman.

This amazing fucking woman, who's falling apart beneath me. Who's unraveling under my touch.

"Look at me," I demand.

Her eyes flutter.

"Nicole. Look at me."

I'm overcome with the need to connect with her.

She opens her eyes as if it's the hardest thing to do. She meets my gaze and a surge of pleasure barrels down my spine. Hot and electric—a warning sign. "I want to watch you come again. I want to watch your beautiful face when you fall apart."

She grabs the covers and moans my name. It sounds filthy and beautiful at the same fucking time. I can't believe I'm lucky enough to be here again. I can't believe I'm with her once more. And most of all, I can't imagine being anywhere else but with her.

"Come with me, baby." I lean over her, letting go of her hips, pressing my palms on the bed. I'm careful with her, making sure not to crush her, but I need to be closer. "Come with me."

She grabs my shoulders, and she's already there. I see it on her face. In the twist of her features. In the shudder of her shoulders. In the way she trembles. In how she thrusts against me.

I follow her, and my orgasm seems to last for minutes. It knocks out wires; it fries circuit breakers. It shocks my whole system with pleasure. I'm louder than I've ever been as I groan and grunt, and I can't seem to stop as I find my own release deep inside this woman I have missed wildly.

I nearly collapse on her, but I remember my manners. I slide to her side, running my hand down her arm. "It's good to be back here."

"You're telling me."

"I don't know how we managed without that," I say. Only I do know—we've never officially been a *we*, but in some ways, I've felt like a *we* the entire time.

"I think the constant barfing killed my sex drive for the first several weeks, so we can blame that."

"Glad your appetite is back."

She nods several times. "Oh, it's back, and it's a hungry beast."

"I'll feed it," I say, and then nip her earlobe.

She meows.

My hand drifts to her belly. "Think the baby is okay? Hope I didn't knock Papaya out of place."

She laughs and rolls her eyes. "*Men.* The baby is just fine. Besides, the baby likes it when the mama is happy."

"Orgasms are the key to your happiness. Duly noted."

She laughs and whispers something I can't make out.

"What did you say?"

She shakes her head.

I furrow my brow, doubting her. Or maybe I'm just wishing she'd said I make her happy, too.

But I'll take what I can get. I bring her closer, and I don't know what the fuck has gotten into me, but I can't get enough of her. I smell her hair, running my nose through the lush strands. I cup her breasts, holding them, feeling their weight. They are bigger than before, and I want to spend my time with these beauties, sucking them, biting her nipples, licking the soft, sweet flesh of her breasts. "I think I might be obsessed with your body."

"Really?" Her lips curve into a grin.

"Yeah. Maybe that makes me a freak, but you've never been more beautiful." I sigh happily.

"I see orgasms fry your brain, too."

"I mean it. You're gorgeous. All your curves. All your bumps. Everything." I run my hand over her stomach. "Everything about you is perfect."

And the moment becomes more perfect when her belly moves against my hand. Like a little roller coaster. A wave.

"I felt a kick," I say, in absolute awe. Our child is moving in her body. It feels like a complete and utter miracle, and I get to witness it. She mentioned in her texts that the baby had started kicking, but I didn't expect him or her to show off for me so soon.

"Isn't it incredible?"

I nod. "Will it kick again?"

"Maybe."

I don't move my hand from her stomach. I keep my palm curved over her warm flesh, saying nothing, as if silence will recreate this moment. Then it happens, like an alien pushing against me. Another little miracle, and I want to experience every single one with her.

I kiss Nicole, tender and gentle, full of so much emotion. So much more than I've felt before. I am so far gone.

* * *

Sometime in the middle of the night, I wake to find her hands on me. We're face to face, and her fingers explore my pecs then trail down to my abs. She reaches between my legs. She strokes me, and her breath catches. Mine does, too.

Gently, I set my hands on her shoulders, and flip her to the other side. I tug her against me, her back to my chest.

We are spoons.

We speak wordlessly, with slow touches and tender moans. With her soft wetness and my hard length. And as she pushes her rear against me, she's telling me *more*.

I reach for her knee, nudge it up to her belly, making room to ease into her like this.

She murmurs as I enter her.

I do, too.

In the dark, I make love to her.

Her soft cries float across the night, mixing with my groans, creating a new harmony of sex and need and want and desire, and most of all, absolute clarity in my heart.

We might still fuck.

We might still like it hard, and wild, and dirty.

But I'm making love to her now, and she's doing the same to me. The world fragments around us as we come together. And I know without a shadow of a doubt that I'm in love with the mother of my child.

But I know, too, that I haven't a clue if she wants the same things I do.

Chapter Thirty-Four

Nicole

In my job, I've encountered nearly every topic known to the modern woman. I've written about shaving styles (for the record—I'm a landing strip kind of gal), how to politely turn down a pegging request while still maintaining a relationship with the man (fair warning—it's not easy), and whether ghosting is ever acceptable (people, please. Be adults and use your words).

But this is a virgin territory I've crossed into.

I'm not sure what to do when you fall in love with your sperm donor.

I've fallen for his tender touch, his huge heart, his protective soul, his quick mind, and most of all, how he takes care of me. He melts me. He makes me weak in the knees. He treats me like a queen.

In the early pink light of the dawn, with Ryder still sound asleep, I contemplate what I would advise a caller who approached me with this dilemma.

Hey there! I asked a man to donate his swimmers to make me a baby and guess what? Oops! I fell for him, too.

Yeah, I've got nothing to tell that crazy caller.

I choose the age-old method of dealing with complicated stuff. I fall back asleep.

When I wake a little later, I pull on a loose T-shirt, visit the bathroom, brush my teeth, and wander into my kitchen. Ryder stands at the fridge, and Ruby's curled up in a little dog ball at his feet. She's not pacing. He must have walked her.

He took care of my dog. Dear Lord, I'm falling in love in a big way. This is it. I've no antibodies to him, and there's no question I'm feeling all the zings. Oh God, I hope he feels the same. Please, please, let him be zinging, too.

Ryder's in jeans and his shirt from last night, and he's staring at the fridge. When I pad closer, I see he's not just staring at the door. I've hung my various ultrasound pictures to the silvery surface, and he's studying them. His index finger is poised over my recent twenty-week one, and he's tracing the outline of the baby's legs.

"Hi," I say, clearing my throat.

He straightens and then smiles. It's a sheepish look, as if he's been caught. "Just checking out Papaya."

I love that the name Papaya has stuck. That must be a sign he feels the same. I gesture to the thirteen-week picture, when I first heard the heartbeat. "I think Papaya was a fig in that one. Funny thing—when I was so sick, Papaya was only a kidney bean."

"Kidney beans are known to be troublemakers." He steps closer, drops a strangely chaste kiss to my forehead, and sets his hands on my belly. "And I think Papaya is almost a mango now, right?"

I nod. "How did you know?"

"I might have googled pregnancy-to-fruit comparisons. Papaya will be an eggplant in a little while."

I blink. Holy shit. He really knows his pregnancy fruits. Better than I do. If he was researching pregnancy in that detailed a fashion, he's not just interested in how *I'm* doing. He's interested in the baby.

"When's your next appointment?"

"A week and a half. But they won't be doing another ultrasound at it."

He snaps his fingers in an *aw shucks* gesture.

Make that *very interested*. I can't stop the next words from coming out of my mouth. I need to know something. Something important. "Would you have wanted to come along if they were doing an ultrasound?"

His eyes light up, and he nods. "Yes. I'd love to take you," he says, and my heart dares to soar for the briefest moment. He'd want to take me. He'd want to be there for me. Everything feels possible. Until he winks. "And if I were there, I could do my damnedest to convince the doc to give you an ultrasound anyway. I'm dying to see it live again. Not just in photos."

He turns back to the pictures on the fridge.

Taking me for me, and taking me to convince the doctor to snap a pic of the baby are two entirely different things. My heart doesn't just fall back to earth. It slams to the ground, as everything snaps into place. It's both beautiful and terrible, what I now know to be true.

"Would you want me to come along?" he asks.

I say yes, then I point to the clock on the microwave and choke out, "I should shower and get to work."

I need to be alone right now.

He nods. "I should get Romeo. I bet he misses me like crazy. I miss him, that's for sure." He cups my cheek. "But can I see you tonight?"

"Yes."

The door clinks shut behind him, and I gulp for air. I try to breathe, and it's suddenly the most difficult thing to do. How could I have missed it? How could I have failed to see what's so clearly happening to this man?

As I shower, my chest aching the whole time, I rewind to all the obvious signs.

He's not looking for romance. He's not interested in love. He never has been, and he's always been upfront about it.

That kind of love is different, but I try not to think about it. Or to let myself feel it.

But he's grown quite interested in something else—fatherhood.

It really is magical, he'd said of the heartbeat.

Anyway, got pics of the papaya?

I might have googled pregnancy-to-fruit comparisons.

He nearly cried when he heard the heartbeat. He practically swooned when he felt the baby kick.

There's no doubt in my mind that his feelings for the baby have completely transformed. He's all in now when it comes to Papaya.

But as for me, well, I'm still everything I originally was to him—a sexual creature. Sure, he likes sleeping with me, and yes, I'm something else to him now, too—the mother of his child. But the third thing I want to be—*his*—isn't in the cards for Ryder Lockhart. He hung up the closed sign on his heart after Maggie ransacked that organ, and he made it clear he doesn't want to re-open it.

Tears mix with the New York City water.

Who am I to blame him? I went into this ready to raise the baby without a man in my life. I can't blame him for wanting to help raise the baby he helped make.

He's in love with the baby, and only the baby.

I sniffle and hold my chin up as water sluices over my body. I tell myself to be tough, to be strong. I have to be, for the baby.

It doesn't matter that I'm falling in love with him. I can't let these new and fragile emotions get the better of me.

Besides, you can't lose something that was never yours to begin with.

* * *

"You were right." I sink down into the booth across from my mom. I'd called an emergency lunch.

"Of course I'm right." She smiles as she tucks a strand of auburn hair behind her ear. "But what am I right about this time?"

I heave a sigh. "It's become . . . quite complicated."

She reaches across the Formica table for my hand and clasps it. "Oh, sweetie. What's going on?"

I breathe out carefully, as if respiration is a bodily function I'm relearning. I lift my chin. Square my shoulders. "I think Ryder wants to be part of the baby's life."

My mother nods sympathetically. She takes her time before she speaks. "And how do you feel about that?"

I try to stay strong. What do I have to cry over anyway? The fleeting notion that we might have become an insta-family? How ridiculous was it to even contemplate that? I won't shed a tear. Instead, I will plaster on a smile. If he wants to be part of his kid's life, that's not a bad thing.

In fact, growing up with an involved father could be a very good thing.

How many women who use sperm donors have the chance to offer some sort of involvement to the father? Hardly any. I should count myself as a lucky one.

"I feel like it could be a good thing for the baby. To know his or her . . . father." My voice catches on that word. "I wish I had known mine."

My mother's lips quiver. "He was a good man. Your father loved you so much."

The fire hydrant cranks on. My eyes leak fat, salty tears. My mother joins me on my side of the table, wraps her arm around me, and squeezes. "I believe in you—whatever you decide. If you choose to have him involved, and if he wants to be involved, it will be for the best."

I nod as a sob hovers near my lips. "It will," I say, choking on the words.

"It will be for the best for your child. What a gift for your baby to know such a good man is his or her father." Her tone is so warm, so loving, so full of motherly wisdom. I know she's right. I just wish that good man wanted me, too.

But only a fool would think she could have it all.

I bury my face in my mother's shoulder, and I cry like a baby in the diner. If I get out all the tears now, I can keep calm tonight, and I absolutely must remain calm. If I can't have all of Ryder, I want to have the part of him in my life that is keen to know his child. It's such a gift, to be able to know your family. It's a gift I didn't think I'd be able to give my child.

Now, it's possible, and I have to stay strong for Papaya.

Chapter Thirty-Five

Ryder

After all my travels, I have the day off.

I spend it with my boy. I take Romeo to Central Park and toss tennis balls to him in the off-leash section until he flops down on his belly, panting in the unseasonably warm March.

We leave, and as I wander through the park, I stop at the bridge over the lake. I stare into the distance, past the water, my eyes landing on the tall buildings framing each side of this oasis in Manhattan.

I'm not here by chance.

I'm here by design.

Maggie and I had our first date in Central Park. Our first kiss on this bridge. As I stand here, I wait for the familiar sensations to pummel me. For the tightening in my chest, the twist in my gut.

It comes, but it fades just as quickly.

"C'mon, boy," I say to my dog. He trots beside me as I head to the park exit then cut across the brownstones and pre-war buildings toward Lincoln Center.

Tension winds through me as I bound up the steps to the fountain. Maggie and I kissed here after I took her to a ballet, the lights from the fountain like candlelight against the dark night.

But when I let go of thoughts of my ex, and focus on Nicole, the tension flickers away.

Next, my dog and I cut a diagonal swath down the city, walking and walking, all the way to the Union Square Farmers' Market. It's open tonight, and I wander around the edges, remembering the times I came here with my ex-wife.

This was our stomping ground, so I brace myself for a slice, a nick, a fresh new cut.

But as I make another lap, I don't bleed.

I don't hurt.

I might not enjoy the reminders of Maggie, but they don't hobble me like they used to. They are part of my past, part of my history.

They don't have to control my present.

Romeo and I walk to Chelsea, and I park myself on the stoop of my building. Romeo, now exhausted from the long trek, slumps on the steps and rests his snout on my leg.

"What do you think?"

He raises an ear.

"Time to move on?"

He raises his other ear. I cycle back to the night of the hookup seminar that Cal's son surreptitiously attended, and remember the thoughts that swirled in my head then. *Hap-*

pily ever after is a cycle of bullshit, love is a medley of lies, and marriage is a thing that can only go wrong.

But maybe not.

Maybe love isn't a collection of falsehoods.

Maybe happiness isn't a farce.

Maybe being together *can* go right, if you trust yourself to try again.

I pat my dog's head, and we go inside.

* * *

A cupcake is a good start.

I grab a strawberry one from her favorite bakery, and a bouquet of red tulips from a florist near her home. My heart skitters as I walk along her block.

I've traveled this block so many times en route to a night of baby-making, and more recently, to taking her home after the Ping-Pong fall.

But tonight feels different.

Because it *is* different.

It's the start of what I hope will be all the things I never thought I wanted from this arrangement and now I can't imagine living without.

When she opens the door, her smile is so bright it nearly blinds me.

"Hi!" Her voice rises at the end as if she's been practicing the greeting all day.

"Hey, beautiful," I say, and dip my mouth to hers to kiss her lips. I catch more cheek than lip.

"Come in." She shuts the door behind me, and after a proper dog greeting from Ruby, I hand Nicole the flowers. "For you."

She sniffs them. "They're lovely."

After she grabs a vase and fills it, she sets the flowers on the living room table then sits. I join her on the couch. She crosses her legs, and places her hands on her thighs. She seems more proper tonight. Not in appearance—she wears jeans and a sweater—but in demeanor.

"Everything okay? You seem . . . jumpy?"

She shakes her head. "Everything is great."

"I got you a cupcake." I hand her the box.

She opens it, her eyes lighting up. "I'm going to save it for later. Too nervous to eat."

"Why are you nervous?" I ask, hoping it's for the same reason I am.

She takes a breath, her shoulders rising and falling. She doesn't speak, and I can't fucking exist in this in-between state any longer. I didn't take a journey to the haunts of my broken heart to do nothing.

"I've been thinking about us," I say, ripping off the Band-Aid.

"Me, too."

Relief floods me. "You have?"

"Yes. A lot." Her voice rises, and hope rises in me. She's got to be thinking the same thing. I can't be so goddamn out of touch with emotions that I've misread her.

"At first, I didn't think I would want this, but now I do." I clasp her hand, and she threads her fingers through mine. God, it feels so right. All of this feels so damn right.

Her voice is soft and heartfelt as she speaks. "Everything has changed, hasn't it?"

My heart soars. "Yes. Everything has changed." I squeeze her hand, take a deep breath, and prepare to tell her I love her, I love our baby, and I want it all.

"Ryder?" In her voice, I hear all the hope in the world. "I would love for you to be involved in the baby's life. Would you like that?"

The floor falls out from under me. My jaw comes unhinged. The room topples, turning upside down.

Yes, I want to shout.

No, I want to shout.

I want you, too.

But she didn't offer herself.

She only offered the child.

"I can tell you've fallen for the baby," she says, squeezing my hand again. "And it melts my heart. If I'm wrong, tell me, and I won't be offended. But if I'm right, I would be so happy to have you as part of the baby's life."

I can't answer her. Her words sound foreign to my ears, garbled and muddy. I want to find the rewind button. The redo option.

I blink, trying to make sense of this flipped-around reality. But when I replay her words in my head, they're not muddy. They're crystal clear. She doesn't want love from me. She wants her baby to have a father.

My chest hurts. My heart literally fucking aches. I want to grab her shoulders, stare into her eyes, and ask her to be mine for-fucking-ever.

I open my lips to tell her she's the one, and I want it all with her, but something catches inside of me.

An ancient hurt. Old fears. Or perhaps the stone that blocks my voice is the stark reality that life isn't a fairy tale.

I think back on my chats with Simone, the things I try to teach her. *You get what you get and you don't have a fit.*

Sometimes, you don't get all you want. In fact, you rarely do in life. I don't have all my business back. I have enough of it. I don't have my marriage, but I have the dog. And I don't get the woman. I get the kid.

The kid I desperately want.

I'm being given a great and wonderful gift, and you don't turn away from that.

When I finally speak again, the words sound as if they're coming from someone else. "I would love to be part of Papaya's life."

"We should probably focus on that, then. Do you agree?"

Her meaning is crystal clear. Last night was a last hurrah.

Chapter Thirty-Six

Nicole

Top Five Signs You're a Pathetic, Mopey Idiot

By Nicole Powers

1. You microwave your tea for five minutes instead of one.

2. You drink it anyway, burning your tongue.

3. You put your underwear on inside out.

4. You don't care enough to change them to the correct way.

5. You can't for the life of you figure out how to write a decent column.

* * *

Top Five Ways to Pretend You're a Badass, Even When You're Not

By Nicole Powers

1. Wave when you walk past his office, like you only think of him as your hot-as-fuck co-worker.

2. Make a joke about the Wheelbarrow position. Even if it falls flat and he stares at you like *How could you possibly joke about sex when we're not having it anymore?*

3. Don't let that shit go. Pat your belly and pretend you're the wheelbarrow now because it's the only way to manage the absolutely awkward situation you're in of BEING FUCKING CO-WORKERS WITH THE FATHER OF YOUR CHILD WHO YOU'RE IN LOVE WITH BUT WHO ISN'T IN LOVE WITH YOU.

4. Casually mention the next doctor's appointment and ask him if he wants to go, since you're totally cool with this new arrangement. When he says of course, say "awesome" and head to your office, shut the door, and lock it.

5. Bawl into your double-ply aloe-vera-infused tissues because you miss him so much it hurts.

* * *

Top Five Reasons You're Not Picking Up the Phone and Admitting You Love Him

By Nicole Powers

1. Your fingers are broken.

2. Your phone is broken.

3. Your brain is broken.

4. Your heart is broken.

5. You're scared.

I drag a hand through my hair and toss that last sheet of paper into the trash can along with my other miserable attempts to write a column. I miss the can by a mile. Sighing, I drag myself from the desk chair like it takes the strength of ten thousand men to walk, then bend and grab the crumpled-up paper from the floor. If my life were a rom-com movie—Emma Stone would play me, thank you very much—I'd miss the trash can with the last wad, but I wouldn't realize it. I'd leave my office with that ball of paper parked on the floor, unbeknownst to little old me.

Ryder would pop in later to ask me a question about his upcoming show. He'd spot the paper on the floor. Being the helpful guy he is, he'd pick it up to toss in the trash. But he'd notice the word *love*, and he wouldn't be able to resist unfolding the balled-up wad. He'd read it, and the camera would pan in on his face, on the slow shift from bemused to thrilled. He'd race out of the office, skid on a street corner, dodge a cab—hell, he'd leap over the hood in a mad rush to find me—then vault over a hot dog cart vendor closing up shop for the night, and arrive at my front door, ready to profess his love.

But this is life.

It's not a movie with a giddy happy ending. I stand by the trash can, rip the page to shreds, and stuff the remains in the bottom of the can.

Chapter Thirty-Seven

Ryder

"And that's the field guide to dating and winning the heart of a modern woman."

I deliver the last line of my new seminar with the best smile I can manage. With business picking up, I refuse to fall into old habits. I won't let one loss slow me down. One big, monstrous, painful loss of the woman I love.

But still, Nicole and I remain friends, colleagues, co-parents. I do my best to remain positive, avoiding the trap of my once jaded ways. "Any questions?"

Several arms shoot up in the air. I'm at a Midtown hotel, giving a talk on a Tuesday evening to fifty or sixty guys.

I call on a sturdy fellow with glasses in the front row. His hair is military short, and he stands. "What if you've got baggage? Like from an ex-girlfriend or ex-wife? That's my situation, and I'm trying to figure out how to approach the minefield of dating. Any advice you can give about getting back out there for guys like me?"

"I can definitely talk about that. That's my situation, too," I say, and he blinks, surprised at first. I'm surprised, too. I haven't shared the demise of my marriage in my talks before. But this guy is direct, and he's asking something that matters. Briefly, I think of Cal and what a hard-ass he is, but maybe the old bastard was onto something—speak from the heart, not the dick. "I'm divorced, and let me tell you, it can be hard to get back out there. You think you're going to be blindsided again," I say, and the guy nods vigorously. Several others do, too. "You think you can't possibly ever want anything serious again. Then, sometimes unexpectedly, a woman comes into your life, and she's not like your ex. She's not like anyone you've ever met. And you just know you have to give it a shot."

"That's awesome, man," the guy says with a smile.

"And the best advice I can give you is don't let the past hold you back from the present."

He beams. "And that's what you did? With your new woman?"

I'm silent for a moment. Is that what I did? Did I give it a shot? I'd like to think so. "Yeah, I did do that."

He doesn't need to know the shot didn't quite work out the way I wanted.

* * *

The next night, as I sink into the leather couch in the lounge bar of a swank restaurant, I reflect back on the military dude's question.

And that's what you did?

I ask myself if I answered with complete honesty.

I'm not sure I did.

I'm not convinced I went balls-to-the-wall for Nicole. I took what she offered, and *only* what she offered. I didn't tell her I wanted her to sweeten the deal. To offer herself, too. I sure as hell didn't let her know that she and Papaya are a package deal, and I want the whole package.

But I shelve the thought when Flynn, his identical twin brother, Dylan, and Flynn's divorced friend, Aaron, return with drinks and join me. We're here to celebrate with Aaron, a stocky guy with a baby face and a good heart. Flynn holds a beer to toast his buddy. When Aaron decided he was ready to try the dating scene again, he hired the Consummate Wingman to give him advice. Naturally, the Consummate Wingman's unofficial sidekick, Flynn, has been observing the whole time.

I raise my glass and toast. "You ready?"

Aaron smiles. "Ready or not, here I go."

He takes a drink, inhales deeply, and sets down the glass. He gives us a farewell salute and heads to the hostess stand, then to his table to wait for his date. He's had a crush on a woman at work, and he finally had the guts to ask her out for dinner after a few coaching sessions.

Aaron moves the linen napkin a centimeter, fiddles with a fork, peers at his watch, and looks at the door. His eyes light up, and I follow his gaze.

A blond woman with her hair in a bun walks in, scans the eatery, and sees him. She waves. He waves back.

I look at Flynn. "He's on his own now."

"It's like the first day at school," Flynn says, pretending to wipe a tear from his eye.

Dylan mock sniffles, pushing his black glasses up the bridge of his nose. Thank fuck he wears different colored frames than Flynn—when they're together it's the easiest way I can tell them apart. "He's on the bus. We'll have to be strong and say good-bye."

I toss a few bills on the table, and we leave.

"You're awesome, man," Flynn says, as the three of us amble down the street. "You gave him the confidence he needed to get back out there."

"To just take a risk," Dylan seconds.

Risks. Chances. Shots.

As I consider the men surrounding me, I have to ask myself if they're taking bigger chances than I am.

Honestly, it's not that hard to answer.

And later, it's not that hard to figure out what I need to do to put myself on the line.

Chapter Thirty-Eight

Nicole

My phone rings late on a Tuesday evening.

Late for me, I should say.

It's nearly nine, and I'm tired because, well, I'm baking another person in my oven. I turn down the volume on the basketball game and grab the phone from the table. "Let us in," Penny demands when I answer.

"You're here?"

"Yes, buzz us in now or we'll throw garter belts and stockings at your window."

"Such hooligans." A minute later, I open the door, and Penny and Delaney march into my place. Ruby barks a happy hello.

"Well, hello there," Delaney says to me and then my dog.

"Hello there to you, too. What brings you here at this hour?"

"It's not that late, and we love you." Penny shuts the door behind them and coos at Ruby, who then offers a full flank for proper petting. Naturally, Penny obliges for a minute.

My friends head to my couch and take their spots. I park myself between them as Ruby sprawls on the carpet, watching us with avid interest.

Penny reaches into a canvas bag she has with her. She takes out a pint of Ben & Jerry's. "We're getting you buzzed first."

"On ice cream?"

"Of course," Delaney says. "It's like a pregnant woman's vodka, right?"

"I've no idea where that logic comes from, but I'm not turning down chocolate therapy." I pop open the pint then stretch my arm toward the kitchen and grunt. "Can't. Reach. Spoons. From. Here."

Delaney rolls her brown eyes. "You only have three and a half more months to use that excuse to get us to do things for you."

"Four months," I mutter, thinking that Ryder probably knows precisely how many days are left.

"Besides, I brought spoons." Delaney grabs three metal spoons from the bag, along with a huge dog bone.

I give her a look. "I know I've been hungry, but I'm not *that* hungry."

Ruby leaps from the floor, rearranges herself into a proper sit, and stares unabashedly at the bone.

"Can I give it to her?" Delaney asks.

"You better."

"Good girl." Delaney offers the treat to Ruby, who returns to her bed, the bone in her jaw, and proceeds to bestow all the love in the universe on it.

I dig into the ice cream. After three bites of chocolate, I arch a brow. "Why are you here, again? Besides your boundless love of me."

"Funny you should ask," Penny says as she dives in for a spoonful. "We decided there's something you need to add to your agenda tomorrow."

"At my doctor's appointment?"

They nod in unison, and Delaney goes next. "While you're there, you should tell Ryder you love him."

I nearly spit out my ice cream. "You can't be serious?"

"Honey, you're miserable without him," Penny says sweetly.

I balance the pint on top of my curved belly. "Hey, look at that. No hands."

"*Nicole.*" The admonishment comes from Penny.

"No, seriously." I point with both hands to this amazing feat I've pulled off. "Have you ever seen a pregnant woman balance ice cream on her belly?"

Penny rolls her eyes. "I bet there are tons of YouTube videos of women balancing ice cream on their big bellies."

I harrumph.

Delaney stares at me pointedly. "You are absolutely miserable."

"Define miserable."

Delaney gestures to my belly. "Balancing ice cream pints for amusement because you miss the man you were too scared to say you loved is the definition of miserable."

I scoff.

"You do love him," Delaney adds.

"Duh."

"How much do you love him?" Penny asks.

I glance at my dog, chowing down on her bone. "Like a dog loves a bone."

She smiles and claps with glee. "I love dog analogies."

"I do, too, especially because you can't fast-talk your way out of this," Delaney says with a smirk. She drops a hand to my knee. "And what does a dog do with a bone?"

My eyes stray to Ruby. Her paws grip the bone fiercely. Her jaw is wrapped tight around it. I glare at them and grumble. "You two set me up for that."

They cackle evilly.

"A dog doesn't let go," I answer.

Delaney squeezes my knee. "Don't you let go, either."

Penny pats my shoulder. "Go get your bone. Or, in this case, your man."

"But what if he doesn't love me back? And what if telling him I love him scares him away from the baby?" A new worry takes root. "I never thought I needed a father for my baby, but now that he wants to be involved, I don't want to freak him out."

Delaney shoots me a gentle smile. "If this frightens him away from the baby, then he was never going to be a great dad in the first place. And I can't imagine a man like him would be that kind of a pansy."

I manage a small laugh. "Pansy he is not." But my laughter fades quickly. Delaney didn't answer my other question, and this one gnaws at me. "What if he doesn't love me?" My voice is tiny, stretched with the threat of tears.

She grabs my hand. "What if he doesn't? You have us, and Ruby, and an ice cream-balancing belly. You'll be no worse off than you are now. And you have your baby."

I do have so much in my life. Is it possible I might have more? I close my eyes and rewind to my last night with Ryder, to the way he touched me, how he held me, the way he worshipped me. Maybe it wasn't only me, the mother of this child, that he was attracted to. Maybe it's me, all of me, the woman and the mother-to-be.

I remember his words . . . the ones about me.

Missed you. Missed this.

It's the only place I wanted to be.

Look at me.

Can I see you tonight?

I've changed. I now want someone in my life as more than a donor, so is it possible he's changed, too? A stupid grin forms on my face. Could a girl be this lucky in real life?

* * *

Katherine's opens at nine a.m. I'm here at three minutes before the hour. The second the doors swing in, I race to the counter where I bought the key chain many months ago. Alongside its gorgeous platinum rings and stunning necklaces, this classy store also carries a handful of little novelty key chains, like the tadpole. When I bought that one, I spotted the key chain I want now.

I squeal when I see it's in stock—a woman in silver, like the sexy silhouettes of women's bodies on the mud flaps of trucks. It's classy kitsch, and I love it. It's exactly what I want to say to Ryder.

I want you to have the woman, too.

A saleswoman strides up to me. "Can I help you?"

I bounce on my toes as I point. "I'll take that."

Twenty minutes later, I carry the box into work as my stomach tries to crawl up my esophagus.

Oh wait. That's nerves. I'm a cauldron of churning emotions—hope and fear and happiness and doubt. But I'm going to do this anyway. I'm going to pursue the impossible dream, and there are tons of top five reasons why this might rank as the craziest thing I've ever done. But there's one reason why this might be the best choice I've ever made.

Top Reason to Tell Him You Love Him

1. He's the one.

I knock on his open office door, but he's not in there. Then, I remember. Right. He's probably recording right now. Damn my baby brain. But I don't leave the box on his desk this time. He doesn't like surprises, and this is something I need to do face-to-face. Clutching it tight in one hand, I'm heading to my office when my phone pings.

His name flashes on my screen, and my stomach dips.

My belly flips upside down as I open the message.

Ryder: Tune in to my show in five minutes.

They are the longest five minutes in the history of the world. Especially because at four minutes and thirty seconds, I have to pee.

Chapter Thirty-Nine

Ryder

"It's the end of this episode on dating and mating, and before I sign off, I have something to say."

Across from me, Jason gives a nod, a sign that he's ready. I tug the mic closer as if I'm getting intimate with it.

I suppose *intimacy* is a fitting word. It's the thing I've shunned. The thing I fear. The thing I want desperately.

"In the last several months, the show has changed. You might have noticed. Did you notice, Jason?"

"Absolutely. You've gotten funnier."

I laugh. "Dude, I was always funny. Take that back."

"Fine," he says in mock indignation. "You've gone soft, then."

I smile. "Some might call it soft. I like to think I've become less of an ass."

I glance at my watch, hoping that a certain someone is listening. Hoping she'll come stand outside the studio window any second.

Jason snaps his fingers. "Ah, yes. That's another way to put it. You've had a jackass-ectomy."

I shake my head in amusement. "And it was a painful process, man. Let me tell you. I went kicking and screaming most of the way. But then . . ."

He picks up the thread. "And then?"

I picture Nicole at the diner asking me to give her half the ingredients she needed, and it's like a bulb glows in my chest. "A certain someone came into my life."

Jason hums an impromptu romantic tune.

"Our listeners might recall the series we did on ten dates to winning a woman's heart," I say, sneaking a peek at the window once more. A co-worker walks past us on the other side of the glass, head bent over his phone. No sign of Nicole.

"Start with a trapeze, and you never know where it might lead," Jason tosses out.

I glance at the window again. Where is she? "You might very well wind up where I am, several months later," I say, keeping my voice cool and calm.

"And where is that, Ryder? Tell us where you are."

She's still not here, but I've got to jump off the cliff regardless.

"I'm in love," I say, holding my arms out wide. "I'm madly in love with the woman I took on the trapeze. She turned my world upside down."

Jason smiles, but he's quiet now because the time for banter is over. It's all soliloquy as I put my heart on the line, for everyone to hear.

"And I want to tell our listeners a little bit about how I fell in love with her."

Out of the corner of my eye, I see a flash of red. A curve of purple.

I turn the chair, moving the hanging mic with me, and I see her. Her cheeks are flushed, like she just ran down the hall. Now she's staring into the window of the studio with a wild grin that tells me to keep going. She wants to hear what I have to say. Her earbuds are in her ears, her phone is in her hand, and the stage is mine, and mine alone.

I can do this. I can say this. The chance to be with her is worth the risk.

"Falling in love with her was different than falling in love with our baby," I say, and Jason's jaw comes unhinged, and he points to Nicole's stomach and to me, the question in his eyes.

I nod a yes to him, but keep my eyes on her.

"Yes, that's right. The woman I took on the dates with me is having a baby. She's having *our* baby, and I couldn't be happier about that"—I pause for a second, realizing I don't need to go into detail about the timing—"*development*. With the baby, it was love at first heartbeat. As soon as I heard the galloping horses, I was done for. No holding back. That kid is mine, and I'd do anything for my baby."

Nicole's lips quiver, and I feel a starburst of emotions—love, happiness, excitement.

"But falling for the mother of my unborn child? I'm not going to lie. When you've had your heart eviscerated, it's a little harder to love again. I tried to fight it. I tried to pretend it was something else, but I'm not some unaware fool who doesn't know better."

Nicole brings her hand to her mouth, pressing her fingers against her trembling lips. Her eyes widen, brimming with tears. My heart grows bigger in my chest.

"Every day, I fell a little deeper. For her mind, her soul, her body, and, most of all, her heart. Her wonderful, huge, amazing heart that cared for me, looked out for me, and has this endless well of love." My throat swells with emotion as I profess my deepest feelings for the woman on the other side of the window. She is stunning with her beautiful round belly, the tears streaking down her lovely face, and her fingers pressed to the glass as if she's trying to reach me. To touch me. But she already has. "Her love, you see—it's limitless. And I want her to know I'm not just in love with the baby—I'm in love with the woman. Mad, passionate, she's-the-one love." I point to her, and she clasps her hands to her heart and mouths *I love you, too*. Nothing in the whole wide world can contain my grin as I finish, "I am wildly in love with the mother of my child, with the woman I took on the trapeze lesson, to the cupcake shop, on the geocaching date. With the love of my life. And that's how you love a woman. With your whole heart. Thanks for tuning in."

I turn off the mic, and Jason gives me a standing ovation as I leave the booth, yank open the door, and stand face-to-face with Nicole. I cup her cheeks in my hands. She is an open book. I can see how she feels written in her blue eyes. Her wet, tear-stained eyes.

"I love you so incredibly much." I kiss her tears.

"And I love you so much," she says, her voice breaking.

We are surrounded by clapping. Loud, ear-splitting whistles. But nothing could tear my gaze away from her. "I love you, and I love Papaya, and I want us to be a family. Do you?"

I hold a breath as I wait, but she doesn't take more than a second to answer. Her shoulders rise, and she gasps. "So much, Ryder. So much. I want that more than anything."

"Kiss her!"

The command comes from Cal, and as I glance briefly away from Nicole, I see my geometric boss, whose face is a circle of satisfaction amid the crowd. Seems everyone in the office heard what was going on, and the hallway by the studio is packed with our co-workers. They hoot, holler, and cheer us on.

As I dip my mouth to hers, someone else shouts, "It was you who knocked her up?"

I kiss Nicole, and give a thumbs-up affirmative to whoever asked.

As our lips touch, everyone else fades away. I have all I want right here in my arms. Sometimes you get more than you get, and you don't stop kissing the girl.

Eventually we do, though. When I finally wrench apart from her, nearly everyone's gone, but Cal's still here.

He claps my back then extends a hand. "Congratulations. Nothing could make me happier than seeing this transformation in you."

Nicole wraps her arm around me possessively. "He's like a new man in some ways. But, if you ask me, he was always pretty amazing."

I kiss her cheek, and a final thumbs-up from Cal is the last I see of him before he retreats down the hall.

We're alone and she hands me a small box, like the one she gave me the day she told me she was pregnant.

"What's this?"

"It's what I was planning to give to you this morning, to tell you I feel the same. But you beat me to it." She swats my shoulder.

"I still like your gifts." I open the box and tug out a silver key chain. A sexy silhouette of a woman dangles from it.

She reaches for my hand and threads her fingers through mine. "The other week, I thought you had only fallen in love with the baby, and I wanted you to be part of his or her life so badly. I'm so glad you want that. But I came in here today, determined to ask for more. Because I'm greedy, and I want all of you. You made my knees weak the first time you kissed me, and you still do," she says, and I feel ten feet tall. "When I'm with you, I feel that zing. That zing that I've never felt before." She reaches for my hand and tugs it to her heart. "I feel it all the time with you. And I bought you this gift because I want you to have the baby and the woman."

I slide my hand down her chest, splaying my palm over her belly. "You're a package deal, Nicole. I want the whole package. And I want to spend the rest of my life making sure you always feel that zing."

Her eyes shine with happiness, then they spark with mischief. "I kind of want to skip work the rest of the day."

"Now, Nicole," I say, playfully chiding her, "I've got a woman and a child to provide for. I can't just go around skipping out on my responsibilities."

"Such an upstanding man." She brings her mouth to my ear. "It makes me want you even more."

I'm honestly not sure how I make it through the next few hours until her doctor's appointment. But somehow, I manage, and we both leave early.

Inside the exam room, the doctor blinks when she sees me. "Hello, I'm Dr. Robinson. And you are?"

I shake her hand. "I'm the one who made her your patient."

Nicole laughs. "This is Ryder. He belongs to me."

I look at my pregnant woman. "I'm hers."

The doctor gives us a nod. "All righty, then. Let's see how everything's going with the mango."

And the mango is just fine.

Epilogue

Nicole

We have epic sex that night.

Obviously.

A man doesn't just tell a woman he's wildly in love with her and then not send her soaring to the heavens.

Ryder sends me flying, all right.

I go off the cliff three or four times. Honestly, I lose track of how many orgasms I have, and that's fine with me. The first time, he puts me on my hands and knees, and it's to die for.

Next, he bends me over the edge of the bed, biting my ass before he drives into me again. Then, in the middle of the night, I wake up to find his traveling hands all over me, and with my skin sizzling, I beg him to kiss me between my legs.

He heeds the call. And after I scream his name, he moves behind me like we're spoons, and we do it slow and tender, like the night I knew I'd fallen in love with the father of my child.

But it's even better because he whispers in my ear as he makes love to me. He tells me he loves me. Tells me he's crazy for me. Tells me he'll always take care of me.

And really, that's better than an orgasm.

But I still have one more.

Like I said, the second trimester rocks.

* * *

The next night, we have a ceremony of sorts. We take the baby contract, and we rip it up. At my living room table, we tear it into as many shreds as possible, and we toss it in the trash can.

"I'm all in," Ryder says.

"You better be." I tug his shirt, pulling him close to me.

"That's a promise. In fact," he says, lacing his fingers through mine, "what do you say we go shopping?"

"Shopping? Now? It's late."

He shakes his head then strokes my ring finger. "This weekend. Katherine's. You got me two key chains. Seems I'm due to get you a ring."

I shriek.

That weekend, I cry happy tears as I pick out a gorgeous diamond solitaire.

"It looks great with my two key chains."

"A tadpole, a woman, and a ring," I say.

He sweeps one hand over my stomach. "Good things come in threes."

* * *

The third trimester, though?

It's rough going.

I'm bigger, more tired, and a little grumpier.

But I'm also less cranky, since I have help. He helps me walk my dog. When I feel like I can barely bend to feed Ruby anymore, he takes over and gives her kibble. He cooks for me, and he makes sure I don't just eat jars of artichoke hearts.

Oh, and he handles the entire move to our new apartment.

I don't need to redo the closet since my mom finds us a new place, suitable for a new family and two medium dogs. Ryder insists I spend the entire moving day at the spa, getting pampered with my best friends.

If this isn't love, I don't know what is.

* * *

I wear a white dress that billows over the pumpkin inside me one month before I'm due to pop. As *Pachelbel's Canon in D* plays, I walk down the aisle at a small church in Manhattan. I'm barefoot and loving it.

Ryder wears a charcoal-gray suit, a pressed white shirt, and a sky-blue tie that I gave him. On the tie is a silver pin in the shape of a papaya. I gave him that, too.

I hold a bouquet of yellow daffodils, and when I reach the groom I'm struck once more by the realization of how lucky I am. This wonderful, witty, handsome man is mine.

We say our vows, and before God, my mom, my brother, Delaney and Tyler, Penny and Gabriel, Ryder's parents, his sister Claire, his brother Devon and his husband

Paul, their daughter Simone, and Ryder's friend Flynn, I promise to love him for the rest of my life.

He pledges to do the same.

When he slides a platinum band on my finger, the baby kicks.

When I give him his ring, the baby does a little jig, and then I kiss my husband. Later, I throw the bouquet, and Simone catches it.

Her dads look terrified.

"Someday," I say with a wild grin.

* * *

"You're almost there, Nicole. You can do it."

Dr. Robinson shouts her encouragement, and I'm sweating, panting, and swearing.

Nineteen hours of labor sucks. She was right. Morning sickness is nothing compared to pushing a watermelon out of your body.

"I can see the head. One more push," she says, her cheerleader voice ringing in my ears.

Ryder squeezes my hand. "You're almost there."

I'm exhausted, and everything hurts, but I want this baby out of me so badly. Machines beep, and nurses encourage me, and Ryder tells me I can do it. I stare at my monster belly, and I imagine that finally, after nine hard, wonderful, amazing months, I will at last get to meet my child.

I bear down and push and push and push until . . .

I hear a wail.

A loud, gorgeous, beautiful cry that fills my heart with joy.

"You did it!"

Tears spill down my cheeks as the doctor announces, "You have a son. And he's perfect."

I'm bawling, too, just like my baby boy and my husband. As the doctor hands me my son, I cradle him in my arms for the first time. It is magic and moonlight and all the stars in the sky, and I am flooded with a love that I know is infinite. Tears streak down my husband's gorgeous face as he plants a sweet daddy kiss on our little boy's head. "Hi, Papaya."

I cry and I smile at the same time. "He's not Papaya anymore."

"He has a new name." Ryder's deep, sexy voice is thick with emotion. We already picked one. He meets my eyes, and then gazes at our baby. "Hey there, Robert Powers Lockhart."

My father's and both of ours.

Another Epilogue

Ryder

"Do you want to grab the sage?"

Robert takes a wobbly step across the concrete. He doesn't actually know what sage is. At least, I don't think so. But he follows my pointing finger and swipes at the herb with his chubby hand. He misses.

I help my one-year-old son and grab some from the plant.

"Now, what about some thyme? Mommy likes that in her pasta, doesn't she?"

"Doggie."

That's Robert's answer for nearly everything these days. He can say mommy, daddy, and doggie. Oh, he can say Ruby, too. But Romeo? No way. That name vexes him.

"Where's the doggie?" I ask.

My blond-haired, blue-eyed son points to my white and brown collie mix. Romeo lounges in the August sun that shines brightly here in the communal rooftop gardens of our apartment building.

"Yes, that's right. That's our doggie. Can you say Romeo?"

"Doggie."

I laugh, then snip some thyme from a miniature potted wheelbarrow where we grow herbs. The mini wheelbarrow was a gift from my wife for my last birthday. We'd tried the Wheelbarrow, and I'm loathe to admit this, but she was right. It didn't work for far too many reasons. Mostly because she hated being upside down in what she called a ridiculously awkward and uncomfortable position. She rode me like a Crouching Cowgirl instead, and that was fine with me.

The next day, she gave me this ceramic mini wheelbarrow, and we planted some herbs in it.

Win some, lose some.

But honestly, I'm winning at pretty much everything.

I'm still working at Hanky Panky Love with my wife, but I'm there as a freelancer now, and so is she. She cut back her hours and started working from home more, and somehow we make it all fit, taking turns caring for our son. We still do our shows, and she writes her columns, too. I've cut back on those since my consulting business picked up. After Aaron, I nabbed a few more guys, and word spread. Now the Consummate Wingman has found a specialty niche in helping divorced guys get back out there.

It makes me feel damn good to give these men strategies that help them build confidence to put their hearts on the line again, especially since I can walk the walk and talk the talk. I'm writing a book on the topic. I don't have a title yet, but my publisher wants to call it *Got Your Back Again*. Maybe it'll stick. The bio, though, was easy to write.

Ryder Lockhart and his lovely wife Nicole have a son, two dogs, and a very happy ever after.

It's the truth, the whole truth, and nothing but the truth.

I also have a date with my wife tonight, so after the little man and I head inside and I mix up a pasta dish for my wife, I answer the door. Her friends are here, since both Penny and Delaney said they'd babysit tonight.

Penny scoops my son into her arms and coos at him. She loves kids and Delaney does, too. Nicole and I have a running bet on who will be the first among her friends to follow in her footsteps. I say Penny, but Nicole says Delaney.

"You are the cutest little guy in the entire universe," Penny says, then plants a huge kiss on his forehead.

Robert squeals with laughter. "Doggie!"

Penny cracks up. Ruby races over to greet Penny, and my son mixes in another word. "Ruby!"

Delaney leans in to kiss him, too. "Are you ready to go shopping with your aunts?"

I groan. "You're taking him shopping?"

"We need to train him early to be a good boy when the ladies shop," Penny says. "Besides, Delaney needs shoes."

"It's true," Delaney says with a straight face. "I do need shoes."

After they leave, I take my wife for a round of mini golf, since we still try to find interesting dates. After she wins, she suggests we grab a drink at the bar at Grand Central.

But she doesn't order champagne. She orders lemonade. After she finishes it, I learn why. She takes me to the Whispering Arch, and when she's on the other side, I hear some of my favorite words from her.

"I'm pregnant."

And I'm the happiest man on the face of the earth.

Nine months later, we have a girl, and we name her Rosemary.

She is an absolute angel.

THE END

Did you enjoy getting to know Flynn? Stay tuned for his story in COME AS YOU ARE! Also, his twin brother Dylan has a story to tell too in STUD FINDER!

COME AS YOU ARE....

The great thing about masquerade parties is no one knows who I am. I can pretend to be whoever I want. For one evening, I'm not the millionaire everyone wants a piece of.

And when I come across the most intriguing woman I've ever met, and it turns out she likes hot, passionate up-against-the-wall sex as much as I do, there's no need for names or numbers.

It's a perfect night.

Until the next day when she walks into my office with a proposal I didn't see coming.

Also by Lauren Blakely

FULL PACKAGE, the #1 New York Times
Bestselling romantic comedy!

BIG ROCK, the hit New York Times
Bestselling standalone romantic comedy!

MISTER O, also a New York Times Bestselling
standalone romantic comedy!

WELL HUNG, a New York Times Bestselling
standalone romantic comedy!

JOY RIDE, a USA Today Bestselling
standalone romantic comedy!

THE SEXY ONE, a swoony New York Times
Bestselling standalone romance!

THE HOT ONE, a sexy second chance
USA Today Bestselling standalone romance!

The New York Times and USA Today Bestselling Seductive
Nights series including *Night After Night*, *After This Night*,
and *One More Night*

And the two standalone romance novels, *Nights With Him*
and *Forbidden Nights*, both New York Times and
USA Today Bestsellers!

Sweet Sinful Nights, *Sinful Desire*, *Sinful Longing* and *Sinful Love*,
the complete New York Times Bestselling high-heat romantic
suspense series that spins off from Seductive Nights!

Playing With Her Heart, a USA Today bestseller, and a sexy Seductive Nights spin-off standalone! (Davis and Jill's romance)

21 Stolen Kisses, the USA Today Bestselling forbidden new adult romance!

Caught Up In Us, a New York Times and USA Today Bestseller! (Kat and Bryan's romance!)

Pretending He's Mine, a Barnes & Noble and iBooks Bestseller! (Reeve & Sutton's romance)

Trophy Husband, a New York Times and USA Today Bestseller! (Chris & McKenna's romance)

Far Too Tempting, the USA Today Bestselling standalone romance! (Matthew and Jane's romance)

Stars in Their Eyes, an iBooks bestseller! (William and Jess' romance)

My USA Today bestselling No Regrets series that includes *The Thrill of It* (Meet Harley and Trey) and its sequel *Every Second With You*

My New York Times and USA Today Bestselling Fighting Fire series that includes *Burn For Me* (Smith and Jamie's romance!) *Melt for Him* (Megan and Becker's romance!) and *Consumed by You* (Travis and Cara's romance!)

The Sapphire Affair series…
The Sapphire Affair
The Sapphire Heist
Out of Bounds

A New York Times Bestselling sexy sports romance
The Only One
A second chance love story!

Acknowledgements

I'm grateful to Lauren McKellar for all she sees. I owe so much to my early readers — Jen, Dena and Kim. You ladies are my inside gals and I'm so lucky to have you. I'm not letting you three go! Karen, Tiffany, Janice, Virginia and Marion provided eagle eyes, and I appreciate them immensely. Nelle O'Brien serves as my New York City eyes and ears. Katie Ashley checked the tadpole details! Huge thanks to Helen Williams for the amazingly stunning cover. This woman knows hot men and what to do with them. I am always grateful for KP Simmon for strategy, insight, guidance and friendship. Thank you to Kelley, Keyanna and Candi for everything every day. I am delighted to have the daily support of writer friends like Laurelin Paige, Kristy Bromberg, CD Reiss, Marie Force, and Lili Valente. Big love to my husband, children and four-legged family members.

Contact

I love hearing from readers! You can find me on Twitter at LaurenBlakely3, or Facebook at LaurenBlakelyBooks, or online at LaurenBlakely.com. You can also email me at laurenblakelybooks@gmail.com.

Printed in Great Britain
by Amazon